WITHDRAWN

To Catch a
Highlander

TO CATCH A HIGHLANDER

KAREN HAWKINS

THORNDIKE
CHIVERS

This Large Print edition is published by Thorndike Press, Waterville, Maine, USA, and by BBC Audiobooks Ltd, Bath, England.
Thorndike Press, a part of Gale, Cengage Learning.
Copyright © 2008 by Karen Hawkins.
The moral right of the author has been asserted.
The MacLean Family Series #3.

The text of this Large Print edition is unabridged.
Other aspects of the book may vary from the original edition.
Set in 16 pt. Plantin.
Printed on permanent paper.

LIBRARY OF CONGRESS CATALOGING-IN-PUBLICATION DATA

Hawkins, Karen.
   To catch a Highlander / by Karen Hawkins.
     p. cm. — (The MacLean family series ; #3) (Thorndike Press large print basic)
   ISBN-13: 978-1-4104-0401-5 (hardcover : alk. paper)
   ISBN-10: 1-4104-0401-3 (hardcover : alk. paper)
   1. Scotland — Fiction. 2. Large type books. I. Title.
PS3558.A8231647T55 2008
813'.54—dc22   2008001831

BRITISH LIBRARY CATALOGUING-IN-PUBLICATION DATA AVAILABLE

Published in 2008 in the U.S. by arrangement with Pocket Books, a division of Simon & Schuster, Inc.
Published in 2008 in the U.K. by arrangement with Pocket Books, a division of Simon & Schuster, Inc.

U.K. Hardcover: 978 1 405 64562 1 (Chivers Large Print)
U.K. Softcover: 978 1 405 64563 8 (Camden Large Print)

Printed in the United States of America
1 2 3 4 5 6 7 12 11 10 09 08

To Ron Chapman
A tall, handsome, broad-shouldered
hero with steely blue eyes.
Umh, that *was* how you asked me to
describe you, wasn't it?

And his beautiful wife, TJ
(aka "Goldilocks"),
who does a great job keeping
"Ole Steely eyes" in line.

CHAPTER 1

Och, me lassies! The fun ye'll have when ye've a man of yer own to torment!
Old Woman Nora from Loch Lomond
to her three wee granddaughters
one cold evening

"You lost *everything?*" Sophia MacFarlane's voice cracked on the last word.

Robert MacFarlane, known as "Red" to his daughter and his gambling companions, winced. "Aye, lass. I — I lost it all."

Sophia sank into her chair, her face ashen. "Even . . . even the house?"

Red swallowed with difficulty. He'd always thought it best to get bad news out fast, but looking at his daughter's quivering bottom lip, he questioned his own advice.

Her wide, light blue eyes and thick lashes were wet with unshed tears. "But how? You were to go to Edinburgh and sell Mother's diamonds for the new roof. How did you end up in a game of chance?"

"I stopped in Stirling, though now I wish to God I hadn't. I'd heard on the road that there was to be a race between the fastest horses in England. At first, I just thought to watch, but Andrew MacGregor was there, and —"

Sophia's lips twisted. "MacGregor has always been trouble."

"*Psht.* 'Tis my own bloody fault and no one else's. Lass, I only thought to help you —"

"*Help* me? By losing the house that I love?"

"I didn't plan it that way!" Distress poured through his voice. "I thought if I could win just once, I could pay for the repairs on the roof, and you wouldn't be forced to sell your mother's diamond set." His brow lowered. "I didn't like the idea of selling it to begin with."

She pressed her fists to her forehead. "I *told* you I didn't care a feather for the diamonds. I only wanted the roof fixed!"

He set his jaw. "Beatrice wished you to wear those diamonds when you married, just as she wore them when I married her."

Sophia's eyes flashed. "Once the roof began to leak, Mama would have been the first to say the diamonds had to go."

Red reluctantly admitted to himself that

Sophie was right. Except when she was caught up in a challenge, Beatrice had been the pinnacle of solid common sense — despite growing up in one of the largest manor houses in Scotland, surrounded by servants with nothing to do but spoil her rotten and do her thinking for her.

But Beatrice was not the sort of woman to let others do for her what she could easily do for herself. She was strong and independent, character traits her own father had deplored.

Every time she had attempted to act on her own, her father would furiously clamp down on her freedoms. Back and forth the two went — until, at the tender age of seventeen, Beatrice had kicked off the family traces and eloped with an unknown adventurer named Robert MacFarlane.

It had been the greatest stroke of luck Red had ever experienced, and it had changed him forever. Life before Beatrice was exciting, but life with Beatrice was exciting and warm and damned near perfect. She made every inn, no matter how sordid and cold, feel like home. In return, Red filled her life with excitement and romance and love. Not once had either of them regretted their impulsive marriage.

Red wished for the millionth time that

9

Beatrice were still with him today. "Sophie, I just couldn't let your mama's diamonds go without a fight. I meant no harm, but now . . . I've lost it all." He swiped at his eyes angrily. "But I'll find a way to fix this, see if I don't!"

Sophia's expression softened as she took his hand between hers. "We'll just have to think of a way out of this mess." She sat silently, her brows knitted.

Red looked at her hopefully. If anyone could think of a way out of this mess, it was Sophie. She'd do it; he knew she would. He watched her face, noting how the sun gleamed through the curtains to gild her already golden curls. The light warmed her skin to cream and traced the delicate line of her heart-shaped face. With her thick lashes, sparkling eyes, and perfect nose, it was hard to imagine a more beautiful woman.

But her obvious beauty and delicate appearance were misleading; from early on, Sophie had her parents' rapacious appetite for excitement. The three had followed the game and traveled from inn to inn across all of Europe without complaint, delighting in each new location, every leaky inn. While Red had plied his trade, Beatrice had made their daughter's life as normal as possible, serving as governess, tutor, and mother all in one.

Beatrice had kept them all safe and sane, laughing at muddy roads and mocking ill-tempered innkeepers until Sophie and Red would dissolve into laughter. She made certain their clothes were dry and clean, their rooms organized and welcoming. Red's and Sophie's entire world had revolved around merry, never-weary Beatrice — which was why her unexpected death years ago had been so devastating.

Sophie was so like Beatrice, it made Red's heart ache. Though society might say a lass of twenty-seven was firmly on the shelf, any man who saw her gold and pink loveliness would think otherwise. While she carried herself with a mature air that clearly told her years, she didn't look a day over eighteen.

Sophia's expression grew graver, and her tender lips pursed as she tapped a slender finger on her chin.

Red silently cursed his friend MacGregor, cursed the ill luck of the cards, and especially cursed the circumstances that had made him hope.

Hope for most people was a good thing, something to carry them through a difficult time. Hope for a gambler was ruin.

One should never wager what one couldn't

afford to lose. Yet in the heat of this game, his heart had swelled with insidious hope at the chance to fix things for his Sophie. Of course he'd lost; gambling was not a game to be based on feelings. He, of all men, knew that. For years, he and his lovely Beatrice had made their livelihood on his ability to turn the cards and play on other men's hopes.

How she would have scolded him for taking chances with the only two things she'd left their daughter. It had been her fondest wish that their Sophie should have a proper home. So she'd tucked away the deed to a house that had been tossed onto a table by a desperate nobleman during one of Red's games and had refused to part with it even when times were lean.

Unfortunately, fortune was a fickle lady and poor Beatrice didn't live to see the house she'd guarded for her daughter.

After Beatrice's death, Red and Sophia had left Italy and traveled to Scotland to take possession of the house on the hill. They'd arrived on a chilled, blustery day, when clouds gathered over the tall, square stone house, the closed doors and windows cold and unwelcoming, a heavy growth of vines almost hiding it from view.

Sophia had immediately set about making

the house into MacFarlane House. Together, they scrubbed and polished, hammered and nailed, fixed and cleaned, until the place was something to behold. Slowly, as they worked, their hearts began to heal, and the house became a real home. Thus it had been for eleven years.

Sophia straightened her shoulders with a determined air, and Red looked at her hopefully.

"We can't just sit back and let a stranger take our home." Her gaze flickered past him to encompass the sitting room. "I couldn't bear to see such a thing."

Red followed her gaze. The wood paneling gleamed softly, and thick Oriental rugs carpeted the room, softening the glossy wood floors. An intricate carving decorated the fireplace, where a large mantelpiece held a carved ormolu clock and a pair of charming brass and crystal candelabras. Several decorative chairs sat before the fireplace, simple yet elegant, covered with red and gold striped velvet and flanked by glossy Chippendale side tables. In one corner stood a small escritoire carved in the French fashion, flanked by intricately carved curio cabinets holding an assortment of china. Sunlight streamed past red velvet curtains and warmed the wood paneling, suffusing the chamber with the rich scents of beeswax and lemon.

With a small fire to offset the spring chill, it was difficult to imagine a more welcoming and beautiful room.

But the centerpiece of it all was sitting in the chair opposite him now: his beautiful daughter. Sophie, with her gold hair, heart-shaped face, just like her mother. The only similarity between Sophie and her father was their unusual eyes, a liquid pale blue fringed with a wealth of curling dark brown lashes.

As a youth, tough and streetwise Red had gotten into many a fight with larger lads who had made the error of laughing at the length of his lashes. Red's fists had been hard even at the young age of eight, so few made the mistake of laughing twice. He wished he could solve his current difficulties so easily. It would take a keener head than his to get out of their current difficulties. "If anyone can find a way out of this mess, it'd be you," Red said stoutly.

Sophia smiled, her heart buoyed by her father's obvious belief in her abilities. She glanced out the window to where the gentle breeze rustled among the roses in the garden. The new path wound through the pink, red, yellow, and lavender flowers to the swaying green trees beyond, passing the white stone fountain where a pink marble angel perched on the edge of a large basin, its fingers forever trailing in the splashing water. Soon someone else would be standing here, taking solace in the garden, instead of her.

The thought ignited her anger. How *dare* someone sit in *her* garden without her permission, especially after all of the work she'd done! There had to be a way . . . Sophia drummed her fingers on the arm of her chair. How could they turn this horrid tide of ill fortune? They had no money and less credit. She didn't know anyone who could help, either; their only wealthy acquaintance was the squire and his fortune was tied up in his own estate, as it should be.

No, if they wished to win back their house, then — She froze, her mind whirling at a sudden thought. "We have neither the money nor the credit to buy back the house, but we *do* have talent and luck. Since the house was lost in a game, I'll simply win it back in one."

"You?"

"Aye. No one would think I could play cards as well as you."

"That's true," Red said slowly. When she

15

was young, he'd taught her how to palm a card, deal from the bottom of the deck, mark the face cards with her hairpin — a thousand little tricks that, when put together, meant that one rarely lost.

But the *real* trick was her brain. Knowing when to play which card, remembering who held what — those were the talents that made a player great, and Sophie had mastered them all by the time she was twelve.

He'd also taught her about the mind-set of the game, of how winning could mean one thing to one person and something entirely different to another; how to read a man and tell if he was desperate and thus close to making an error; and how wanting something very badly could distract a person until he'd lost it all.

Red rubbed his chin. "It might work, lass, but it could prove dangerous. Men like Dougal MacLean may look as soft as a goose's backside, but they're cold and hard if they think they've been cheated. Your mother wouldn't have liked the thought of your playing a game for real stakes, either."

Sophia's heart tightened. She couldn't let MacFarlane House go. It was all she had left of Mama.

She pushed the emotion away, her voice

hardening. "What do you know of this man?"

"Dougal MacLean? Not much. Mostly rumor." Red ran a hand through his hair. Once a bright red, now it was threaded with white and had faded to auburn. "He is known as a rake and handsome as the day is long. You'd need to keep your wits about you."

"I've met handsome men before," Sophia said confidently.

Red didn't look convinced. "Aye, but there's something different about this one. And he's a proud man; his whole family is soaked with it." Red pursed his lips. "I'd say he has a bit of a temper, too."

"How do you know?"

"The earl of Stirling made some very unflattering comments about one of MacLean's brothers during the game, and I saw the anger in his eyes."

"Did he say anything?"

"No, for there was a sudden flash of lightning, and a gust of wind blew the shutters wide open, and we were all scrambling about, trying to close the window and gather the cards." Red chuckled a bit. "The earl tried to blame that on MacLean. Seems there's a rumor the MacLean family is cursed and when they lose their temper, storms gather."

Sophia smiled faintly. "Do you know anything else about MacLean?"

Red's eyes narrowed. "He seemed a mite taken with his position. He travels in a coach and eight, and a prettier string of horses you'd be hard pressed to find."

That was promising. A vain man could be led. "Do you think he'll come here?"

"He said he wished to give the house to his nephew or such and would come see it beforehand."

She nodded. "Good. Do you remember anything else?"

Red made a face. "He dresses like a Frenchman, all lace cuffs and whatnot."

Sophia curled her lip. "A dandy."

"Yes . . . and no. There's more to him than his trappings. He's quick, and blasted good at covering his emotions, which is how he bested me. You'll need to be ready to meet this man, lassie," Red warned. "You've not played cards in a while, and he's uncommon intelligent."

"Then we will practice every day until he arrives."

"It will be a week, at least. The races won't be over until then." Red regarded Sophia. "You'll need a new gown or two, as well."

She looked down at her morning gown of

pink muslin. "Why?"

"A man will wager more if he thinks you don't need his blunt."

"Very well. I will order some new gowns from the seamstress in the village. She just made a trousseau for the baron's daughter. I'll also need some paste jewels — he'll never be close enough to know the difference. Perhaps I'll win back both the jewels and the deed."

"It's worth a try." Red looked around the room, a twisted smile on his lips. "The house may be a problem. You've done too good a job with her; she's beautiful. I doubt MacLean will wish to part with her once he sees her."

Sophia frowned. "True. Once he sees it, he'll never want to wager it. I wish —" An idea popped into her head, one so dazzlingly brilliant that it froze her mind for a full moment.

"Sophie?" Red's voice broke through her thoughts.

"Do you think it will be an *entire* week before MacLean arrives to view" — she couldn't get the word *his* through her lips — "the house?"

"At least. Maybe longer if he stays after the races for the revelries."

Then it could work! She would need help,

but with enough willing and able hands, she could —

"Sophie?" A crease rested deep on Red's brow. "I don't like that look. What are you thinking?"

She stood and rubbed her hands together. "I know exactly how to make MacLean wish to be rid of our house. We'll just undo all of the work."

"What?"

She waved a hand, too busy thinking to explain more. "Leave it to me. I will see to it all."

"Whatever 'tis you're planning, have a care. If MacLean decides you are out to trick him, he'll not rest 'til he's gained blood for blood."

"I'll be cautious," she replied absently, her mind whirling with plans.

"No, you won't. You've too much of your mother in you. Once she set her mind to a path, she wouldn't be turned, come hell or high water."

Sophia grinned. "Determination is a good thing."

"That depends on the cost, lass."

Sensing his worry, Sophia changed the subject by asking Red about the specific plays in the game that had lost the house. Eager to absolve himself, he described the hands he'd been dealt and how he'd been fooled into wagering everything.

Sophia listened with half an ear. Once she was done with her beloved house, the foppish MacLean would *beg* someone to take it from him. No soft-skinned, lace-covered, dandified profligate would ever take this house and make it his.

Ever.

CHAPTER 2

Careful how ye speak o' others, me dearies. Ye never know when yer words may come back and bite ye in the arse.
Old Woman Nora from Loch Lomond
to her three wee granddaughters
one cold evening

Despite Red's prediction, it was more than a month before Dougal MacLean arrived. He'd met a lovely young widow in Stirling, and the enticement of pouty lips and an overflowing bodice had persuaded Dougal to linger.

Not that he'd needed much persuading. He'd been on his way to his sister's house, and it was difficult to stomach her husband. Though Fiona seemed to love the blackguard, Dougal only tolerated him because Jack Kincaid was clearly as mad about Fiona as she was about him. Which meant that Dougal was forced to "play nice," as

Fiona so inelegantly expressed it.

Dougal didn't like to play nice, but neither was he immune to his only sister's pleas to visit her.

Now, Dougal turned his large black gelding into the lane leading to the house. It had taken him a while to find the entry marker, hidden between two large oak trees on the long and lonely stretch of road.

The lane was narrow and overgrown, though it grew wider and more favorable as it twined down a long line of graceful trees that arched pleasantly, making a lace canvas of the blue sky.

"It's a pretty bit of land, eh, me lord?"

Dougal glanced back at Shelton, his groom, who followed on a large bay. "It's passable." In truth, he was a bit surprised. It was rare when a deed won over a card table held real value. All too often, the lands were gone to waste, the house (if there was one) a leaky mess, and the title encumbered to the hilt. So far, these lands had the look of being maintained, if a little rugged. That was something, anyway.

As a flock of pigeons took wing from the field and swooped toward a small, picturesque lake, the groom nodded his appreciation. "Excellent hunting, I'd say. Might want to reconsider givin' the place to yer nephew and keep it fer yerself. Maybe put a huntin' box on it."

"It would be a waste; I rarely use the hunting lands I have."

The groom sighed with envy. "If 'n I was ye, I'd do nothin' else but hunt."

"I've no doubt you'd do just that, for a more lazy individual I've yet to meet — other than myself, of course."

Shelton beamed. "Thank ye, me lord! 'Tis a rare day I can consider meself an equal with ye on any grounds."

"You're welcome," Dougal returned gravely.

"Aye, ye've made bein' lazy a form o' art that few — look!" The groom pointed eagerly at the soft shoulder of the road, where a fox print appeared. "Cooee, looks fresh, too!"

Dougal eyed the thicket beyond. "Fresh or no, it would take a better man than me to get a horse over this uneven ground without breaking a leg."

Shelton shot him a sharp look. "Ye're many things, me lord, but unskilled on a horse ain't one of 'em."

"You unman me, Shelton. I don't know how to react to such excessive praise."

The groom's expression turned to one of long suffering. "There ye go ag'in with the nonsense, me lord. Are ye sure ye ain't a bit Irish?"

Dougal grinned. "Not that my mother would admit to." He turned in the saddle to admire the vista. The scent of clean, damp earth and fresh grass rose to meet him, the sunlight dappling the world through the trees. Birds sang overhead, while the horses' hooves clopped pleasantly along the level path.

The land alone would make an excellent present for his new nephew, though Mac-Farlane had vowed the house was the jewel of the property. However, as the man had been attempting to offer the deed in lieu of a considerable sum of money, Dougal doubted that as truth.

Dougal urged his horse onward, cleared the last curve of the drive, and found himself pleasantly surprised again. The house rose before him, large and square, the mullioned windows sparkling in the late-afternoon sun. MacFarlane House — soon to be renamed Kincaid Manor — was a pleasant redbrick structure with a graceful façade brightened by a wide portico held by eight grand Ionic columns. Large windows framed a set of double white doors topped by an arch of stained glass depicting a sunburst over a set of hills very like those on which the house stood. A smaller wing extended from each side of the main structure, the brick covered with a romantic swath of deep green vines.

MacFarlane — a charlatan and professional ivory turner if Dougal had ever seen one — had said that the house was elegant. But it wasn't quite that. It was more . . . charming.

His nephew would enjoy this when he grew to majority. The lad would need a residence of his own, a place where he could come and be his own man without the hen cackling of his mother and the barking of his stern father.

Dougal grinned. Black Jack Kincaid had been the rakehell of all rakehells before Fiona had tamed him. It would gall the man to watch his own son follow the same path — which he would, if his uncle Dougal had anything to say about it.

Jack would hate that Dougal was gifting the lad with the house, which would make it all the sweeter. Ah, yes, there was some compensation in being an uncle, after all.

Dougal turned his horse through the neat stone and iron gates near the house. He'd take a quick look around, and if it appeared reasonably sound, he'd hire workmen to make whatever repairs were necessary.

As he turned his horse down the final bend in the long drive, the horse whickered and pranced, stopping abruptly.

"Gor!" Shelton said, pulling his horse to one side of the drive as he looked down. "The drive has done been torn to hell!"

Dougal frowned. Before him, the nicely smooth drive had given way to a morass of huge holes. Unlike the usual wear and tear one found in a drive from years of use and neglect, these appeared freshly dug.

"I'll be a weaver's mother," Shelton said with horror. "Who in the world would dig holes in a perfectly good lane?"

"I have no idea, though it does seem a wasted effort." Dougal guided Poseidon around the holes and finally halted at the steps that led to the front portico.

Though some of the windows were thrown open to the cooling evening air, no one seemed aware he'd arrived. He swung down, handing his reins to Shelton before climbing the steps. He paused at the top and removed his gloves.

The groom tied the mounts to the ornate iron hitching post and hurried after Dougal. "Me lord, shall I knock on the door?"

"By all means." Dougal tucked his gloves into a pocket and looked up at the large columns. They were well placed and seemed solid, the ornamental work of high quality.

Shelton knocked, but no answer came.

Dougal looked back down the lane from the portico, wondering anew at the fresh holes. Perchance some large stones had recently been removed; that might cause such havoc.

Shelton knocked again, a bit harder, but still no answer was forthcoming.

After a moment's silence, the groom puffed out an irritated sigh. "Me lord, no one's answering. Shall I —"

Dougal held up his hand, and the groom obediently silenced. Voices, low and murmuring, came from one of the open windows at the far end of the portico.

Dougal gestured toward the window. "The servants must be busy in other rooms and are unable to hear your knocking."

Shelton scowled. "Lazy is what they are. I'll wager a month's wages they heard me and jus' don't wish to do their duty!" He turned as if to march to the window and accost whoever might be inside.

"No," Dougal said softly.

He walked down the portico to the open window and peered in. As his vision adjusted to the darkened room, he realized he was looking into a sitting room. Large, with well-placed windows, the chamber should have been airy and bright but instead appeared unkempt and dingy. A stained settee and two chairs — one without an arm and one sitting rather drunkenly to one side — decreased the room's natural charm, as did the other mismatched pieces of furniture.

Even worse were the walls, which were papered in a sadly faded red and cream striped pattern. This might not have been so evident, but empty, large portrait-shaped spots proclaimed how bright the paper once had been.

From inside the room, someone yelped, "Ouch!"

Dougal leaned to his left and saw two people kneeling by one of the large fireplaces at the far end of the room. One was a large, burly man with arms bulging with muscles, his hands clutched about a mortar board and trowel, his gray head tilted to one side as he peered up the chimney shaft. Beside him was a woman in a faded blue gown, her hair pinned beneath a kerchief, though Dougal detected a strand of gleaming blond several shades lighter than his.

She turned her elbow to examine it. "I scraped it on the edge of the brick."

Her assistant grunted. "Ye need to be careful."

"I know, I know. I won't have any skin left

by the time we finish." She bent over and looked up the chimney. "Angus, I don't think it'll smoke the way it is now." Soft as butter, her sweet voice slid over Dougal's senses with the delight of fresh cream.

Bloody hell, if this woman looked even half as attractive as her voice, he might be enticed to stay away from his sister's a bit longer.

Her companion snorted. "Trust me, miss. I think it will smoke, and badly."

Miss? Then she wasn't a servant.

"I don't know, Angus," the woman replied, her cultured, silky voice at odds with the man's rough country tones. "I want this chimney to smoke worse than Lucifer's own fire. Let's add another brick to be certain."

Dougal stiffened. He'd thought they were repairing the chimney, but they *wanted* it to smoke. What in the hell was going on?

The woman rubbed her neck with a gloved hand, black ash smearing her skin. "Goodness, I'm going to be sore tomorrow."

"Not as sore as ye were after we spent three days smearin' ash and wax over the panelin' in the library," the man returned evenly, scooping some mortar from a bucket and preparing to insert a brick into the chimney.

Dougal's hands curled into fists. They

ments." The woman gave a delicious chuckle and then said in a falsetto, *"Oh, Lord MacLean, your voice is so manly! Oh, Lord MacLean, I've never seen such clean hands! Oh, Lord MacLean, I've never felt this way about a man before!"*

Dougal's eyes narrowed, heat simmering his stomach. The wind lifted a bit, swirling the curtains at the window and ruffling woman's clothes.

Miss!" the servant said. "Ye shouldn't be n' of taproom wenches."

coughed as the wind blew some of sh into the air. "No, I shouldn't," she , waving away the ash cloud, "though hat I've heard of him, he's the sort and with whoever is available."

t bad fer the plan?"

leaned forward, his gaze riveted man's slim back.

k her head, the strand of golden ing where it curled down her it's a good thing. A man who is ted is easy to fool."

wered, gripping the window tly his fingers went white. So hood-wink him into giving y, did they? But how? He'd e'd part with the deed for significant as mismatched

were bricking up his chimney and had already smeared ash over his library paneling? B'god, he'd put a stop to this foolishness right now. He moved to step over the low windowsill, when the woman stood, her back still to him, and sighed. "Angus, when you're done with the brick, I shall add some oiled rags. That will make it smoke even worse."

Angus turned an admiring glance at his partner in crime. "Miss, ye've a gift fer this, ye do."

She chuckled, the sound just as seductive, except for the hint of mockery. "I'm becoming as adept at this as the new owner is at shirking his duty."

"Now, miss, he might have a good reason not to rush here."

"Like what?"

"I don't know. Perhaps he won several houses at the card game and has been visitin' them all."

"It's far more likely he was waylaid by a lass with loose morals. From what I hear, the man's a lace-bedecked profligate."

Blast the woman and her rude assumptions! He may have stayed in Stirling to sample the charms of a widow, but that did not make him a lace-bedecked profligate. What burned the most was that she was correct in her assumptions about what had kept him away from his new acquisition.

The large man stood, ash and soot falling to the floor about him. Huge as a barn door, he spread his hands wide. "Och, miss, it smokes good enough now. Come, we've worked hard today. If there's more to do tomorrow, we'll do it then."

"If there's time. We don't know when MacLean will bother to arrive." She sighed and stripped off her gloves. "I shouldn't complain, for the man's lateness has been a boon — we've been able to get so much done."

"Aye," the man agreed. "The house has never looked so poorly."

"Indeed," the woman said, her voice tinged with pride. "We've put all of the good furniture in the attic and brought down the old odds and ends, hid all of the good portraits and replaced them with the horrid ones stored beneath the stairs, loosened the railing on the staircase, pried up some floorboards, and packed away the good dishes, leaving only the old and broken pieces."

Dougal blinked. *Good God!*

The rough man chuckled. "Going to serve the new owner on a bared table, are ye?"

"There's far more to this scheme than

even you know. Wait until you see all tha Red and I've done to the place!" The wom an's voice shimmered warm and generov with laughter, sending Dougal's imagir tion tumbling into a silk-sheeted bed.

A woman with a voice like that s' have the face of an angel, the boc Greek sculpture, and the skills of san. Chances were, she was a ha crone.

The hulking workman began tools. "I hope ye and yer pa k doin'. Fop or no, no man ta his belongings."

"Psht," the woman said if we plan on knocking peeling his pockets."

That was someth thought grimly.

The workman fer yer sake, mis

"Yes. Then until she shi placed a ha voice. "I w but we h arrives

"I d MacLea tying him to

were bricking up his chimney and had already smeared ash over his library paneling? B'god, he'd put a stop to this foolishness right now. He moved to step over the low windowsill, when the woman stood, her back still to him, and sighed. "Angus, when you're done with the brick, I shall add some oiled rags. That will make it smoke even worse."

Angus turned an admiring glance at his partner in crime. "Miss, ye've a gift fer this, ye do."

She chuckled, the sound just as seductive, except for the hint of mockery. "I'm becoming as adept at this as the new owner is at shirking his duty."

"Now, miss, he might have a good reason not to rush here."

"Like what?"

"I don't know. Perhaps he won several houses at the card game and has been visitin' them all."

"It's far more likely he was waylaid by a lass with loose morals. From what I hear, the man's a lace-bedecked profligate."

Blast the woman and her rude assumptions! He may have stayed in Stirling to sample the charms of a widow, but that did not make him a lace-bedecked profligate. What burned the most was that she was correct in her assumptions about what had kept him away from his new acquisition.

The large man stood, ash and soot falling to the floor about him. Huge as a barn door, he spread his hands wide. "Och, miss, it smokes good enough now. Come, we've worked hard today. If there's more to do tomorrow, we'll do it then."

"If there's time. We don't know when MacLean will bother to arrive." She sighed and stripped off her gloves. "I shouldn't complain, for the man's lateness has been a boon — we've been able to get so much done."

"Aye," the man agreed. "The house has never looked so poorly."

"Indeed," the woman said, her voice tinged with pride. "We've put all of the good furniture in the attic and brought down the old odds and ends, hid all of the good portraits and replaced them with the horrid ones stored beneath the stairs, loosened the railing on the staircase, pried up some floorboards, and packed away the good dishes, leaving only the old and broken pieces."

Dougal blinked. *Good God!*

The rough man chuckled. "Going to serve the new owner on a bared table, are ye?"

"There's far more to this scheme than

even you know. Wait until you see all that Red and I've done to the place!" The woman's voice shimmered warm and generous with laughter, sending Dougal's imagination tumbling into a silk-sheeted bed.

A woman with a voice like that should have the face of an angel, the body of a Greek sculpture, and the skills of a courtesan. Chances were, she was a haggard old crone.

The hulking workman began to gather his tools. "I hope ye and yer pa know what ye're doin'. Fop or no, no man takes well to losin' his belongings."

"Psht," the woman said airily. "It's not as if we plan on knocking him in the head and peeling his pockets."

That was something, at least, Dougal thought grimly.

The workman grunted. "I hope it works, fer yer sake, miss."

"Yes. Then I can clean my lovely house until she shines once again." The woman placed a hand on the mantel, regret in her voice. "I wish we hadn't been forced to this, but we had no choice. I hope the new owner arrives soon to see our work.

"I daresay some taproom wench has kept MacLean a prisoner to his oversated palate, tying him to her by paying him compliments." The woman gave a delicious chuckle and then said in a falsetto, *"Oh, Lord Mac-Lean, your voice is so manly! Oh, Lord Mac-Lean, I've never seen such clean hands! Oh, Lord MacLean, I've never felt this way about a man before!"*

Dougal's eyes narrowed, heat simmering in his stomach. The wind lifted a bit, swirling the curtains at the window and ruffling the woman's clothes.

"Miss!" the servant said. "Ye shouldn't be talkin' of taproom wenches."

She coughed as the wind blew some of the ash into the air. "No, I shouldn't," she agreed, waving away the ash cloud, "though from what I've heard of him, he's the sort to dally and with whoever is available."

"Is that bad fer the plan?"

Dougal leaned forward, his gaze riveted on the woman's slim back.

She shook her head, the strand of golden hair gleaming where it curled down her back. "No, it's a good thing. A man who is easily distracted is easy to fool."

Dougal glowered, gripping the window frame so tightly his fingers went white. So they wished to hood-wink him into giving up the property, did they? But how? He'd be damned if he'd part with the deed for something so insignificant as mismatched furnishings and smoking chimneys. There had to be more to this scheme.

He quietly stepped back out onto the portico and strode to where the horses were tied. Jaw tight, he turned to his groom. "Did you hear that?"

"Some of it." Shelton shook his head. "Lordy, but it do look as if ye're not wanted."

"It's my house, damn it. I shall toss these charlatans out on their ears!"

"And then?"

"I shall leave and send Simmons, my man of business, to repair what's been ruined." Dougal scowled at the open windows. "What idiots, to think they could fool me with such nonsense."

Shelton nodded. "Shall I stable the horses?"

"No. I won't be long. If I am not out in twenty minutes, come inside and inform me that the horses have been watered and are ready for the road."

Shelton's weathered face split into a grin. "Thinkin' ye might need a rescue, me lord?"

Dougal raised his brows. "Have I ever needed to be rescued? I merely wish to make a clean exit once I've exposed their ruse."

He grimly turned and walked back up the

steps, the groom following. "Knock, Shelton, and don't stop until the knocker falls from the door. I'm going to deal with this insurgency once and for all."

Sophia whirled toward the door. The pounding thud came again, so loud the hall echoed with it.

Angus blinked up at her from where he was stooped beside the fireplace, a damp rag in one hand as he cleaned the ashes from the floor. "Gor, miss! Do ye think 'tis the new master?"

She shook her head. "I didn't hear a carriage."

Relief flooded Angus's face. "Aye, yer pa said the new owner drives a coach and six, don't he?"

"Eight," she corrected absently as the banging came yet again. "It must be the boy from town with the wood."

"It's about time."

She nodded. Over the past month, her plan had grown by leaps and bounds. Still, the delay had irked Sophia. Apparently, winning her lovely house was so unimportant that the high and mighty Lord MacLean couldn't be bothered even to visit it.

Her chest tightened as if she couldn't quite catch her breath. He *had* to visit the house. If he didn't, then all of her efforts would be for naught. All of the work she'd done by day, all of the card practice she'd been doing by night.

Red had said she possessed a natural talent with the cards, and most evenings she could beat him. She could win back her house by counting the cards and outwitting MacLean. All she needed was the chance.

The loud knocking came again, and Angus threw down his rag in disgust. "That lad needs a thrashin', he does." Angus stood and wiped his hands on his pants, leaving long ashy streaks, then turned toward the door.

"Wait! You should wear your coat."

Angus blinked his astonishment. "Fer the lad?"

"As practice. When MacLean arrives, you'll need to present yourself as my butler." She held up a rag. "Wipe your hands, and put on the coat. For our plan to work, MacLean must think we're wealthy, which means that the butler would know how to answer the door properly."

"The lad'll mock me," Angus said darkly, though he took the rag and scrubbed at his hands.

"Not once he sees your fancy coat." She assisted Angus into the waiting coat of black broadcloth. He knotted a muslin cravat about his neck, muttering.

Sophia looked him over. With a bath and the black trousers that went with the coat, Angus would make an impressive butler. "Go on, now. You know what to do."

"Aye, answer the door and look bored. I've seen Poole do it time 'n' again fer the squire, but I'd never thought I'd be doin' it meself."

Sophia nodded encouragingly. She'd borrowed Angus and his wife, Mary, from the squire. Sophia and her father had very simple needs, and she had only two maids from the village who came once a week to help with the cleaning and cooking. With just Red and herself living here, most of the rooms had been kept in shrouds, the curtains drawn to keep out the damaging light and dust.

She smoothed Angus's coat and smiled. "If Jimmy teases you, he will have to answer to me."

"Very well, miss." Angus turned to the doorway. He took a step forward and then froze.

Something about his stance made Sophia pause, too. She followed his gaze to the glazed windows that flanked the front doors. Outlined in the bright sunlight was no short, scrawny lad but the figure of someone tall, broad-shouldered, and unmistakably masculine.

"He's come," she breathed, her heart thudding so loudly she was certain it was as audible as the thundering knock upon the door.

"Blast it," Angus swore. "And yer pa's nowhere to be found."

Red had gone to borrow a good coat from the squire. The local seamstress had worked night and day to produce six new gowns for Sophia, along with chemises, petticoats, and pelisses, and she hadn't had time to sew up a new coat for Red.

The knock thundered again.

Angus tossed her a glance over his shoulder. "Upstairs, miss! Ye can't see him like that."

Sophia looked down at her worn, ash-dusted gown. "Dear me, no! But . . . what about you?" She gestured toward his black-streaked breeches.

"If he says aught about it, I'll tell him I fell into the coal bin chasin' after a cat."

"It will have to do." She turned toward the stairs, ordering over her shoulder, "As we've practiced it, Angus! Let him in, and fetch him a glass of that horrid port we purchased in the village. When you're done, send Mary upstairs right away with a bucket of water. I need to wash."

Angus paused, one large hand on the doorknob. "Now? But MacLean's already here."

She lifted her chin. "I waited for Mac-Lean; now *he* can wait for *me*."

Angus grinned, "Very well, miss."

She swept up the stairs, turned down the hall to her room, and entered swiftly, undressing as she went.

Downstairs, she heard the sound of voices murmuring. Soon Mary was at the door, carrying a bucket of water. Sophia washed vigorously, shivering while Mary clicked her tongue in disapproval.

"Ohhh," Sophia said, wincing as she bent down to pick up her dropped towel. "My sore back."

Mary, plump and gray, shook her head. "I dinna know what ye are thinkin', miss. 'Tisn't right fer a lady of yer standin' to be doin' such work."

"Someone has to do it," Sophia said firmly. She dried off, glad she'd washed her hair the night before.

As soon as she was dressed in her chemise and stockings, Mary worked her magic with brush and pins. In an amazingly short time, Sophia's hair was twisted into a sophisticated style, one thick ringlet dangling before each ear. That done, Mary opened the new jewelry box Red had given Sophia. It contained what looked like a king's ransom in jewels but in reality would barely have paid the fine to spring a pickpocket.

Mary pulled out an ostentatious set of fake sapphires and clasped the necklace around Sophia's neck. Twin earrings soon hung from her ears, and a wide bracelet glittered from her wrist. That done, Mary crossed to the wardrobe and removed a silk gown of palest yellow, trimmed with ribbons and tiny flowers of Regent blue.

As Mary tied the last bow, Sophia turned to regard herself in the mirror. She was a small woman, smaller than most. Her pale yellow gown was smooth over her shoulders, the small sleeves topping her slender arms, the bodice decorated with tiny blue rosettes. The gown was fastened below her full breasts with a wide blue sash, her skirts a graceful drape of yellow silk.

Sophia wished her heart weren't thudding so hard. It was a pity MacLean had come today, when Red wasn't nearby to lend his support. Still, it was up to her to lure her victim to the rocky shore of loss by appealing to his vanity and challenging his manly pride. She smiled at herself in the mirror.

"It isn't perfect, but 'twill have to do."

"Och, miss! Ye look as pretty as a princess." Mary opened the door and stood to one side. "Careful going down the stairs; yer pa pried up a board in the third step."

"On the *steps?* Someone could get injured."

"So he's hopin'."

Sophia frowned. "I'll have Angus fix it. I want MacLean to hate the house, not die in it."

"Men never think, miss. 'Tis a sad fact o' life."

"Tell me about it," Sophia muttered. "Wish me luck. I've heard a lot about Mac-Lean, none of it good."

"Good luck, miss. Ye'll be able to deal with the likes o' him, I've no doubts about that. Now, off with ye! The man's waiting."

"Thank you, Mary." Sophia went to join their guest, her stiff back protesting. She paused on the top step and took a deep breath, willing away her anxiety. *I can do this,* she told herself. But another part of her whispered, *If I fail, I'll lose Mother's house — my house.*

Her throat tightened, then she straightened her shoulders and continued down the stairs, careful to avoid the loosened board.

What Sophia didn't know was that her

guest had seen it all: her graceful approach down the hallway, her pause at the top of the landing, her hesitation at the first step, and her change from tense to calm in the space of one movement.

Dougal stood beside the library door, which was back from the stairs, so while he could not see her face, he could easily enjoy her graceful descent down the stairs. And he found himself enthralled by the sight of the one thing he hadn't expected — an extraordinarily well-designed woman. He'd almost hoped, when he'd first caught sight of her on the landing, that she would not be his hostess, the woman who only thirty minutes before had been sabotaging his house.

But as he watched her float down the stairs, her face turned away at a regal angle, her blond hair piled high on her head, he couldn't help but wonder how she'd be in bed. A pocket Venus, she was tiny, made just for a man's pleasure.

Oh, yes, he was going to enjoy this encounter very, very much.

All of his earlier irritation gone, Dougal waited until she reached the bottom step, then coughed lightly.

She slowly turned to face him. If Dougal had been entranced before, nothing had

43

prepared him for this.

Her face was that of an angel, her lips pink and full, her nose small and up-tilted. But her eyes truly entrapped him. Thickly fringed by dark brown lashes that curled extravagantly, her eyes were a shimmery pale turquoise, light and yet vivid. It was as if he were looking into an especially pure pool.

By God, he would have this woman in his bed — he knew it with a fierceness that burned his blood.

The woman flushed, her hand coming up to her throat, a wary expression entering her eyes.

Dougal bowed, saying in his usual bored voice, "Miss MacFarlane, I presume."

She dipped into a curtsey, visibly gathering herself as she spoke in a rich, husky voice he instantly recognized. "Yes, and you are Lord MacLean, I believe. My father was so vague when he explained how he'd finally gotten rid of —" She stopped as if she'd said something wrong, then laughed lightly and shrugged. "That is, welcome to Mac-Farlane House!"

CHAPTER 3

Och, me dearies! If ye must fight with the one ye love, it'll save ye all sorts of trouble if ye begin from the winnin' side.
                    Old Woman Nora from Loch Lomond
                        to her three wee granddaughters
                                    one cold evening

Sophia fought the urge to step back. Mac-Lean was nothing like what she'd expected. His hair was the gold of a lion's mane and he was so tall that if she went up on her tiptoes, her head would barely reach his shoulder. She'd expected the lace that adorned his cuffs and edged his cravat but not the dangerously masculine air that accompanied it. All the silk and satin in the world couldn't soften the harsh edges that made him what he was — sensually handsome, boldly masculine, and temptingly dangerous.

Yet all of that faded before the impact of

his vivid green gaze. His eyes seemed to burn through her, sending answering quivers through her body.

She flushed as he continued to look at her, his deep green eyes traveling over her face. His gaze touched her lips and eyes, slipped down to her shoulders, lingered on her breasts, then fell to her waist and lower. The insolence of his gaze made her want both to hide and to throw back her head and dare him to continue.

But more than that, his arrogant stare made her want to best him, to take back not only her house but some of his confidence, as well.

"I suppose you know why I've come," he said, his voice deep and rich, with a hint of superiority that raked across her nerves. "I wish to view my new property."

Sophia kept her smile firmly on her lips. "My father informed me that you would be coming, my lord. We expected you much sooner."

His gaze dropped to her mouth. "I was detained."

Sophia curled her fingers into her palms. "How unfortunate. I am afraid my father is not here at the moment and won't return for some hours."

MacLean smiled, his sensual lips parting

to reveal white teeth, his eyes twinkling lazily. "Then we shall have to do without him."

"So we shall. I suppose you wish to see the house now?"

He gave an indifferent look around that set her teeth on edge, before turning his gaze back to her. "Later, perhaps. For now, I'd rather speak with you."

"Oh?" She inwardly winced at the squeak in her voice. She was not a woman to rattle easily, yet there was something heady and dangerous about this man, something sensually lethal.

"I must admit that I never expected to find such beauty here." His gaze raked her again. "It quite takes my breath away."

Sophia quirked a brow. He didn't look breathless. He looked calm and collected — a bit predatory, perhaps, but nothing to suggest that her appearance had been anything more than a pleasant surprise.

She wasn't vain, but men had been reacting to her strongly for a long time, and it was annoying that the one time it would actually be beneficial to make a man breathless, that wasn't happening.

Something glinted in his gaze, and he slowly looked her up . . . and down, his lips curving into a smile as heated as his look.

Sophia's breasts tightened as if she stood nude in a cold room, and she had to fight the urge to cover herself.

Good God, *she* was reacting to *him!* Never once in her twenty-seven years had that happened.

His gaze was as hot and immediate as a touch. "Had I known *you* were waiting, Miss MacFarlane, I would not have lingered, I assure you."

Flattery was something she knew how to deal with, and it was much better than this odd heat that simmered between them. "What a pretty compliment, Lord Mac-Lean. I don't know what to say."

He bowed. "I merely speak the truth. I daresay you've heard such before."

"And I'm certain you've spoken such before."

Amusement twitched his lips, though he said gravely, "I am sorry if you were left waiting on my arrival. I hope you were not bored."

"Oh, I managed to keep busy."

"I'm certain you did," he replied, almost under his breath.

Sophia cast a sharp glance at MacLean. Something about his manner made her wonder if he knew of her efforts to disguise the value of her house. The thought was

completely ridiculous, of course; there was simply no way he could know.

He smiled blandly, came forward, and took her hand in his. His fingers closed over hers in a firm clasp. "I apologize that some important business held me in Stirling longer than I anticipated." His gaze glinted almost challengingly. "I own quite a bit of property in that area. I would be remiss if I did not tend to it whenever I was in town."

Perhaps he hadn't been carousing, after all. Not that it mattered. What did matter was the way her skin tingled at his touch, as if the casual contact were something far more intimate. "I hope your business was profitable."

He bowed. "More than you know."

His voice was low, wickedly so. Sophia realized that her heart was thudding against her chest, her hands damp, an odd quiver in her knees. So this was what Red had meant when he'd warned her that MacLean was dangerous. Good God.

Enough of this! She freed her hand with light laugh. "I am sorry Red is not here t welcome you."

He raised his brows. "You call your fath by his given name?"

"I was raised on the Continent, so I da say my manners are somewhat differe

49

from those of the average London miss's. My mother and I accompanied my father from game to game. There are times when I miss traveling."

"You don't travel now?"

"Not often enough." Funny, she hadn't really allowed herself to think about it since Mama's death. But sometimes a picture in a newspaper or the mention of a far-away place would set her imagination flying, and an unfamiliar longing would engulf her. Red called it wanderlust. She called it silliness.

"Red should arrive in time for dinner." She sent MacLean a flirtatious glance from beneath her lashes. "You *are* staying for dinner, aren't you?"

MacLean's gaze narrowed with a considering look before he bowed. "Of course. I couldn't imagine doing else."

"Wonderful! Then you must also spend the night. We are miles from an inn, and I can promise that the sheets are fresh and clean." *And the beds lumpier than those at any posting house.*

She gestured toward the library. "Would you like some refreshment? There is sherry in the library."

He stepped beside her and captured her hand, tucking it into the crook of his arm.

His fingers tightened on hers ever so

slightly, and a jolt of awareness blazed through her. She caught her breath and glanced up at him, wondering if he felt the same.

His dark gaze flickered over her face, lingering on her mouth, before he smiled and increased the pressure a bit more. "I must thank you for being here. It would have been a cold welcome to arrive to an empty house."

She couldn't imagine MacLean being disturbed by anything, much less an empty house. She was going to have to rethink her plans a bit. Worse, she had to rethink her own reactions.

She was cold and hot at the same time, her stomach knotted, her heart pounding in the most curious fashion. She'd been prepared for a handsome man but not for such a *physical* one.

The lace and ruffles at his wrist and throat merely emphasized his bold masculinity. No fop had ever moved with MacLean's lithe animal grace, and certainly no wastrel had ever looked at her with eyes that burned with such promise.

He might be more than she'd expected, but she was certain she could handle him. She removed her hand from his arm and entered the library. "Here we are." She glanced around the almost bare room, noting with pleasure that it was chilly and rather damp.

She and Angus had dulled the paneled walls with a coating of wax and soot, removed the welcoming rugs and replaced them with torn and threadbare ones from the older parts of the house, taken all of the lovely furnishings to the attic and replaced them with bits and pieces from other rooms, none of which matched and which lamentably failed to fill the huge space.

She hadn't removed the books, fearing they might get moldy if she packed them away. Instead, she'd reorganized them, putting the odder, less readable ones at eye level and hiding the better, leather-bound tomes on the top shelves where they could be viewed only with a ladder. Or could have been, if she hadn't sent the ladder to the attic, leaving half the shelves out of reach.

She glanced at her guest, wondering what he thought of the dreary surroundings.

MacLean's gaze slowly encompassed the room, yet no expression crossed his face. Obviously, the poor man was trying to be polite.

She hid a smile as she walked to the sideboard. "I don't know why Red kept this old house. I daresay it was sentiment.

Mother always wanted to make it into a home, but she grew ill, and . . ." Sophia waved a hand. "As you can see, it would require a monumental effort just to make it livable."

MacLean turned his gaze her way. "Is the rest of the residence in such ill condition?"

"Some of it's worse." She turned up two sherry glasses and removed the glass top from the decanter. "I suppose you are disappointed in the house."

"It's not what I was led to believe. Your father described it quite differently when we were playing cards. He implied that the house was in impeccable shape."

Sophia gave a merry peal of laughter. "He didn't!"

"Yes, he did."

"I'm so sorry he misled you. Red can be quite . . . enthusiastic when gambling."

"I've since been told that he is one of the most notorious gamblers in Scotland. Had I known that, I would never have allowed him into the game."

"You outwitted him," she pointed out, pouring a good measure of sherry into each glass.

"*Luck* outwitted him. I had nothing to do with it."

"He hasn't played seriously since my

mother's death and isn't as adept as he once was."

While she, on the other hand, was better than ever. To her surprise, she'd enjoyed the hours of practice immensely. There was something about the game, the feel of the crisp cards beneath her fingers, the flicker of candlelight, and the breathtaking challenge of attempting to read her opponent's expressions and guess the strength of his hand.

As if MacLean could read her thoughts, he crossed his arms over his chest and regarded her with a faint smile. "What about you, Miss MacFarlane? Do *you* play?"

"Sometimes." She brought him one of the glasses of sherry and handed it to him, smiling up at him. "And sometimes not."

"Do you win?" he asked, cupping the delicate glass in his large hand.

"I win more often than I lose."

"That's quite a feat."

"I'm quite a good player." She returned to the sideboard and retrieved her own glass.

"Considering the fact that your father made his way as a gambler —"

"Pardon me, but Red prefers to call himself an 'arbiter of good fortune.' "

"I'm sure he does." He swirled the sherry in his glass, his gaze considering. "Miss

MacFarlane, pardon me for mentioning this, but you don't look like your father."

"I am said to favor my mother."

"She must have been a beautiful woman."

"She was," Sophia replied coolly. "She died more than ten years ago."

"I'm sorry to hear that," he said gravely, then tilted his head to one side. "I don't detect a Scottish accent, either. Your father's is quite strong at times."

"You have a bit of an accent yourself."

"My brothers and sister and I grew up here."

"Ah. I have no siblings."

"You're to be congratulated," MacLean replied dryly.

She smiled and drew one finger along the rim of her sherry glass, noting how MacLean's gaze followed the move intently. "Lord MacLean, you seem more interested in my history than in the house."

His brows rose. "You've been asking questions, as well."

So she had. Red always said an intelligent player knew his opponent's weaknesses. "I suppose I have been. Ask whatever you will; I have nothing to hide."

"We all have something to hide." He sent her a secretive smile and crossed to the small grouping of mismatched furniture before the fireplace. "Miss MacFarlane, you still haven't answered my question about your accent." He turned to face her. "You sound like every other London miss I've met, and yet you're here, in the middle of Scotland."

"My mother was English and quite well educated. She saw to it that I was, too."

"Mothers always worry about that, don't they?" He took a sip of sherry and grimaced.

Sophia did the same, wrinkling her nose. "It's atrocious, I know, but that's all that's left in the cellar besides a bottle or two of weak port."

MacLean set his glass on a nearby table. It slowly rocked to one side as if to topple over, then stopped. Then the glass began to slide. It moved slowly to the edge, where it came to rest, precariously perched at an angle.

MacLean's glance was surprisingly filled with laughter. "I thought I'd have to ask for another glass."

Sophia's breath caught in her throat, and she found herself drawn by the warmth that lit his green eyes, by the way his well-cut mouth curled as if beckoning her forward. She caught herself leaning toward him — actually leaning — and hurried to turn away, her skirts swirling as she did. She went to a small, chipped Sheraton chair by the fire. "Pray have a seat. I daresay you're tired from traveling."

"A little, perhaps." He moved to the faded red chair she'd indicated. As he lowered himself into it, there was a loud crack. One of the wooden legs snapped and broke, just as Sophia and Angus had planned when they'd sawed it half-through.

A normal man would have been tossed to the floor, but with a lithe twist, MacLean shifted his weight forward and managed to remain upright, turning to regard the chair as it collapsed.

Sophia swept to her feet. "Goodness! How horrid!" She narrowed her gaze accusingly at the chair. There was nothing like a little humiliation to set a man against a location, and it was a pity MacLean hadn't been thrown to the floor as she'd planned.

MacLean bent and picked up a piece of the broken chair, his expression unfathomable. "Horrid, indeed."

Her desire to smile fled. Did he suspect something? Could he see where Angus had cut the chair leg partway through?

MacLean hefted the leg in his hand, his mouth thinned.

Sophia cleared her throat. "I'll call the butler to remove that."

His gaze locked with hers. The chair leg still in his hand, he walked toward her.

Sophia licked her suddenly dry lips. She didn't know this man, not really. What was he going to do?

She gripped the arms of her chair. Should she run for help? Surely not. Nothing she'd heard had indicated MacLean was a man of violence. Of course, everything she knew of him was mere hearsay —

He stopped before her and stood looking down into her face with the faintest of smiles. He didn't look angry; he looked *knowing.* As if he understood exactly what she'd done and why.

A fear of another kind gripped her. Surely, he didn't. There was no way he could —

MacLean leaned forward. Sophia's heart jumped, her skin warming oddly when his arm brushed her shoulder as he leaned past her . . . and tossed the chair leg onto the unlit fireplace.

Sophia closed her eyes, inhaling the scent of his cologne, a subtle masculine mixture that sent a shiver up her spine. As her pulse eased, she slanted a look up at MacLean.

He smiled darkly. "It's a shame to waste good wood."

Sophia sent a resentful glare toward the broken chair leg. It was a shame to waste her and Angus's efforts, too.

She forced herself to shrug. "I'm sorry your chair collapsed, but the furnishings are in as poor repair as the roof."

He retrieved his abandoned glass of sherry.

"I assume the roof leaks."

"Only when it rains."

His eyes warmed with laughter as he watched her over the rim of his glass. "I'm surprised you countenance this place."

"I'm here for my father. Once he returns and you take the house, I will be on my way."

"May I ask where?"

"Italy, perhaps. Or France." She shrugged. "I haven't yet decided."

"I love Italy." His voice deepened the faintest bit. "I imagine Italy would love you, too."

To her surprise, Sophia's cheeks warmed. She had been the object of admiration for as long as she could remember, yet with this man, mere compliments seemed to be more. They were suggestions, enticements, blatant invitations. All without an improper word.

The men she'd known were mere pale imitations of the man before her.

It was more than the masculine beauty of his face. It was the powerful lines of his body, from his muscled thighs encased in knit breeches to his broad, commanding shoulders. He stood at ease, one hand in his pocket, yet she could sense the power that reverberated from him.

He was a man coiled to spring, to devour anything that might get in his way. And that, Sophia realized with some alarm, included her. Which was why she needed to regain control of the situation, and quickly.

She sank into the center of the lumpy settee, then gestured toward the small, rickety seat she'd vacated moments before. "Lord MacLean, pray have a seat. That chair is safe." And half the size of a regular seat. She *dared* him to be comfortable in it.

He eyed the chair and shook his head. "I believe I'll stand."

"As you wish." She smoothed her skirts, the movement of her slender hands drawing Dougal's gaze. She had the most kissable mouth and the most intriguing — and challenging — blue eyes he'd ever seen.

She was an intoxicating mixture, this woman who dared to trick him. She was beautiful beyond compare; he'd never met a woman so intoxicatingly appealing, her voice and movements matching the perfection of her face and form. It was a joy just watching her. Yet she was more than a beautiful face and body: she was intelligent and challenging, possessed a quick mind, and, unless he were mistaken, an even quicker sense of humor.

He had to know more about this woman. She was lovely, amazingly graceful — and damned sure of herself.

It was this last that intrigued him the most.

She regarded him now, calm and yet faintly challenging. "Do you have any questions about the house that I —"

"I have changed my mind."

She blinked. "I beg your pardon?"

"I believe I will sit, but not on this chair. The settee is the most welcoming piece in the room, especially with you sitting on it."

"Yes, but —"

He sat, his hip brushing hers.

She scrambled to move to one side, but he'd deliberately sat on the edge of her skirt.

Her gaze narrowed, and she said stiffly, "I beg your pardon, but you are sitting on my skirt."

Dougal smiled and leaned back, resting his arms along the back of the settee so that she was closed in by him. He found himself charmed by the thought.

"Lord MacLean, I have asked you kindly to remove yourself from my skirt. Please do so, or I will be forced to take more drastic measures."

"Such as?"

"Calling for Angus," she said flatly. "In case you didn't notice, my butler is larger than the average servant. He could easily pick you up and break you in two."

Dougal quirked a brow. "While that behemoth you call a butler could easily pick me up, he'd have to get close to me first."

She smiled smugly, setting Dougal's pride on edge. "I wouldn't try him; he's faster than he looks." She cast a glance down at Dougal's boots. "Plus, you'd have to race through the barnyard, which could prove fatal to your shine."

Damn this woman! She taunted with every phrase, teased with every look. He shifted so that his hip was even more firmly pressed to hers. "Miss MacFarlane, I believe —"

A knock sounded on the door, and Angus stuck his head in. "Excuse me, miss, but —" His brows lowered as he realized how close Dougal was to Miss MacFarlane.

Inwardly sighing, Dougal moved slightly, releasing the edge of her skirt.

She was up in a trice, sending him a glare before turning to her butler and saying in a firm voice, "Yes, Angus. What is it?"

The butler scowled, jerking his thumb

irritation.

He turned on his heel and left.

back over his shoulder. "Lord MacLean's man insists he be allowed to come in and —"

"Move out o' the way, ye jabber jaw!" came a rough voice behind Angus.

Eyes squinting with irritation, Angus said stiffly, "Just one moment, miss." With that cryptic statement, he disappeared into the hallway.

There was a bit of scuffle, and Angus's head lurched in through the opening, then disappeared. More scuffling sounded, then a loud *"Oof!"* followed by the appearancc of a man Sophia didn't know. He was short and square, with bow legs and a large, square head from which flowed a mass of salt-and-pepper hair. He was dressed in the height of fashion for a servant, his black coat and breeches neatly pressed, silver buckles at his boots and belt, a nicely starched neck piece stuck into his waistcoat.

"There ye are, me lord —" The servant's gaze dartcd from MacLean to her . . . and there it stayed, his eyes wide, his mouth half open.

"This is my groom, Shelton." MacLean flicked a cool glance at his man. "What is it?"

The groom collected himself by gulping

loudly. "Aye, me lord. Sorry fer —" He straightened his shoulders and said in a singsong manner, much as if he had memorized his lines, "What I meant to say was that the horses have been watered. They're ready to go, me lord."

"Stable them."

Shelton blinked. "Stable them? But, me lord, ye tol' me to —"

"Shelton," Dougal said softly, standing.

The groom snapped his mouth closed and bowed. "Yes, me lord. I'll stable them right away. How long will we be?"

Sophia was aware of MacLean's gaze on her face.

"I will need to stay a day or two in order to evaluate the house," he said.

Sophia said a short prayer of thanksgiving. She'd have time to persuade him to wager the house in a game of chance. Yet she had the uneasy feeling that perhaps it would be safer to let him go.

She shook off the ominous thought. Such ridiculous emotions! She needed to watch herself; her feelings for her home were already affecting her judgment.

"Of course, you'll need to stay for two nights — perhaps more, if you wish to see all of the lands."

MacLean looked at his groom. "We're

staying, then."

The man's shoulders slumped. "Aye, me lord." With an accusing glare at Sophia, the groom left.

Sophia dipped a curtsey and smiled up into MacLean's eyes, saying huskily, "I will be pleased for the company, my lord."

It was a trite but effective way to capture a man's attention. For some reason, they all seemed to fall for it. And for a second, so did MacLean. His gaze darkened, and he leaned forward ever so slightly, his expression intent.

But as quickly as he'd reacted, he also recovered, his face going smooth and blank. It was with a decidedly cool voice that he said, "So will I, Miss MacFarlane."

"There are still several hours until dinner. Perhaps we can while away the time with a walk in the gardens or a game of cards something." She looked up at him with a hopeful smile.

"I wish I could, but if I'm to stay the night, I will need to speak to my man and my portmanteau. I assume meals are set on country hours?"

"Dinner is at seven."

"Excellent." He bowed deeply. "Until evening, Miss MacFarlane."

She curtsied in return, fighting to hide

CHAPTER 4

Ne'er pass the point o' no return without bein' certain 'tis exactly where ye wish to be.

> Old Woman Nora from Loch Lomond
> to her three wee granddaughters
> one cold evening

Red shook his head. "I don't like this."

They were in the large storeroom beside the kitchen, where Mary had bustled Red after he'd returned from the squire's carrying the borrowed coat. Once there, he'd questioned Sophia about every detail of MacLean's arrival and their conversation in the library.

"I don't like it, either," Sophia agreed. It had been two hours since MacLean had excused himself from the library. He'd sent his groom to fetch his clothing, and Angus had escorted MacLean to the guest bedchamber.

Sophia had been hard pressed not to laugh when MacLean had tripped over one of the floorboards she and Angus had pried loose. Better yet, MacLean had ripped his lace-edged sleeve on a broken nail in the door-frame of his bedchamber. She knew because she'd heard his loud curse from the hallway.

Sophia had expected him to roar at the servants and demand things be repaired, but all he did was ask Angus for a hammer to protect himself from the loose boards and stray nails that seemed to plague Mac-Farlane House.

To Sophia's delight, Angus had gloomily replied that there weren't enough hammers in the whole of Scotland to do that.

Since Angus had left MacLean in his bedchamber, they hadn't heard a word from him. Perhaps the man was sleeping, although how could anyone sleep in such a damp room and with such a lumpy mattress and smoky chimney?

More likely, he was awake and seething at being forced to endure such horrid conditions. She wished she had been there to witness his reaction to the threadbare furniture with broken springs and flat cushions, the inadequate bed coverings for the chilly chamber (it faced north, where the wind was fiercest), a window that was nailed slightly open, and more.

Red turned to her, his brows lowered. "Something's wrong. I can feel it."

"You and your premonitions! Nothing's wrong."

"Then why do you look worried, too?"

"I'm not. Everything is fine. MacLean is just a bit more . . ." She paused to consider. "A bit more *everything* than I thought he'd be. It's as if everything he says has another meaning. I feel as if I'm at cross-purposes with him with every word."

"He's mocking us," Red said darkly.

"It's more as if he's looking for something, or trying to decipher a set of clues — though I don't know what, exactly. He can't know our plan, so it must be something else."

Red turned to look at her, his gaze steady. "Perhaps he's trying to decipher you."

That was possible, she supposed. He *had* reacted to her flirtation with interest, though he'd attempted to hide it.

Perhaps that was it. A curious wash of pleasure raced through her. And here she'd thought him indifferent to her. "He's used to the best London has to offer."

Red snorted. "There's not a woman in London who could hold a candle to ye, lass."

"You," Sophia absently corrected.

"You," Red agreed just as absently. He crossed his arms and sank his chin into his chest, mulling over the situation. "MacLean is sharper than I gave him credit for; I let his lace and silks cloud my vision. No wonder I lost to him."

Sophia shrugged. "MacLean's quick, Red, but so am I."

He beamed, his worry melting before her confidence. "That you are, lassie. I only worry that you don't realize the sort of man MacLean is."

"I know enough to be cautious."

"That's good." Red paced between the rows of dried herbs. "Angus said the man could hardly keep his eyes off you."

"Aye," Mary said, coming into the storeroom and pulling a sack from the wall. She tugged the cord, removed an onion, and rehung the sack. "I saw the way he looked at you, too. As if he might devour ye whole, like a bread puddin'."

The power to drive a man like MacLean wild with desire sent a dangerous thrill through Sophia, one she hadn't felt in years.

That was why her reaction to MacLean had been so strong. It hadn't been an answering attraction, just the thrill of controlling the passions of such an obviously powerful man.

Of course, it wouldn't last; such hot passions rarely did. But it only had to last long enough for her to entice him into a card game. Which meant she had to keep him at a deep simmer, at arm's length, but no more . . .

A pleasurable shiver raced through her. He was hot enough now to scald her fingers. That would work to her advantage, but she had to keep her wits about her more firmly than she had today. "This will work, Red. We just have to go carefully."

He placed a hand over hers and said in a bracing voice, "Ye'll beat him, lass, fer ye've the skill. I know we'd planned to stretch the game out over several nights to drive up the stakes, but I think we'd best do the trick and get it over."

"He may not throw the deed out the first night. He doesn't seem like a man who would let go of anything that's his."

"Perhaps I can goad him into it. He'll not want to look foolish in front of you; no man with pride would."

Sophia nodded slowly. "He has pride. A lot of it." She turned to Mary. "Is everything ready for this evening?"

"Yes, miss. The pork will be salted 'til it's hard, the soup peppered and cold, the lamb burned on one side, raw on t'other." Mary sighed. "It near broke my heart to treat such a good piece of meat in such a way."

"Aye," Red said with feeling. "I watched ye do it, and it near made me cry, too."

Sophia laughed and hugged her father. "When this is over, Mary will cook you an entire leg of mutton, perfectly roasted and seasoned."

His eyes brightened. "With mint sauce?"

"Aye," Mary said, beaming.

Red sighed happily. "Thank you, Mary." He placed an arm about Sophia and walked into the hallway and up the stairs to the main floor. "Just be cautious, lass. He's a charmer. I saw the way the women looked at him in Stirling. I don't wish to see you moping about the house, going into a decline after he's gone," Red teased.

"If I have a house when this is over, I shall be far too happy to mope," she returned with asperity.

Red chuckled, opening the door to the foyer. "That's my lass. I don't know what I was worried about; you'll never lose your heart."

Something about Red's certainty gave her pause. "Are you suggesting that I'm cold-hearted?"

"Nay, never think it. I only meant that

you're less emotional than most women, and —" He blinked at her expression. "Don't look like that — I didn't mean to upset ye."

She forced a smile. "Of course not." Still, a niggling worry pressed against her chest. It was true she'd never come close to losing her heart before, yet her contact with eligible suitors had been limited, since MacFarlane House was out in the middle of the Scottish countryside.

Then again, she probably wouldn't have come into contact with many eligible suitors if she'd been traveling the inns and taverns of Europe, either.

Red patted her shoulder, worry in his gaze. "Lass, I didn't think o' what I was saying. You've too much of your mother in you to be anything but passionate."

Reassured, Sophia smiled. "Mama was passionate about many things, wasn't she?"

"Och, your mother was a woman like no other. Logical and capable on one hand, yet on the other —" He stopped.

"On the other?"

"Nothing, lass. Just speaking off the top o' me head again."

"My," she corrected.

"My." He took her hand and patted it. "Just have a care with your heart. That's all

I'm asking."

"There's nothing to worry about. Mac-Lean is not the sort of man I'd be attracted to. He's far too arrogant."

"Glad to hear it."

She kissed his cheek. "Now, if you'll excuse me, I'm off to take my bath."

Sophia dashed upstairs, almost putting her foot down on the loose third step. "That could have been ugly," she murmured, hurrying on past.

She made her way down the hallway, deftly hopping over the loosened boards and pausing beside MacLean's door to listen a moment. She heard nothing, so she continued to her own bedchamber, where a hot bath steamed invitingly. Sighing with anticipation, she disrobed and was soon soaking in a hot tub, her feet propped up on one side as she ran a washcloth over her shoulders.

The hot water soothed her spirits and helped her mind to focus. MacLean's unexpected sensuality had disconcerted her, but now, the steam from her bath rising about her, her sore muscles relaxing as she soaked, she realized that she could turn the entire episode to her benefit.

"One battle does not a war make," she told herself firmly. Cheered by this, she rinsed off and climbed from her bath just as Mary arrived to help her dress.

When Mary had scurried back to the kitchen, Sophia sat before her mirror, a bronze silk gown framing her shoulders, paste diamonds gleaming at her throat and ears.

She collected her silk fan and a matching reticule, then went out to the hallway and down the steps, avoiding the loose board. She ran through her agenda for the evening, ticking off the items on her fingers. *Horrid meal, smoking fireplace, rattly windows, guttering candles, broken furniture, lopsided dining table and chairs, mismatched china —*

Caught up in her thoughts, she didn't see Dougal until she reached the bottom step.

He was standing beside the door to the dining room, arms crossed over his broad chest. He was dressed in formal clothes, his black coat smooth over his muscled arms and shoulders, his knitted breeches molded to his muscular legs. For some reason, the sight of those powerful thighs made her heart speed up and her body grow warm.

Dougal had already thought his hostess astoundingly beautiful, but her bronze silk gown was made to make a man's mouth water. The décolletage was low, revealing the full, rounded tops of her breasts over a scrap of cream-colored lace. A cream ribbon was tied beneath those breasts, the long ends fluttering down over her hips as if unable to stop caressing her delicious curves. The skirt was cut long in the back, so that it hung on the steps behind her and outlined the front of her legs in stark relief.

Every curve was accented, and the deep color of the gown made her hair appear more golden than ever.

God, he loved her hair. He burned to see it unbound, falling past her waist in a glorious sweep to her hips. His body tightened at the thought, and it was with a decidedly forceful move that he pushed himself from the wall and strode toward her.

She paused with an expression of . . . not fear, but perhaps . . . excitement?

The idea pleased him, and he grinned. "That's a lovely fan."

She looked down, blinking as if surprised to discover an exquisitely painted fan in her hand, then shot him a rueful look. "Oh, this. I'd forgotten I carried it."

"Distracted, are you?"

"Yes, and I'm sure you know why."

A pleased smile curved his mouth. "Because of me?"

"No," she returned smoothly. "Because

76

my father returned but a half an hour ago, and I'm worried he'll be late for dinner."

"I see. And here I had hopes that you might have missed me."

She sent him a dismissive smile. "I saw you not three hours ago."

Dougal knew a set-down when he heard one, though it was rare he was on the receiving end. It was an unpleasant sensation. "Yes, I was thinking about a nap, then . . ." He shrugged and glanced away. He didn't have to wait long.

"Oh, dear! The mattress was too lumpy, wasn't it?" Her rich voice lowered with false compassion. "I'm so sorry about that. Red refuses to purchase new mattress ticking when —"

"You misunderstand," Dougal said. "I didn't intend to take a nap, just to rest. However, the bed was so comfortable that I fell asleep anyway."

Sophia opened her mouth, then closed it. She'd spent *hours* stuffing his feather mattress with straw, wood chips, stones, and sticks. How could he possibly have slept? "How . . . how fortunate for you. My bed is as hard as a rock."

He leaned forward, so close that his lapel brushed her cheek, the scent of sandalwood engulfing her as he whispered in her ear, "Perhaps you need another opinion . . . about your bed."

His warm breath teased her ear, and she shivered but rolled her eyes. "No, thank you." She glanced up the stairs. "I hope Red hurries; I am famished."

"I am famished, as well." He tucked her hand into the crook of his arm. "Perhaps we should await your father in the dining room?"

"Of course." His casual touch was playing havoc with her equilibrium, her skin tingling as if he'd stroked her, but she managed a credible smile. "Perhaps we can find some sherry and —"

At the top of the steps, Red's door opened, and he came out, turning his head to one side as if listening.

Sophia took a step forward, releasing MacLean's arm. "Red! Lord MacLean and I were just going into the dining room."

Red turned a startled look their way and hurried down the steps. "Och! MacLean, I didn't realize you'd already come downstairs. I was going to escort you to the dining hall myself and —" His foot hit the third step, his boot catching the loose board.

Sophia started forward, but it was too late. With a loud yelp, Red toppled down in a blur of tangled arms and legs, landing at the bottom of the stairs with a sickening thud.

CHAPTER 5

Since the time of Eve, women've born the brunt of takin' care o' the ill. Meanwhile, men have done what they could to be the worst ill folk in the world. Life's simply not fair to the fairer sex.
                    Old Woman Nora from Loch Lomond
                         to her three wee granddaughters
                                    one cold evening

More than an hour later, Sophia came downstairs, pausing at the loose third step. She regarded it sullenly, then lifted her skirts to kick it. She pulled back her foot and —

"That won't fix it, you know." MacLean stood at the bottom of the stairs, arms crossed over his broad chest, amusement in his green eyes, his dark blond hair falling over his brow.

She dropped her skirts back over her ankles. "I know, but it might make me feel better." She came the rest of the way down the steps. "Thank you for riding for the doctor."

"It was the least I could do. How is your father?"

"He's asleep now, thanks to the laudanum." She peeped up at MacLean. "I suppose you heard him yelling as the doctor set his leg."

"I never knew there were so many rude words in the English language. Or French, German, Italian, Latin, or . . . there was another language I didn't quite recognize."

"Greek."

He paused, his eyes dark. "I daresay he is not happy that his daughter is now unchaperoned. A gentleman would bid his adieu."

"You can't leave!"

The words hung in the air. Sophia hid a wince and said again, in a more measured tone, "I'm sorry. I'm distraught over my father."

MacLean gave her a devastatingly sexy half-smile. "You misunderstood me; I said, a *gentleman* would bid his adieu." His voice, low and soft, rolled over her senses like liquid silk. "Fortunately for us both, I am not a gentleman."

"No?" She flicked a finger at the lace on his wrist. "You dress like one."

"I dress like a dandy. Or, as my oldest brother, Alexander, often says, like a 'damned dandy.' "

Her lips quirked. "Your brother sounds a bit harsh."

"You have no idea." He smiled. "As I was saying, dressing fashionably does not make me a gentleman."

"Fine. You are not a gentleman, and I am far from a child," she returned with a lofty wave of her hand. "I don't need my father's presence for protection."

"But perhaps I do."

She had to smile. "You don't need protection from me, Lord MacLean. I don't bite — though if I don't get something to eat soon, I may change my mind."

His eyes sparkled with laughter. "By all means, then, let us eat." He led the way to the dining room, standing aside to allow her to enter.

As she brushed past him, a hot sensation told her that his gaze was lingering on her posterior. She glanced back and found that she was correct. "Lord MacLean!"

He reluctantly lifted his gaze. "Yes?"

"Is something wrong with my gown?"

"No. There's absolutely nothing wrong with your gown. Or what's in it."

She should have been shocked by his

impropriety but instead was pleased he'd noticed. "Thank you. I must say . . ." She allowed her gaze to travel across him. "You fill your clothes well, too."

She'd thought to shake him, but Mac-Lean's green gaze heated, and he took a determined step toward her.

Sophia spun on her heel and whipped around the table, sliding into her seat. "I hear Mary in the hallway, so dinner will be served shortly. The soup course is already on the table." She gestured toward a soup tureen that sat, steam seeping from the lipped edge.

His gaze dark, MacLean nodded and took the chair across from hers.

She watched beneath her lashes as his chair rocked with his weight. MacLean scowled and grabbed the edge of the table. Angus had cut varying lengths from each chair so that some rocked, while others were at a distinct forward slant so that you had to press back to keep from sliding into the floor.

"Is something wrong, Lord MacLean?"

"This chair." He scooted forward and slipped a little. With a scowl, he stood and pushed his chair to one side, selecting another.

"Lord MacLean —"

"Dougal," he said firmly, sitting down in the new chair. This one rocked backward, and he lurched, as if afraid it would topple over completely.

Sophia coughed to cover her amusement. From the dark scowl turned her way, she hadn't succeeded.

"That's it." Dougal shoved back the chair and stood, glancing about the room. "Ah!" He strode forward and picked out a thin book of sermons from a set on a side table. He lifted the back of his chair, placed a book beneath one leg, and sat down. "Much better."

Sophia wished he weren't quite so enterprising. She and Angus had worked for hours to make every chair a uniquely uncomfortable experience.

Dougal peered into the soup tureen. "This looks interesting."

His foot came to rest beside hers beneath the table, his boot pressing along her slipper. Was it intentional or an accident? She moved her foot back.

His followed.

She moved her foot a bit to the right.

Again his followed, only this time he slowly, with feather-light precision, rubbed the edge of his boot along her foot. To her surprise, her skin prickled with awareness.

He caught her gaze. "Sophia?"

"Yes?" She realized he'd used her given name and stiffened. "I haven't given you leave to address me in that way."

"Since we've established that I'm not a gentleman, I thought we could dispense with all of society's silly rules."

Alarm fluttered through her. "Some of society's rules are necessary." For her peace of mind, if nothing else.

"Surely not the use of your name. That one lone rule can be tossed away. At least, until your father is well enough to join us."

Did that mean MacLean would stay longer than one night? She almost gave a bounce of exultation. *I could bring this to a close in three nights, if he'll give it to me.*

He smiled across the table, a wicked, knowing smile. "Would you care for some soup, Sophia?"

Her gaze dropped to where he held the soup tureen toward her dish, the ladle filled. She forced her mind to focus. "Yes, please."

"Yes, please, *Dougal*," he said, ladling soup into her bowl. "How much soup would you like, Sophia?"

The way he said her name made her think of a crackling fire. One might be drawn to the flame, but that didn't make it scorch any less.

She considered pretending outrage at his use of her given name, but didn't she wish to create more intimacy? Fan his desire so that he'd be at her mercy when she manipulated him into playing cards?

She offered him a fleeting smile. "Very well, Dougal." The name slid over her lips delightfully.

"Sophia suits you. Is that your full name?"

"Sophia Beatrice MacFarlane. Beatrice was my mother's name."

"It's lovely. My full name is Dougal Charles Alistair Donald MacLean." He gave her a rueful smile as he ladled soup into his bowl. "I inherited both of my grandfathers' names, as well as the name of one of my great-uncles."

"How sad." She peered into her bowl, noting with satisfaction the murky color and the globs of congealed fat that floated among half-cooked carrots and huge chunks of onion. The smell was even more unappetizing. "I'm fortunate that I never knew my grandfathers. They died before I was born, and from what I hear, neither of them was very pleasant."

Dougal lifted his spoon and slid it into his mouth. Immediately, a frozen look came over his face.

Sophia tensed.

He removed the spoon from his mouth.

Sophia gripped her own spoon tighter.

A slow red crept up his face, his eyes watering slightly.

Ha! Mary's soup was working its magic. Pleased, Sophia pretended to eat some soup.

Dougal slapped a hand on the table.

The dishes and Sophia jumped. "What's wrong?"

He pointed to his bowl with his spoon. *"That."*

"The soup? Why, whatever's wrong with it?"

"Nothing. That is the best soup I've ever had."

Sophia blinked. Surely, he hadn't just said —

He dipped his spoon back into his bowl and took another large bite. Though his eyes watered and his face turned a deeper red, he continued to eat, murmuring, "Excellent!" every third bite or so.

Sophia looked at her own soup, which reeked of garlic and pepper and onion. Mary had added a large amount of salt, as well. But watching MacLean eat with gusto made her question her perceptions.

What if Mary's natural ability to cook had overcome her attempts to provide an inedible meal?

Sophia dipped her spoon into her bowl and gingerly sniffed the contents, grimacing at the strong odor. Casting a puzzled look at MacLean, who was about finished with his soup, she put the spoon into her mouth.

The burning sensation of pepper mingled with the rancid taste of uncooked garlic and what could only have been salted dishwater. She jerked the spoon from her mouth and grabbed her water goblet, pouring it into her mouth to wash down the horrid taste.

Gasping, she glared with watery, accusing eyes at MacLean.

He seemed not to have noticed anything, too busy scraping the bottom of his bowl, as if afraid some succulent tidbit might have escaped him. Finding nothing more, he placed his spoon on the table and sat back, wiping his mouth with his napkin. "That was the best soup I've ever been served. I believe I'll have more."

"More? Are you . . . are you certain?"

"I'm positive."

Unable to believe her ears, Sophia placed her own spoon on the table and watched as Dougal refilled his bowl. Within moments, he was eating yet more of the soup, making appreciative comments as he went.

Sophia looked at the soup in her own bowl. Maybe the soup on the *top* of the bowl was not as good as the soup from the *bottom,* where all of the more edible layers might be hiding. Her stomach growled, and she wished she'd remembered to eat something earlier. Her father's accident had gotten in the way of that, too.

She picked up her spoon again and dipped it into the bottom of her bowl, trolling for a better sample. She lifted the spoon and took a hurried bite. This time, a sweltering fire began to simmer, a slow burn tickling her tongue. It simmered through her nose to her eyes, which watered as if she was standing in smoke. Choking, she gulped the soup down. Now her throat and stomach were also on fire. She dropped the spoon and grabbed at her water goblet, gulping as fast as she could.

As her eyes cleared, she caught Dougal's amused gaze. "My dear Sophia, whatever is the matter? You look a bit flushed."

"It went down the wrong way," she croaked.

His lips quirked.

The door opened, and Mary bustled in, followed by Angus. They carried an assortment of platters and plates, which they set on the table unceremoniously. Mary collected the used dishes, pausing when she saw the soup bowls. "Gor," she breathed when she picked up the nearly empty tureen. "Someone done eat the soup!"

"Never!" Angus said, his eyes as wide as saucers.

"All of it," she said, holding the tureen toward Angus.

He peered into it as if expecting to see a hole in the bottom. "Well, I'll be."

"It was excellent," Dougal said.

Angus sent Dougal a look of respect. "Ye must have an iron stomach."

"Indeed," Mary said, a worried look on her face. "I beg yer pardon, me lord, but do ye feel well? There was a bit of pepper in that soup."

Dougal shrugged. "I'm fine. And I must get that recipe to give to my own chef."

"Gor!" Mary blinked at him, unable to look away.

Angus did the same.

Dougal smiled inquiringly at Sophia. "I feel as if I've become an exhibit at the British Museum."

Sophia sent Mary a warning glance. "That will be all, Mary."

Mary placed the soup dishes and tureen on a tray, the heavy crockery rattling pleasantly. She turned to regard the large salver in the middle of the table with a doubtful air. "Shall I serve the meat before I leave?"

"No, thank you," Sophia said. "We will serve ourselves."

"I'm quite adept with a carving knife," Dougal said, eyeing the covered platters with evident curiosity.

Mary gave a reluctant curtsey. "Very well, me lord." She turned and followed Angus to the door. "We'll be right outside if ye need us."

"Thank you, Mary."

Angus couldn't seem to tear his gaze from MacLean's soup bowl as he made his way after his wife into the hall. "He ate it all, Mary," he repeated, as if he couldn't believe it. "He ate every drop."

Dougal waited until they'd closed the door behind them before saying in a reflective voice, "They certainly seem concerned about my predilection for soup."

"They are an amusing couple, aren't they? I never know what they'll say next."

"Indeed." Dougal turned his attention to the salvers on the table and lifted the cover from the first one.

On the platter sat the roast, half of it black, the other half bloody. A wilted sprig of parsley sat beside it, as if Mary couldn't quite allow the roast to leave her kitchen without trying to disguise it.

Silence hung over the table.

Dougal set the cover to one side and removed the covers from the other dishes: a bowl of something green that sat in an oily liquid; a thick slab of pork in the middle of a large, chipped platter; some turnips floating unappetizingly in water; and a basket of undercooked bread.

Sophia thought the turnips were a nice touch. *No one* liked turnips.

Dougal picked up the carving knife. "Well, my dear?" he asked pleasantly, an amused glint in his eyes. "How do you like your meat? Raw? Or burned to a charred mess?"

Sophia sighed. "The kitchen is in such poor condition that it's almost impossible to make a good meal. I don't know how Mary manages as well as she does." She picked up the closest dish and held it out to Dougal. "Turnips?"

"Of course I'll have some." He took the dish from her hands. "As will you."

"Oh, I don't think —"

A large spoonful of turnips plopped onto her plate.

She started to protest, but Dougal put even more onto his own plate.

To make matters worse, he added in a deep voice that made her shiver, "I love turnips."

It was indecent that the man could make

a sentence as abhorrent as "I love turnips" sound like an improper proposition.

But Dougal MacLean managed it.

"It's a pity about the kitchen," Dougal said. "I'll have to look at it. Do you think you might give me a tour of the house in the morning?"

Her heart lifted immediately. "Of course. We can do it first thing after breakfast." Oh, could she give him a tour! She couldn't wait.

Dougal picked up the carving knife and pointed at the roast. "Do you prefer burned or raw?"

"I'll have the burned portion, thank you."

"Excellent choice. The turnips will complement them perfectly." He winked at her and filled their plates with such amused spirits that Sophia found herself watching him through her lashes.

What was wrong with this man? Surely he wasn't used to such horrid meals? Yet to watch him eat with such enthusiasm, you'd think he was starving.

Perhaps that was it. He'd said he was hungry after his journey, then there had been the delay after Red's accident. No wonder the man was able to eat the horrid meal!

Dinner progressed, with Dougal asking questions about the house and lands. Sophia kept her answers as disparaging as possible, mixing in just enough actual facts to make her comments seem truthful.

Finally, Dougal placed his fork on his plate. "Are you finished? You haven't taken a bite."

"I had some bread and butter earlier, when Mary brought a tray for Red," Sophia lied. "I fear it quite spoiled my appetite. But you haven't eaten much, either."

"I ate so much soup, it filled me up."

Dougal stood and moved to her side of the table. "Allow me," he said, helping her slide back her chair. As she stood, his hands brushed against her shoulders, and her skin tingled.

She glanced at him, wondering if he felt the same, and found him standing close. Much too close.

He bent, his lips by her ear. "My dear Sophia, I realize you must spend some time with your father, but can I entice you to have a glass of sherry with me before you retire?" He traced a finger down her cheek. "It would make the horror of the library almost bearable."

It would also provide a chance to test his boundaries and discover his feelings about a game of chance. *Keep your eyes on the prize, Sophia.*

She smiled up at Dougal. "A bit of sherry would be just the thing. I can imagine nothing more pleasant."

His lips were but a few inches from hers. She found herself looking directly into his eyes, dark green with faint swirls of gray, his lashes shadowing them mysteriously.

Sophia's breath caught in her throat. She had to fight the urge to lean forward, ever so slightly, and press her lips to his hard, carved ones.

Her chest tightened. All she had to do was —

The door banged open, and Sophia jumped as Mary swept in, Angus hard on her heels. He gave Sophia an apologetic gesture. "Mary thought ye might be finished with dinner."

"Mary is correct. Lord MacLean and I will have some sherry in the library." She looked meaningfully at Angus. "I trust the fireplace has been prepared?"

Angus beamed. "Aye, it should just be catching proper-like now. Yes, indeed." He gave her a broad wink.

She almost winced at his obvious hint, glancing back to find Dougal regarding her with an urbane smile, nothing in his expression showing that he had understood Angus.

Relieved, she allowed him to escort her to the library. Her fingers rested on his arm, and she was amazed at the muscles she felt through the fine cloth of his coat. Were all men of fashion so strong?

Dougal looked down on Sophia's golden curls as she kept her gaze pinned on his forearm. In all his days, he couldn't remember being so amused. He still wasn't certain what MacFarlane and his tempting daughter were trying to do, begging him to stay and then making his visit so inhospitable, but he'd be damned if he'd leave before he found out.

His gaze dropped to the line of her neck and down to the tempting breasts mounded above that cream-colored lace. Whoever had made her bronze gown had known how to tempt a man; it showed just enough — and hid just enough — to make a man yearn to rip it off.

They entered the library, where a small fire was just catching in the fireplace. The room was still inordinately chilly, the colors and furnishings still dark and oppressive. But as Sophia entered, it seemed as if the gleam of her bronze dress and the diamonds flashing at her throat and ears lit up the entire chamber with a new, warmer light.

"Oh, dear. The fire isn't very well laid." She peeped up at him through her lashes in an endearing manner. "Would you mind?"

He reluctantly released her arm and bowed. "Of course." He crossed to the fireplace, his arm still tingling from her touch. He could almost taste the tension whenever she was near, and it was growing stronger.

Dougal's entire body was aflame. God, he loved the chase, the feint and parry as potential lovers fought for control of each other and themselves. And that was what he wanted from Sophia MacFarlane. Before he left, he was determined to have Sophia in his bed.

He looked at the fireplace and noted that even with a small flame, smoke was already seeping into the room. He grasped the rusty poker and stirred the small flame, scattering and weakening the blaze rather than making it grow higher. Though his efforts dimmed the fire, a thick curl of smoke immediately lifted up from the front of the fireplace.

From behind him, Sophia said. "Oh, dear. I forgot about that chimney. Actually, all the chimneys in the house are in disarray."

"Yes," he agreed. "Almost as if someone had bricked them partway up."

97

Her gaze darted to him, a crease on her brow.

He smoothly added, "I daresay it's nothing but age. My oldest brother lives in a castle built in the twelfth century, and every chimney smokes." He took a deep breath. "Ah, the scent of wood smoke! It reminds me of home."

She didn't look pleased.

Smiling to himself, Dougal moved to the small table holding the decanter and glasses. "Shall I pour the sherry? If you think you can stomach it."

She raised her chin. "I would love some."

"Excellent." He poured them each a glass and returned to her side. Their fingers brushed as he handed her the glass. He watched as she placed her lips delicately on the edge of the glass and slowly tipped it, letting the ruby liquid barely touch her lips before tilting it back down.

She wasn't drinking the sherry, just as she hadn't eaten dinner.

Dougal took a sip. It was acidic, but he'd had worse. "I hope your father is not too uncomfortable."

"He'll still be sleeping. I wish he'd watched himself coming down those stairs. He knew about that board, because he's the one who —" She stopped, then finished smoothly, "Who knows all of the loose boards in the house, and running down the stairs was foolish."

"I almost tripped over that step myself."

Her gaze flew to his. "You did?"

It amazed him how pale her eyes were. Set in such dark, thick lashes, they seemed almost to glow. "Yes," he said slowly. "I did."

Her cheeks flushed, and she looked genuinely unhappy. "I'm sorry about that. I'll have Angus fix it."

"I already asked him to do it when the doctor was with your father."

"Oh." She frowned a moment. She sighed impatiently, as if shaking off an unwelcome thought, then set down her glass and crossed to a small table by the window. "Goodness, I am restless tonight."

"Perhaps we should do something to distract your mind from your father's condition." He took a reflective sip of sherry. "Do you have a chess set? We could play that, I suppose."

"There's no chess set here. However," her voice quickened slightly, "I do believe there are some cards."

"I had no doubt there would be," he returned.

She shot him a sharp look. "What do you mean?"

"Since your father is a notorious gambler, naturally there would be a pack of cards somewhere in the house."

"Very true." She turned to the small table and opened a drawer, removing a deck of cards, the evening light caressing her cheek. "This will be just the thing to keep my mind from my troubles."

He crossed to join her at the table. "Excellent! I never turn from a game, myself." He set down his sherry and pulled back a chair for her, waiting until she seated herself and then taking the chair opposite hers.

She watched him from beneath her lashes, noting his athletic grace and the way the lace at his cuffs dropped over his masculine hands with such effect.

Idly, she shuffled the deck, her fingers moving nimbly over the cards.

Dougal found himself watching her hands, the way her slender fingers caressed the cards. He thought of those fingers caressing him, sliding over his —

"Dougal?"

His name slid through her lips like velvet over bared skin. His heart thundered in his ears; his body tightened. "Yes?"

Her eyes, so pale and yet so bright, met his. "I was wondering . . ." The sound of the cards flipping through her lissome fingers

100

filled the quiet.

He leaned forward, impatient. "Yes?"

"Did you bring money with you, or shall we play for markers?" She flipped the stack of cards to the table with a professional twist of her wrist. "I don't play for less than a guinea a hand."

His lips twitched. "The question is not if I have money. The question is, do you?"

"I don't need funds, as I don't plan on losing," she said, her gaze mocking.

For a moment, he thought he'd heard her incorrectly. Slowly, he said, "I beg your pardon, but are you saying you could *beat* me at a game of chance?"

A dismissive smile rested on her lips. "Please, Dougal, let's speak frankly," she drawled softly. "Naturally, I expect to win; I was taught by a master."

Dougal was entranced. He'd been challenged to many things before, but no one had so blatantly dismissed his chances of winning. "A guinea a hand?"

"At least."

"I didn't realize I'd need a note from my banker, or I'd have brought one with me."

Her eyes sparkled with pure mischief, which inflamed him more. "If you've no money with you, then perhaps there are other things we can play for."

The words hung in the room, as thick as the smoke that seeped from the fireplace. Like a blinding bolt of light from a storm-black sky, everything fell into place. *This* was why she and her minions had worked so hard to convince him that the house was worthless. If he thought it of low value, he'd be eager to wager the deed.

Of all the devious plots!

Yet Dougal found himself fighting a grin. He'd been feted and petted, fawned upon and sought out, but until now, no one had gone to such lengths to *fleece* him.

Dougal couldn't look away from Sophia. He knew his own worth; women had paid attention to him for so long that he took it for granted. He'd dallied and toyed, taken and enjoyed. But never, in all of his years, had he so desired any woman as he did this one. The irony of it was that she desired him, too — but only for the contents of his pocket.

Dougal didn't know whether to laugh or fume. He should be insulted, but instead he found himself watching her with new appreciation.

Who was this woman? She was such a mixture of question and half-answer that he might never know her. While her appearance and behavior were those of a gently bred woman, he couldn't forget his first sight of her, dressed in soot-smeared clothes, helping Angus brick up the chimney.

There was so much about Sophia Mac-Farlane that intrigued him — and it dawned on him that perhaps this was why the women of London had palled. He needed someone less concerned about propriety and more willing to bend rules. Someone deceptive. Someone more like himself.

"Sophia, what are you offering as a wager?"

"You first," she said calmly, bold amusement glimmering in her gaze. "What do *you* have to offer?"

He was even more aware of the seductive line of her shoulders and the tantalizing curve of her breasts, hidden by that damned piece of lace. "I have funds in my London bank. I could draw markers against that."

"No, thank you."

He raised his brows.

"I have no plans to travel to London anytime soon, to gather the funds from a marker."

"So you won't take my markers."

"No, but . . ." Her gaze sharpened, though her voice remained soft. "You could use the deed to this house, such as it is. I'm sure you must still have that in your possession?"

There it was. "Of course."

Sophia deftly shuffled the cards, her fingers flying. "Well, MacLean? Will you play for the house?"

He crossed his arms and leaned back. "I might, *if* you are willing to offer something of equal value."

"Equal to this house?" She flicked her fingers in the air. "Considering its condition, I think I might come up with something." Her fingers came to rest on her necklace. It sparkled against her pale skin, like dew on a flower. "What about this?"

He eyed it from across the table. Though it sparkled beguilingly, he knew better than to trust mere flash. "No."

She smiled serenely. "Why not? It's a lovely piece."

He regarded her through narrowed eyes, considering this, then held out his hand. "Let me see it."

Her fingers tightened over the necklace, her smile faltering. "You don't trust me."

"No. And you'd be wise not to trust me."

Her hand dropped from the necklace, and she said stiffly, "I have changed my mind. I don't wish to wager my necklace after all."

"Because it's fake?"

Her eyes flashed. "No. Because my father

gave it to me, and it's precious."

Dougal crossed his arms over his chest. "Well, then. If you won't wager your necklace, what *will* you wager?"

"I suppose a marker is out of the question."

He shrugged. "You wouldn't take mine."

"But I don't have any jewelry I wish to part with."

"Not unless you'll allow me to examine it. I have quite a good eye for jewelry."

"I'm certain you've bought many pieces." Her voice held delicate sarcasm.

"I like a woman in diamonds," he replied softly. "And nothing else." He pursed his lips, regarding her through half-closed eyes. "I wonder if . . ."

"If what?"

"I'm not willing to wager the house . . . yet."

Her eyes sharpened. "Yet?"

"I need to see more of it, get a better sense of its worth. Once that's done —" He shrugged. "I might be willing to wager it."

She tried to look disinterested but couldn't mask her disappointment. "I suppose that makes sense."

"However, I have something else to wager: the necklace from the diamond set your father lost to me."

Her eyes glittered with interest. "Against?" she asked quietly.

"The sight of you wearing it — naked."

A delicate blush touched her cheeks, but her gaze never wavered. "You were right; you aren't a gentleman," she said huskily.

"And you aren't a lady of quality. I'd say that makes us a matched pair."

"I may not be the daughter of a duke, but neither am I a light skirt. I won't wager my virtue," she said sharply.

"I wasn't asking for your virtue. Just a moment to appreciate your charms in their natural state. But if the thought frightens you —" He waved a hand in the air dismissively.

Sophia regarded him stonily. She would not fall for the oldest manipulation in the book; she was no child to be double-dared into doing something she'd regret.

But neither was she the sort of woman to quit. If she wished to win back her house, she had to inflame this man, make him desire her beyond the bounds of common sense.

Her heart thudded as she dropped her gaze to the cards beneath her fingertips. "I won't disrobe."

His gaze locked with hers. "No?"

One word had never sounded so persuasive. She shook her head. "Not for a mere necklace."

"I see. What will you do for a mere necklace?"

She considered this a moment. "I will let down my hair."

His gaze locked on her hair, a stillness to him that made her uneasy. Finally, to her surprise, he nodded. "Very well."

She blinked. "You agree?"

A smile flickered across his face. "I love a woman's hair — it is one of my weaknesses. I think seeing yours unbound, streaming over your shoulders, would be one of the most sensual things I've ever witnessed."

Well, when he put it like *that,* it made her wish she'd held out for the entire set, not just the necklace. "We are decided, then: the necklace against my hair. Only . . . you must promise you won't touch. That's not permitted."

She wasn't certain why she added that caveat. Perhaps because she was afraid of herself, of the effects if she touched *him.* One of them had to be in control, and she was determined that it be her.

He didn't move, but she sensed a change in him. He was intent, focused on her as never before, his green eyes burning brightly. "I would never touch you unless you desired it."

Sophia's fingers trembled. Could she do this? Did she dare?

She felt a strange exhilaration, almost a hunger. He was playing right into her hands. "I agree, then." The words feathered over her lips, a breath and yet more. "The diamonds were my mother's."

"And of exceptional quality, I might add. I was quite pleased with them."

She nodded and shuffled the cards once more. Oddly, she felt no fear, only a wild desire to see what might come of this madness. If she wished to win back the house, she had to become bolder, had to prove to him that she was his equal in daring, as well as everything else.

She straightened her shoulders, the gesture lifting her bosom and drawing his attention. "Shall I deal, MacLean? Or will you?"

He chuckled, the sound low and seductive. "You are an intriguing woman, Sophia Beatrice MacFarlane."

"But not a lady, as you so eagerly pointed out," she said with a sniff.

"There are many definitions of the word *lady*."

"Yet I doubt any of them apply to me."

Dougal raised his brows. There was something exquisitely provoking in the way she said that, looking like every man's image of an angel, all blond beauty and angelically sweet smile. Yet in her eyes lurked an entrancing gleam of deviltry.

His body leapt at the sight, not just in response but in recognition. He was so bored with London's amusements, women, wagers and cards and brandy. Bored with following a mindless cow path of propriety, that stifled the air and attempted to rob him of his sensual nature.

More than anyone else he knew, he luxuriated in the niceties of life. He enjoyed the sultry fragrance of an unlit cigar, the warm tincture of good brandy as it slid over his tongue, the silky slide of satin sheets, the crisp outline of a woman's naked figure reclining against his pillows, the seductive clink of ice in a waiting glass . . .

When he'd first arrived in London, he'd experienced such a wealth of sensory stimulations he'd thought they'd never pall.

Yet less than a year later, he knew his error: newness wasn't enough — he needed originality, as well. With Sophia, he might have found both.

She was breathtakingly beautiful to behold, her hair soft as silk, her voice rich and melodious, her skin exotically scented with rose and jasmine, her body lushly formed.

She was the perfect woman in all ways but one: she was doing her damnedest to fleece him out of MacFarlane House.

Thank God he'd discovered her devious plans; he wasn't certain he'd have escaped whole, otherwise. She drew him in as effortlessly as a candle draws a moth, just by being. Had he ridden in unaware, he could have been duped. The thought stung a bit more than he'd have liked.

She laid the cards on the table before him, her eyes aglow in the candlelight, a faint tremble in her voice. "Well, MacLean?" she asked, her voice teasing, daring, and excited all in the same breath. "Do you dare?"

CHAPTER 6

So there he was, the laird of Clan Mac-Lean, facin' the dreaded White Witch. She'd already placed her curse upon him, but he hadn't given up yet, thinkin' he could sweet-talk her into takin' back the curse. What he didn't take into account was that he might talk sweet, but she tasted sweet. And that's another power altogether.

Old Woman Nora from Loch Lomond
to her three wee granddaughters
one cold evening

Sophia's entire body tingled, her gaze drawn to MacLean's lips. She placed her elbows on the table and rested her chin against the back of one of her hands. "Do you have my mother's diamonds with you?"

"I do." He reached into his pocket and pulled out a velvet pouch, untied the string, and tipped it over. A river of diamonds and gold spilled onto the table.

Sophia reached for her mother's necklace, but his large, warm hand covered hers.

"*Tsk, tsk,*" he drawled, his eyes bright. "You know the rules."

"I do," she said pertly. "And the first one was no touching. I wish to examine the set in the light — unless you fear I might discover you've traded them out for fakes?"

He grinned and placed a kiss on the back of her fingers. "Very well. You may examine the items."

She'd never felt so alive and so amazingly clear-headed. It was as if she'd been asleep for years and was only now awakening.

Was this how Red felt when he gambled? If so, it was a wonder he'd been able to quit when Mama had died. For the first time, Sophia wondered what else her father might have given up all those years ago.

She picked up the necklace and trailed it between her fingers. The metal was warm from resting in Dougal's pocket.

"So?" Dougal's deep voice broke into her thoughts. "Are you satisfied it is your mother's necklace?"

She gently set the necklace back on the table. "Yes."

"You might want to look at the whole set — in case we make an additional wager."

Her heart skipped a beat. *Please, make an additional wager!* "I don't need to examine the rest of the set. I can see it's all there."

"Very well." He scooped up the diamond set and placed it on top of the pouch, a glittering mass of diamonds and gold on the crushed red velvet. He slid it to the center of the table.

She slid the cards toward him. "Shall we play *Vingt-et-un?*"

His brows rose. "Twenty-one? I thought you'd pick something more prone to strategy."

"Tonight I feel like wagering it all on the flip of a card."

Something glimmered in his eyes. "As you wish. Do you want to deal?"

"I don't wish you to think I've cheated, when you've lost."

"Oh, I will watch you too closely to allow that." He waved a hand. "Continue."

Smiling at his bravado, she took the cards and shuffled them, her fingers flying. She loved the feel of the cards in her hands. She would play to lose this first game; she needed to tempt MacLean into wagering more. And then more. Until he was so eager to win that he made a mistake. That's all she needed: one mistake.

She watched her opponent from beneath

113

her lashes, considering him dispassionately. He was a man of jaded tastes. If she wished to capture his attention, she had to be something fresh. Something different.

She placed the cards on the table. "Do you wish to cut the deck?"

After a moment, he shook his head. "Not this time."

A faint smile tickled her lips. "Now you are the one being trusting."

"I don't see that I can lose this wager. On one hand, I get the diamonds. On the other, I get you."

His deep voice sent a shiver up Sophia's back.

For the veriest instant, her hands quivered on the cards. She gathered her composure and dealt out his first card, a five.

His eyes glinted. "Five is my lucky number."

"How fortunate for you." She dealt herself a queen.

"You are ahead, my love."

"For the moment." It seemed as if every object, every bit of light in the room, was focused on them and them alone.

He tapped the table with one finger. "Another."

She flipped over the top card. A six landed beside his five. "Eleven," she said.

"So it is."

Sophia flipped over another card.

"A three," he said. "You have thirteen. I hope you don't believe in luck."

"I don't," she replied coolly. "I believe in ability and effort."

He regarded her somberly. "I don't suppose you might wish to increase our wager?"

Already? This was going to be so easy. "What shall we increase it to?"

He gestured toward the diamond set. "The earrings from the set."

"Against?"

"A touch." His voice held a smoky promise.

Her gaze drifted to the glittering diamonds. One touch — just one — would inflame him all the more.

She knew it would. She knew it because it would also inflame her. "Very well. One touch. For no more than one second."

He frowned. "For the earrings? They are diamonds."

"I know what they are. I also know my worth."

He grinned, his teeth white. "You drive a difficult bargain."

"Are we agreed, then?"

He nodded and leaned back, his gaze hooded as he pointed. "Another."

She flipped over a card. "A two. Now you have thirteen, as well."

Irritation flashed across his face. "It's your turn."

She placed her fingertips on the deck, her heart quivering. So much depended on the next card. She slowly drew it and placed it beside her others. "A four. That gives me seventeen." She forced a pleased smile to her lips; she'd wanted to lose this hand, blast it.

"You can't take another card without going over."

"Perhaps I won't need to." Sophia lifted the top card from the deck and placed it beside Dougal's cards. An eight shined up at him.

There was a moment of silence.

When she looked at him, he was watching her, a smile curving his mouth. "I win."

"Not yet," she said tartly. "I have one more card."

"Yes, but it's highly unlikely you'll draw a four."

"Unlikely but not impossible." She lifted the card from the deck and held it, afraid to look but too excited not to. With a sharp intake of breath, she flipped the card over.

It was a five. She'd lost.

Dougal pushed his chair from the table,

the legs sliding across the rug with a whoosh. "You, my love, have a choice to make. Shall I help you put the necklace on? Or take your hair down?"

Her heart beat faster. "I can do that myself, thank you."

"A pity." He looked around the room, considering every aspect. "Please stand by the window. The light will be better there."

Sophia crossed her arms. "I am not going to stand in front of a window where anyone might see me."

Dougal grinned. "Who would see you? We're in the middle of nowhere."

"Angus might have to go to the barn, or your groom might wander across the front, or —"

"Very well! Stand where you wish." His tone was tight with urgency.

Excellent. She wanted him desperate.

She walked to the darkest corner, turned, and waited. "Here."

"It's pitch dark over there."

"You may bring a candle."

He sighed and carried his chair to her corner. "Fine."

She swept past him, took the necklace from the table, and returned to where he stood. "I assume you want me to wear this now?" She handed him the necklace.

His lips twitched. "This isn't quite the way I'd envisioned this."

"I'm certain you imagined a grand seduction."

"Perhaps."

"For one hand of cards?" She gave him the smallest of smiles. "Be realistic, MacLean." She turned. "Would you fasten the necklace, please?"

The cold necklace draped over his fingers as he looked at the back of Sophia's neck. Its delicate line drew him, the soft hair springing forward, golden and fragile. It was his favorite place to kiss a woman.

Suddenly, he was aware of her scent, a seductive mixture of jasmine and rose that made him think of sunny fields and warm summer days. He closed his eyes and drew in the scent, his fingers tightening over the necklace. It was too much. He instinctively lowered his head to taste her, pausing just shy of touching her.

His mouth hovered over the sweet spot, his breath warm on her skin, the faint scent of her perfume tantalizing him further . . . pulling him . . . drawing him forward . . .

"MacLean?" Sophia's husky voice broke into his thoughts. "You . . . you may touch me for one second."

One second wouldn't be enough. An hour

wouldn't come close. Two weeks? Not even that. He needed a month, two, perhaps ten, to enjoy her fully.

But all he would get was his time here. Once she realized he wasn't about to be cheated out of his house, she'd never want to see him again.

He sighed, straightened, placed the necklace about her elegant neck, and clipped it closed, his body aching with desire.

She turned to face him, her eyes sparkling with excitement.

An answering wave of excitement flooded Dougal. Bringing a candelabra to a small table in the corner, he lit each candle, holding Sophia's gaze from the other side of the flames. The light bathed her in a golden glow, making her look more ethereal than ever before.

He sank into the chair and leaned back, letting the sight warm him more.

She took a deep breath, then reached to pull a pin from the golden hair piled on her head.

"Wait."

She paused.

"Slowly."

She grasped a pin and slowly pulled it free, a thick strand of blond hair falling to her shoulder with a whisper.

She was painfully beautiful in the candle-light as she released golden curl after golden curl, and Dougal's body tightened more with each passing second. Her hair was even longer than he'd imagined; thick and silken, it flowed over her breasts, down to her waist.

Every movement was pure agony and pure delight, her perfectly formed arms casting shadows over her face, then allowing the light to caress her parted lips, her creamy skin.

Dougal couldn't look away.

Finally, the last strand of hair was released. The necklace gleamed against her creamy skin, partially hidden by her hair.

Sophia met his gaze, her voice almost a whisper. "There. I have paid my debt."

"Not yet." He stood. "There is the matter of the touch."

Delicate pink stained her lovely silken skin. "Oh. That."

He stood before her and looked down at her.

She peeped up at him, her thick lashes shadowing her eyes. "Should I . . . should I move?"

"No."

She nervously wet her lips.

Dougal almost groaned, holding his control as tightly as he could. He began at her hip, holding his hand a bare inch from her.

"What are you doing?" she asked, her voice breathless.

"Not touching you . . . yet." Slowly, as if he actually were touching her, he curved his hand over her hip, to her waist, then up. He paused over her breast, cupping his hand to the exact right size, yet he did not touch her.

She swallowed, her breath coming faster. Her breast came perilously close to his hand, and he moved back the tiniest bit.

He could feel the pull of her, an invisible connection so strong it made him want to step away as much as it made him yearn to move forward. He could tell she felt it, too. She was panting as if she'd run a race, her skin flushed and dewy, her eyes locked on his as if she'd never look away.

He slowly lifted his hand beneath the silken mass of her hair to the delicate line of her collarbone, still not touching, his fingers a bare half inch from her skin. The diamond necklace gleamed, and he knew it would feel cool against her warm skin.

Her head tilted back as she unconsciously moved to give him access to her neck. He bent then and pressed his lips to the spot where her pulse beat wildly in her throat, right beside the necklace.

Sophia closed her eyes and grasped his broad shoulders as his feather-soft kiss jolted through her, sending wave after wave of sensual heat.

Her skin tingled, her senses reeled, her heart pounded so loudly she thought she might collapse. Just as her knees wavered, he pulled away, his lips branding her neck as surely as the touch of hot metal.

They looked at each other. Dougal's eyes were so dark they appeared black. His face was set, with deep white lines down either side of his mouth . . . the same mouth that had tasted the tender skin on her neck.

Sophia shivered. She should do something, say something. But what? All she could think were the words that had entered her mind the second he'd touched her: *Don't stop. Don't stop. Don't stop.*

She took a shaking breath. "We are even now." With trembling hands, she tried to lift her hair back into place and pin it, but her hands shook so much that she couldn't.

Dougal stood watching her, his expression unfathomable.

She gave up, letting her hair fall back around her. She could only hope neither Angus nor Mary would see her on her way to her room. "I . . . I should retire now."

All he did was nod, roughly.

Sophia backed toward the door. "I'll — I'll bid you good night and —"

"Wait."

She didn't move, couldn't have if her life depended on it.

He walked toward her, his gaze caressing her hair, her lips, and lower.

Sophia stood statue-still as Dougal stopped before her, reached up, and slid his warm hands about her neck.

Her heart thundered and her lips parted. He stepped back, the backs of his fingers grazing her breast as the necklace slid loose from her neck to drop into his hand.

He tucked the necklace into his pocket. "I believe this is mine."

Sophia's euphoria evaporated in an instant. "I forgot I was wearing your necklace."

He lifted his brows. "It's not an issue now." He walked to the door and swung it open. "Shall I escort you to your room?"

Ha! As if she'd allow him. She lifted her chin and sailed past. "No, thank you," she said over her shoulder. "I know the way quite well."

He followed, his boots loud on the stairs behind her. "I merely thought to enjoy your company a few moments more."

She halted on the top step, forcing her

lips into a smile. "I don't think I could handle any more enjoyment this evening."

He grinned, his eyes twinkling wickedly. "Very well. I suppose it's too much to ask for that tour of the house in the morning?"

"I thought we'd take a look at the lands first and then the house later in the afternoon. It will be easier on the horses if we ride when it is cooler."

"Until morning, then." He gave her a long look of triumph, amusement, and something else that left her strangely breathless. "Good night, Sophia."

A moment later, she was standing alone in the hallway, looking at his closed door.

CHAPTER 7

The moment ye think ye've got a man tight in the palm o' yer hand, he'll slip out 'twixt yer fingers and leave ye wonderin' what happened.

Old Woman Nora from Loch Lomond
to her three wee granddaughters
one cold evening

"MacLean did *what?*" Red struggled to sit upright in bed.

It was early the next morning, and Sophia sat with her father in his bedchamber. She picked up the laudanum bottle and uncorked it. "Yes, MacLean did exactly that. And would have smacked his lips the entire time, if he'd been less well bred."

"That — that — that —" Red sputtered, his white nightcap slipping to one side. He forcefully plopped it back in place. "And he seemed like such a refined fellow!"

Sophia picked up a spoon from the side

table and filled it with laudanum. "I was shocked, too."

Red eyed the spoon of laudanum. Every time he moved, he winced, but except for that, he was fine. "I don't want any laudanum. A man can't think when he's dosed up with that stuff."

"You had two spoonfuls last night, which is why you were so muddled. The doctor said you'd only need one today."

"I won't have any." Red sent her a hard glance. "Tell me more about MacLean. I still can't believe that he — lass, are you certain? He couldn't have eaten that horrid soup!"

"He did, and he even pretended to like it."

"Pretended?"

"No one could have liked that meal." She wrinkled her nose. "Mary was mortified."

"Mary can be mortified all she wishes; we can't have MacLean da—"

Sophia slipped the spoon into his mouth and dumped the contents.

Red choked, his face contorting, and he looked around wildly.

"Do *not* spit that out."

He glared at her, and after what appeared and sounded like a heroic effort, he swallowed the laudanum. "Blech! There! I hope

126

ye're happy!" He grabbed up a hand cloth and began rubbing his tongue vigorously.

She calmly replaced the spoon and recorked the bottle. "As I was saying, Mac-Lean swore that he liked every dish at dinner, even the turnips. They were so hard it almost broke my knife to cut one."

"Hm. That's very odd, it is." Red's sharp gaze rested on her face. "What about after dinner? Was he willing to play cards?"

Sophia began to clean the small table beside the bed. "Yes. We played for Mother's necklace."

Red rubbed his hands together. "I knew you could handle him, Sophie! You'll have him eating out of your hand in no time. You let him win, didn't you?"

"Let" wasn't quite how she'd put it. She *should* have "let" him win, but she'd had to fight off a tremendously competitive impulse, one that had surprised her. "Of course he won. He was quite pleased with himself."

"Perfect." Red lay back against his pillows and smiled. "How I wish I could have seen you play."

"There wasn't much to see. I lost."

"Nonsense. You learn a lot about a person by the way he plays cards."

Then it was a good thing no one had seen

her play.

"How many hands did you play?"

"One. It was an introductory game, so to speak." It had certainly introduced Sophia to the dangers of flirting with a practiced man.

Red regarded her for a long moment. "Ye look a mite pale this morning, lassie. Is something wrong?"

Other than the fact she hadn't slept a wink, her peaceful slumber disturbed by memories of MacLean's warm lips pressed to her naked skin, not a thing. "I'm fine," she said shortly.

Red caught her hand. "Lass, was he rude to you?"

She laughed. "Not at all."

He released her and winced. "I'm sorry if I sound like a worried old man. Must be the laudanum."

"It must be. Now rest." Sophia busied herself smoothing the blankets.

All last night, she'd thought about the smoking gaze Dougal had sent her when he'd left her standing in the hall.

She'd gone to her room feeling short-changed in some way. *She* should have been the one to whisk out of sight, leaving Mac-Lean staring after her with a sense of loss, not the other way around.

Worse, in her dreams, she kept finding herself back in the library, MacLean's warm lips on her neck. She'd wanted to go further, to feel his mouth everywhere. Once he began, she didn't wish him to stop — ever.

It had been like that with the card game, too. She hadn't wanted to stop but had wanted to wager more, risk more.

As she plumped Red's pillows, she saw that the medicine was beginning to take effect.

"I hate leaving you to handle this yourself, Sophie," he murmured.

"Don't worry." Sophia collected the empty breakfast dishes and piled them on the tray. "I can handle MacLean."

The question was whether she could handle her own unexpected desires.

"Aye," Red said through a mighty yawn. "You're nothing like your mother when it comes to gaming."

Sophia paused beside the bed. "I thought you said Mama had the gift."

"Och, she did." Red snuggled down in the sheets. "She was a natural, but she possessed a major flaw: she never knew when to quit. Once she was wound up, it'd take a brick wall to stop her."

"Is that bad?"

Red's sleepy voice came slower and slower.

"No gambler wins who doesn't know when to quit."

His gentle snore filled the room.

Had she inherited Mama's fatal flaw? Sophia remembered the sharp disappointment she'd felt on losing to MacLean last night. Surely that was normal. After all, no one liked to lose.

Her mind whirling with this new information, Sophia quietly left her father's bedchamber. No matter what tendencies she had or didn't have, she was left with no choice: if she wished to win back her house, she had to fight her weaknesses. All of them.

Dougal stepped out through the terrace doors into the sun, the early-morning air nipping at his cheeks.

He buttoned his coat and wished the night hadn't been so damnably cold. His huge bedchamber had a small, badly smoking fire and a very thin blanket. And his mattress had been so lumpy that he couldn't get comfortable.

He strode out through the garden, his head woozy from lack of sleep. Still, he noticed that though the house was in poor shape, the gardens were perfect. The paths were well lined, the flower beds filled with roses and lilacs, the trees well trimmed.

He smiled darkly. His beautiful little angel of trouble must have run out of time.

As he crossed the barnyard, a wide door opened, and Shelton came out, leading Poseidon. The horse pranced as the groom took him to a nearby paddock and released him. As the horse raced off, the groom caught sight of Dougal and froze. "Gor! It can't be ye!"

"Well, it is."

"But it's afore noon!"

Dougal rammed his hands into his pockets. "Pray do not give me more of a headache than I already have."

"It's probably from the shock of bein' up so early."

"I've been up earlier than this before. I have seen many sunrises."

"That was a'cause ye *stayed* up, not a'cause ye *woke* up."

Dougal considered this. "You could be right." He yawned.

"Didn't ye sleep well, me lord?"

"No. The bed was lumpy, the fire smoked so badly I was forced to extinguish it or die, then I froze to death the rest of the night because the blanket was so thin."

"That's a shame. It was right comfortable in the tack room. I've a cot and a neat little pot-bellied stove."

Dougal sent a thoughtful look at the barn. "Can you put up another cot?"

"O' course. Only . . . won't it seem odd that ye're sleeping there?"

"I don't intend on telling anyone." Dougal eyed his retainer a moment. "Has the staff made you welcome?"

"Aye, and that Mary, can she cook! I've never had a better piece o' roast. But it was the apple pie as made the meal. It was flaky and sweet, all buttery, with —"

"Enough!" Dougal's stomach growled loudly. "The food I was given was not fit for consumption. Ride to town today, and fetch some foodstuffs. Some apples, tarts, a few meat pies — whatever will keep well."

"Aye, me lord. Do ye want an apple now? I've one here I was saving fer yer horse."

"Thank you." Dougal pocketed the apple.

"Not very hospitable, giving ye poor victuals and a lumpy bed."

"This is all part of their plan. Mr. Mac-Farlane regrets giving up his house on the gaming table, and his daughter is determined to regain it."

Shelton's eyes narrowed. "Ye aren't goin' daffy over this female, are ye? Ye said we were leavin' yesterday, and now ye're talkin' of stayin' — even with the bad food and bed."

Dougal shook his head. "She is beautiful." Breathtakingly so. "But this is more about accepting a challenge; Miss MacFarlane wishes to play me for the house." The problem was, the delicious Sophia had only one thing to wager against it.

"Play fer the house? But ye've already won it."

"That fact doesn't hold back people as focused as the MacFarlanes." He quirked a brow. "Never fear, Shelton. I am determined to teach the chit a lesson. She's an impudent, outspoken slip of a girl who desperately needs to learn what's what."

"Be careful. Ye might be the one learnin'," the groom said shrewdly.

"Nonsense. I'll tame her, and then we'll be on our way."

Shelton shook his head. "I don't know that anyone can actually tame a woman. They may *think* they can do it, but I've never seen it meself."

"I shall indeed tame the lovely Miss Mac-Farlane," Dougal said, unperturbed. "And I shall begin this morning. Have two horses saddled for a ride. I assume there is a decent horse for a lady?"

"Aye, there's a neatish mare." The groom rubbed his chin. "There's six good mounts in the stables. Ye'd think there'd be fewer, this place being so run-down and all."

"Are the stables in bad condition?"

"They're as solid as can be, with new hardware on the front paddocks. The rest of the place is a bit dusty, as if it hasn't been used in a while." He frowned. "Seems odd someone'd have such a kick-up barn and yet the house be so appallin'."

Indeed, it was. "Perhaps the lady has a softness for horses."

"I'd guess it's the lady's father. Most of the mounts are rather large, and she's knee high to a fairy."

Dougal choked a laugh. "She may be knee high to a fairy, but she's large with determination and willful trickery." It would be pure delight beating Miss MacFarlane at her own game.

He reentered the house through the terrace door and found the breakfast room by following the murmur of voices.

He paused outside the door and heard Sophia's soft voice. "Angus, you did an excellent job last night."

Angus's gloomy voice replied, "I don't know nothin' about coats and gloves and such. I'm a groom, not a butler."

"I know you are, and the best head groom in the entire county. I shall have to take the squire some of that nice London tea in thanks for lending you to me."

"He'll want no thanks. Ye know the squire's partial to ye, as are all of us. He'd give ye the shirt off'n his back if ye asked him."

Was the squire an admirer? Dougal's jaw tightened. The man was probably thick-necked and red-faced. Of course such a lout would be drooling over Sophia — she was beautiful.

"The squire's been so kind," Sophia said in a warm voice. "I should ride over and see him this afternoon."

Dougal realized his hands had tightened into fists, and he stared at them, frowning. Bloody hell, was he actually *jealous?* Over a woman he'd just met?

He shook his head. He was easily irritated until he'd had breakfast. That was what made him so ill tempered, not the thought of some country bumpkin panting after his future mistress.

Dougal paused, one hand on the door-knob. Future mistress? Where had that come from? But the more he thought about it, the more he liked it.

Sophia MacFarlane was clearly no in-nocent; she grew up consorting with gam-blers and other risqué types. And she car-ried herself with the air of a woman of the world, exuding the confidence of the experienced. It was one of her most attractive traits.

Dougal had never been interested in an innocent; he didn't have time for the drama, the tears, and the recriminations. He loved women who knew who they were and what they were and who luxuriated in that fact.

He turned the knob and opened the door. Sophia spun around at the sound, her skirts flaring about her, her eyes bright as they found his.

Good God, she was lovely. It was more than just her golden hair and startlingly blue eyes. It was the way her cheeks rose to meet her temples, the way her full lips curved when she smiled, and the contrast of her milky-white skin against the tan lace at her throat.

She looked fresh and tempting, dressed in a very fashionable morning gown of blue muslin trimmed with lace and adorned with a striped blue and tan sash that tied neatly under her breasts. Her blond hair was put up in a simple manner that left little tendrils curling before each ear. A blue rosette was pinned in her hair, and small pearl earbobs dangled from her lobes.

She dipped a curtsey. "Good morning, Lord MacLean."

He bowed. "Good morning, Miss Mac-Farlane. It's a lovely day."

Last night, he'd wondered at his curiously strong reaction to her, but in the light of day, he realized that it was merely a natural reaction to such an incredibly beautiful woman. Added to that was the shock of discovering what his little angel of trouble had planned.

Yet no matter how he'd met her, or when, he'd have had the same powerful reaction. Any man would.

She turned to Angus and said in a husky voice, "That will be all."

Angus's mouth tightened, but he gathered some empty platters and left.

Dougal waited until the door had closed. "Your servant is . . . quite unusual."

Sophia sighed. "Here in the country, one can't be too choosy. I've had better luck finding help in town."

He'd had better luck in town, too. Or so he'd thought until he'd come to Mac-Farlane House and met a golden angel with nimble fingers waiting to pluck his winnings from his waistcoat pocket.

Sophia took her chair, gesturing for him to do the same.

Dougal eyed the breakfast repast. In addition to burnt toast, there was poorly trimmed ham, eggs that looked rubbery enough to bounce off the floor, pathetically dry scones, and small, smoking pieces of something he suspected had once been kippers.

Sophia noted Dougal's disgusted expression, and her heart lifted.

He looked amazingly handsome this morning, dressed in a blue riding coat and white shirt, his dark blond hair curling over his collar, his green eyes glinting as he began to fill his plate. Two scones, a scoop of eggs, and a large piece of blackened ham all went onto his plate.

Sophia had eaten earlier in the kitchen with Mary, who had served warm muffins with cream and marmalade, some lovely bacon, and crusty toast, complemented by a pot of hot tea.

Sophia hid a smile as Dougal attempted to cut his ham. Too tough for his blade, it tore into uneven pieces under his knife. He lifted a piece and regarded it on the tines of his fork.

Sophia sighed. "It's wretched fare, isn't it? There's no stove, just an old fireplace with a spit. It's not what Mary's used to."

Dougal set down his knife, apparently giving up on the thought of breakfast. "We are to ride out this morning, I hope? I slept so well I've been looking forward to the ride."

Sophia's smile froze. "You . . . you slept well?"

"Better than I have in weeks. It must be the fresh air."

Blast it, that wasn't what she wanted to hear.

"I'm glad you slept well. I suppose, then, that your chimney didn't smoke the way mine does?"

"It did at first, but I put out the fire. It's not healthy to be overly warm when one sleeps."

She frowned. Was that some odd belief he'd gotten from London? If so, it was inconvenient, to say the least.

He glanced out the window. "I am particularly keen to see the vistas and the hunting lands."

"Hunting lands?"

"Yes." He pushed his plate aside and said lazily, "It occurred to me that the best use of this property might be as a hunting box. I could abandon the house and build a smaller, more compact structure somewhere else."

Dougal had to fight a grin when her mouth dropped open, then closed, then opened again, outrage plain on her face.

He couldn't help adding, "*Or* I might turn the place into a horse-breeding farm. I daresay with a little work, I could turn the bottom floor of this house into additional stables and — I'm sorry? Did you say something?"

Sophia choked, her face turning red.

Dougal lifted his brows. "Sophia, are you all right?"

She gasped, saying in a hoarse voice, "Yes! I'm fine. Why wouldn't I be?"

"I don't know. You just seemed . . . upset."

She shook her head, her golden curls dancing in the warm sunlight. "I merely swallowed the wrong way." She took a deep sip of her tea as if to demonstrate.

Dougal found himself mesmerized as her lips touched the delicate porcelain cup. Damn, but she had a lovely mouth, full and red and made for kissing. He imagined what she'd taste like now, a hint of sugar and cream and ripe lust.

His body stirred, and he shifted in his seat, reminding himself to be patient. The longer they lingered on the cusp of the relationship, flirting and testing, advancing and retreating, the more satisfying their joining would be.

In Dougal's experience, it was after passion abated that the spark left and never returned. He'd had many relationships, but none had lasted beyond three months.

His brother Gregor said he couldn't focus on any woman long enough to fall in love. Recently married, Gregor was a fine one to talk about focus, given the leisurely way he'd finally realized he loved Venetia, whom he'd known since they were children.

Still, Dougal wondered if perhaps he was too quick to form relationships. Was it possible that he'd never been more than temporarily attracted to any woman because he didn't take the time to get to know her?

Surely not. He was a normal, healthy man with a normal, healthy appetite — one that was being thoroughly and deliberately whetted by Sophia.

He watched as she bit her lip, her brows drawn as she considered his statement about making her house into a stable. She was no innocent miss, this worldly trickster. Not once had she mentioned the awkwardness of being alone with him; not once had she completely rejected his advances; and, with the exception of one or two moments, she'd shown only the boldest character.

Dougal liked that about her; there were none of the silly games played by so many of London's ladies.

The door rattled, and Sophia sighed. "Angus."

The lout probably had his ear pressed to the door. Time to spirit his lovely hostess away, far from the watchful eyes of her servants.

Dougal stood and captured her hand, gently pulling her to her feet. "Shall we ride?"

She smiled up at him with a warmth that made his body leap in response, tucking her hand into the crook of his arm and leaning against him. "It *is* a lovely morning," she said, her voice dripping over him like honey. "And there are plenty of places we can explore. I want to show you the entire grounds."

Yes, Dougal was discovering that a pretty face crowned with glorious golden hair and gifted with a devious, obviously intelligent mind was irresistible.

In fact, it took him a moment to remember what he'd been going to say before she'd pressed her breast against his arm. Dougal's gaze drifted over her, lingering on her lace-covered breasts. "I'd be delighted to see anything you wish to show me, Sophia."

Delicious color bloomed in her face. "You're quite flirtatious this morning. Are you this way every morning? Or just after a good night's rest?"

Dougal grinned. "Perhaps it's the company."

"Hmm," she said, peeping up at him through her thick lashes. She had the most entrancing habit of doing that, and it inflamed him every time.

She smiled as if aware of the fire raging through him. "I assume you know how to ride."

"Expertly. And you?"

"I can hold my own."

She sent him such a provocative look that he said, "Let me guess. You are actually the offspring of a gypsy princess, and horses hold no fear for you."

"I have many skills," she said airily. "Too many to name."

His heart quickened. "I daresay you do."

"You'll be the most impressed when you see me ride. That is my *true* skill."

Dougal had an instant vision of Sophia riding him. The image was so powerful that for a moment, he couldn't even breathe.

She breezed past him into the foyer, her skirts swishing, her legs outlined for a heartstopping moment as she placed her foot on the lowest step. "I won't be long." With a flirtatious smile over her shoulder, she went up the stairs.

Dougal nodded, totally mesmerized by the delicious sway of Sophia's hips until she disappeared out of sight.

CHAPTER 8

*Once ye make up yer mind to do some-
thin', 'tis better t'stumble o'er the small
hillock of jump-ahead than t'bash yer head
on the jagged rocks of did-nothing.*
Old Woman Nora from Loch Lomond
to her three wee granddaughters
one cold evening

An hour later, Dougal decided that Sophia
MacFarlane was indeed part gypsy. Though
Poseidon clearly outmatched Sophia's bay,
it was all Dougal could do to keep up with
her. She even managed to pull ahead sometimes, damn it all.

If he were more familiar with the terrain,
he would have put an end to such nonsense,
of course. But as tempting as it was to show
the vixen who was the better rider, he
wasn't about to put Poseidon in harm's way.

The sight of Sophia's trim figure galloping ahead had irritated him enough to cause

menacing clouds to gather overhead, but then Dougal realized that there were distinct advantages to allowing the pert Miss Mac-Farlane to ride in front. For one, he was afforded a delightful view of her narrow waist and lushly curved behind.

Dougal allowed his gaze to drift there now. Nice. *Very* nice. His irritation cooled even more as he admired her sapphire-blue riding habit, appreciating the severe lines that molded to her figure, curving lovingly around her hip as she rode before him sidesaddle, her skirts fluttering as she galloped. A rakish hat with a long, floating scarf completed the picture.

Never had Dougal met a woman with such unconscious beauty. She sparkled and shined from within as much as she did from without. He found it increasingly difficult to remember that she was attempting to trick him out of MacFarlane House.

As they rode out of the small forest, she pulled her mare to a walk, allowing Dougal to pull up beside her. She glanced up at the clouds that had gathered but were now sifting away. "For a few moments there, I thought it might rain."

He eyed the white lace that adorned the deep V of the habit, framing her décolletage most temptingly. "I don't think it will."

She glanced at him, her eyes appearing a deeper blue, reflecting the color of her habit. "But the sky —" She glanced up, then frowned. "Why, it's completely clearing! It looked as if it might storm but ten minutes ago."

"The wind has blown all of the clouds away."

"Yes, but —" Her gaze rested on him, suspicion clear in their blue depths.

"But what?" he asked gently.

She opened her mouth, then closed it. "Nothing," she muttered. "We should return; it's getting hot."

So the delicious Sophia had heard of the MacLean curse. It was such a part of Dougal's life that he didn't think about it unless forced to. Ignoring Sophia's evident curiosity, he merely said, "It is getting warmer."

"We'll walk the horses back." She leaned forward and patted her mare's neck.

Dougal enjoyed an even more excellent view of her décolletage. "I was willing to walk the horses the entire way." He nudged Poseidon forward until the two horses were even. "*You* were the one who wanted to canter madly down the road."

Sophia straightened, a delightful smile curving her lips. "Not used to being bested, are you?"

"No," he said bluntly. "Poseidon could outrun your mare, and you know it. But I'm not about to risk galloping over a field I don't know. There could have been rabbit holes."

"Of course. Rabbit holes. I understand."

He frowned, about to defend his actions further, when he noted a twinkle in her gaze. The little minx was taunting him. For some reason, that improved his mood, and he said with a smile, "Sophia, my love, don't tempt a sinner. I am not afraid of you or your horse, and you damn well know it."

"I'm sure you have a *reason* for not wishing to race," she returned in a demure voice, though her eyes sparkled with laughter. "I am just not certain you have a just *cause*."

"I have both. The reason for not racing you is the potential harm to the animals; and the just cause is that I wish to keep you alone for as long as possible. And that will be more difficult to do once we reach the house."

Her brows rose, a faint color touching her cheeks. "Oh."

His lips twitched. "That's all you can say now? After all that posturing? You are a tease, my lady."

"I don't consider myself so."

"No woman does, and yet most are." He gestured toward the stand of trees that covered the hillside across the valley. "Tell me, is the property heavily wooded?"

"There are several stands of trees, and the rest is tenant-farmed. Our tenants do very well. We've made several improvements over the last few years, and the new irrigation system has greatly helped during the dry season."

Her voice was filled with pride, the sort that came with years of ownership. Dougal recognized the tone because his own brother Hugh was fairly eaten up with it. One could hardly speak to the man without hearing how many bushels of this he could produce, how many calves had been thrown, and all sorts of unrequested information. How had the daughter of a gambler become passionate about such things?

"The water system took us almost two years to complete, because the —" She caught Dougal's amused gaze and added hastily, "Or so I've heard."

"I see." He did see, too. Miss Sophia Mac-Farlane held a more than common affection for her land.

He pointed to a small thatched cottage nestled in a glen. "Is that one of the tenant holdings? It appears to be in very good repair."

She flicked a glance at the cottage and shrugged. "I suppose. I hadn't really noticed."

Ah, so she was all cool composure now, her enthusiasm hidden behind a veil of propriety.

A faint flicker of disappointment made him determined to shake her façade. "How many tenants are there?"

"Fourteen families. Several are third-generation."

"Interesting. Since this is my land now, these are important things to know."

Sophia's lovely face lost all expression, and she turned away to regard the vista that spread before them — the purple mountains in the distance, the hazy glen below, the verdant fields stretched in between.

She gestured toward a steep hill, pock-marked with large boulders. "Much of this land is untenable. It's rocky and hard."

"It looks as if it could still be used."

"Well, it can't," she said sharply. "Furthermore, there's marshland on the other side of these hills. No one can even live near it, because the mist produces ill humors."

"Ill humors?"

"Yes. The entire place is encircled in thick

forest, too." She lowered her voice. "They say there are wolves there, the size of humans."

"I like wolves," Dougal said mildly. "The larger, the better."

She blinked.

"They're great sport for hunting. And I am an *avid* hunter." He glanced across her, lingering at certain areas. "As you may have guessed."

Her face bloomed with color, the delicate pink tracing along the creamy line of her cheeks. She looked away, and he was afforded an excellent view of her profile and the full curve of her lower lip. She had a mouth that begged to be tasted, and he was more than willing to do so.

Dougal wasn't used to denying himself. When he wanted something, he got it. It was that easy, and there was no reason to think she was going to be any different. She might have more spirit and a damned bit more mystery to her than most, but he would win. He knew it with a certainty that made him smile.

As they passed under a large oak tree, the brim of her hat cast her eyes into shadow. "I was wondering about something."

"What?"

"What does a man like you want with a

place like MacFarlane House?" At his raised brows, she shrugged. "It's out here in the middle of nowhere."

"My brothers and I were raised in the country. My mother died when I was young, and my father believed that boys needed plenty of fresh air and that the longer they were out of the house, the less likely they were to break anything inside it."

Her eyes crinkled with amusement.

"So my brothers and I spent a good deal of spare time fishing in the streams, riding horses, and getting into trouble whenever we could."

"You mentioned your brothers before. How many do you have?"

"Fo—" He clamped his mouth closed. "Three."

She looked curious. "Three? You seem uncertain."

Poseidon shied to one side, and Dougal realized he was clutching the reins as if his life depended on it. It had been two years since his youngest brother had died, yet still it was difficult to talk about. He forced himself to say in a calmer voice, "I have three brothers."

"Ah." There was nothing but acceptance in her voice.

He hesitated. He wasn't given to making

confidences, and yet . . . why not? Perhaps she would open up more if he gave a little. A very little.

He steeled himself and managed to say, "I had one other brother, Callum. He was the youngest."

She waited quietly.

"He —" *Died.* The word caught in his throat, hanging there until he thought he'd choke. The pounding of emotion shocked him; he'd thought he was over this. But that was the way it was. He'd manage to mention Callum without trouble sometimes, only to have the name slice through him the next.

Damn it all, emotion was the reason Callum had died, and he'd be damned if *he'd* succumb. Dougal said in a cold voice, "My family is no concern of yours."

Sophia stiffened, and she snapped, "Pardon me for making conversation. I must assume you're tired from our long ride." She leaned forward, her cheeks flushed. "Which explains why you have become cranky and ill tempered."

Never in all of Dougal's adult life had anyone dared to call him cranky or ill tempered! A gust of hot wind ruffled across them. "I am sorry if my desire not to discuss my family has upset you, but I don't feel that it's necessary."

Her lips thinned, and she turned away. "None of this is necessary, my lord. We can proceed in silence."

He frowned. "Sophia, I —"

"Since you wish to keep things on a more formal level, it's *Miss* MacFarlane."

She was encircled with chilled politeness, and Dougal's irritation swelled. Overhead, the clouds began to gather yet again. "Don't be missish," he snapped. "Just because I have no desire to speak about —"

She clicked at her horse, and suddenly they were cantering down the path, gone so quickly Dougal had no time to react.

Damn that woman! How dare she? Black and boiling, clouds poured from the north and spread across the sky. Dougal dug his heels into Poseidon's sides and galloped after Sophia.

Sophia heard the thunder of Poseidon's hooves as the horse and its furious rider gained on her. She leaned low and urged her mount on. The sudden wind blew leaves across the road, and the trees overhead swayed madly. Sophia's hat flew from her head, stealing hairpins as it was blown up into the sky, the scarf swirling with it.

Sophia's hair tumbled down. She shoved it back and raced on. Her heart pounded against her throat as the house came into sight. Though Dougal was gaining, she still might reach the safety of the house. She *had* to make it, because if he caught her —

Lightning crashed, and a tree just a pasture away exploded, burning bits of wood showering down. Sophia's little mare ran harder, terror overtaking her.

Good God, was it possible the stories of the curse were true? It had been clear only moments before. Yet when Dougal had grown angry —

Poseidon appeared in the corner of Sophia's sight. He'd caught up to them!

Sophia galloped madly through the gates. Just as she came within view of the barn, a gloved hand reached past her, grabbed the reins, and pulled both Poseidon and her mare to a halt.

The little mare tossed her head in protest, but Dougal held tight, and she soon stood obedient to his control, breathing heavily, her sides heaving.

Her mistress glared at Dougal. "How *dare* you pull up my horse in such a fashion!"

"And how dare you mock me?" He dismounted, holding his temper in check with the greatest effort. The storm that boiled overhead begged to be released; he could feel the pressure, but he refused to bow.

Shelton raced across the yard to meet him. "There ye be, me lord! I seen the storm and thought —" The groom caught the tension between Sophia and Dougal, for he closed his mouth and began to back away, his gaze darting up to the gathering storm.

Dougal tossed the reins for both horses to the groom. "There's a tree on fire in one of the fields. See to it that someone checks on it."

Shelton sighed. "Not again —" He sent a nervous glance at Sophia. "I'll see to it meself."

"Thank you. The horses have been run hard. Please see that they are tended to, as well."

"Yes, me lord."

Dougal reached up to assist Sophia from her saddle. She gripped the pommel and glared at him, daring him to move her. "Come," he said impatiently, reaching for her. "It might rain." Though it wouldn't if she'd just stop being so damned stubborn.

Her knuckles whitened on the pommel. "No."

A blast of lightning crashed behind the house, turning the entire world white for a second. The horses shied, but the groom held them tightly.

"Pardon me, miss," Shelton said nervously. "It'd probably be best if'n ye did as his lordship asks."

"I can get down myself." She met Dougal's glare. "I will *not* be fumed at in such a manner. Furthermore, I refuse to be affected by these cheap theatrics!" She gestured to the boiling sky.

"Gor!" Shelton covered his eyes with one hand.

Dougal instantly went from mad to furious, and the clouds rumbled to life. Yet in that instant, he realized that this tiny little bit of a woman had just reduced centuries of a dramatic and secretive curse to "cheap theatrics." He didn't know whether to rage or laugh, but somehow, looking up into her amazing blue eyes, laughter was beginning to win.

"Furthermore," she continued in high dudgeon, "I won't be cowed by a few damned drops of rain!"

Shelton groaned loudly. "Law, here it comes now."

But it didn't. Instead, a chuckle rippled through Dougal.

Sophia appeared outraged. "Are you laughing at me?"

"No, sweetheart. I'm laughing at *us*. We cannot even ride from the field to the house without racing. We're doomed to challenge

157

each other forever, and if we don't have a care, my temper will fry the two of us like sausages over a spit."

Her lips quivered in response. "I don't particularly care for that image."

"I haven't time for elegance, my love. It *is* getting ready to rain, so sausages are all you'll get."

She laughed then, the light peal dissipating every drop of anger. Dougal laughed, too, and Shelton gave a huge sigh of relief.

Dougal was still laughing as he lifted her to the ground. She was so delicately curvy his hands spanned her waist. She was a miniature. He'd forgotten that when she was in the saddle, for she was a bruising rider.

This once again made him imagine her riding *him,* her firm thighs on his hips, her lush breasts bare, within reach of —

Aroused beyond belief, Dougal set Sophia on her feet rather suddenly.

Dougal was vaguely aware of Shelton leading the horses off to the barn.

Sophia peeped up at him, her hair down around her shoulders. "You have a horrible temper."

"It's the bane of my family."

She glanced past him to the clouds overhead. "So the curse is true?"

Dougal winced inwardly. The family curse was not a topic that could be mentioned lightly; women inevitably wished to know more. And with Sophia so tantalizingly close, talking was the last thing he wished to do.

He shrugged and murmured a dismissive "Perhaps."

He couldn't stop looking at her lips, lush and moist. It was all he could do not to take them with his own. His hands tightened on her waist.

She colored and tried to step back, but Dougal refused to allow her to do so.

Her eyes narrowed, and she said in a cool voice, "At least we managed to tour the property. I'm afraid it hasn't been well managed; you should know that, as you're to take possession."

Suddenly, Dougal was weary of the pretense. He wished she'd just tell him the truth, that she didn't want him to take her house, though he had no idea how he'd reply. He was not a romantic, handing out large gifts merely because a lady's eyes were an unusual shade of turquoise, any more than he was a fool who folded before a woman's tears.

He was a man of reason and common sense, a man who did not allow emotion to move him. Still, for reasons he didn't quite understand, he wished she'd simply be honest with him.

She plopped her fists on her hips, the wind whipping her golden hair about her face. "Any other man would thank me for my honesty."

The word grated on him, and he lashed out, "I must assume the neglect is your father's fault."

Her eyes flashed. "My father is a good steward."

"Oh? Then why is the house in such poor condition?"

She opened her mouth to protest, and he could tell that while she didn't like his question, she couldn't very well refute it. "My father was not here very often."

"*Someone* planted those lovely flowers near the lake. They also spent a lot of time on the garden in the back of the house." At her surprised look, he added in a dry tone, "I'm not blind, you know." His gaze flicked down to her breasts, interestingly encased in her tight riding habit. "I can see *very* well."

Her cheeks flushed, and she tried to pull away again.

Behind Dougal came a bang, like the sound of a large door slamming, and Sophia's eyes widened. "Angus, *no!*" she cried.

"Ye misbegotten bounder!" Angus roared.

Dougal turned just in time to see a huge fist hit him squarely in the eye.

Thanks to Sophia, who'd jumped up and clung tightly to Angus's huge arm, the punch was softened. Otherwise, not only would it have knocked Dougal down (which it did), and not only would it have sent the world dark (which it did), and not only would it have blacked his eye (which it did), but it also might have killed him. Instead, Angus's slowed fist merely smashed into Dougal's face, spun him around, and laid him out as neatly as a piece of firewood.

CHAPTER 9

*So . . . ye made yer da' angry by tellin'
him a fib, did ye? Let that be a lesson to
ye, then. If ye tell a fib, ye'll pay the price,
so make certain it's worth it.*

Old Woman Nora from Loch Lomond
to her three wee granddaughters
one cold evening

"Dougal!" Sophia dropped to her knees
beside his prostrate form and scanned him
anxiously. Though blood ran down his
cheek, his color was good, and he was
breathing.

"I should kick 'im, too," Angus said sourly.

Sophia glared. "What is wrong with you?"

"Yer hair!"

"My hair?" She touched her hair, then
winced. "The wind tore off my hat and the
pins with it. That's all; nothing happened."

"He was holdin' ye, too," Angus growled.
"Had yer father seen it, he would have —"

162

"He would have had the good sense to leave me be! How am I to gain MacLean's trust if you attack him for helping me down from my horse?"

"Yer horse is already in the barn," Angus said stubbornly.

Mary appeared in the doorway, taking in the scene at a glance. "Angus, ye hothead! What have ye done?" She rushed forward, stooping beside Dougal and dabbing at his cut face with the edge of her apron as she castigated her husband. "Ye fool! What did ye think ye were doin'?"

"What I should've done afore," he said. "And I'll do it again once't he rises."

"You will not!" Sophia flew to her feet, her hands on her hips.

"He had his hands on ye," Angus repeated.

"He was doing nothing that I didn't want him to do," Sophia snapped.

Angus growled.

Mary looked up, her brows raised high.

Sophia rubbed her temples, which were beginning to ache. "I didn't mean that the way it sounded. I just meant that he was doing nothing wrong, nothing that Red would object to."

Angus's scowl deepened. "I'm beginning to think yer father don't understand what's at stake."

"My father lost this house, and I must win it back. Do you want to see us tossed into the street, homeless?"

Angus looked uncertainly at Dougal's prostrate form, caught Mary's accusing gaze, and sighed. "Och, now, miss. I dinna wish ye to lose yer home. Ye know I don't."

"I know what sort of a man Dougal is, Angus. Though he may dally with loose women, he's been raised a gentleman. He would never touch me unless I gave him permission." He might use incredibly powerful seduction tactics, but that was her problem, not Angus's.

"Aye," Mary said. "Don't ye remember how the miss took care o' the squire's son when he tried to kiss her in the garden?" She beamed at Sophia. "That was well done."

Sophia grinned. "He limped for a week."

Angus grunted. "The squire's son isn't half the man this one is. This is no boy ye're dealin' with here. He's a man's man; ye can see it in his eyes."

She placed a hand on his arm. "Angus, if it will make you feel better, I promise to call for help if MacLean so much as looks askance at me."

A distressed look filled his broad face. "If'n ye'll promise, miss, then I'll try to —"

Dougal moaned and raised a hand to his forehead.

Sophia dropped to her knees beside him. His left eye was swollen and red and would turn darker soon. Worse was the cut where Angus's knuckle had split the skin on Dougal's cheek.

Mary patted the trickle of blood away with her apron. "There, there, Lord MacLean. Don't move until ye've got yer breath." She glanced up at her husband. "Angus, be of use, and bring us a cold, wet cloth."

Angus nodded and turned toward the house.

Sophia helped Dougal sit upright. He leaned against her but managed to sustain most of his own weight.

His coat rubbed against her cheek, and she was assailed with the faint scent of his cologne and the warmth of him through the fine material. She cleared her throat and said in a slightly husky voice, "How do you feel?"

He touched his eye and winced. "What happened?"

"Angus."

Dougal's brows lowered as the realization flooded through him. "That bloody bull hit me!"

A huge blast of wind suddenly pummeled

them all. Sophia's skirts were flung to one side, her hair streaming across her face until she couldn't see.

Mary paled and crossed herself. "Gor, what was that?"

"Where is Angus now?" Dougal's cold voice cut through the air like a knife.

Sophia eyed him uneasily. She didn't like the way his mouth had hardened, his eyes so dark they were almost black. "Angus is inside fetching a cold cloth for your eye. He's very sorry for what happened."

Dougal touched his rapidly swelling eye. "Bloody hell, what did he hit me with? An anvil?"

"His fist."

"You should put that fool in a bear-baiting pit. You'd make a fortune." Dougal struggled to rise.

Sophia helped him on one side, Mary slipping under his other arm.

The wind swirled a bit harder, sending dust into the air.

"Heavens!" Mary said, glancing over their heads at the sky. "That's the third thunderhead as has passed this way today."

Sophia turned. A huge bank of thunderclouds hung overhead, roiling as if alive.

"We should get inside," she said uneasily.

Dougal didn't even glance at the clouds

as he held a hand over his bruised eye and cheek. "Bloody hell, I can barely see."

"Aye," Mary said. " 'Tis swelling. I'll fetch some ice chips from the icehouse; that'll do better than a wet cloth." The wind gusted heavier still, and Mary coughed as a swirl of leaves and dust kicked up about them. "Miss, you and Lord MacLean had best get inside. The rain is going to be a heavy one; I can taste it." With that warning, she left.

Dougal removed his arm from Sophia and stood on his own, though he swayed.

"Come, MacLean," Sophia said, "you should be lying down."

Dougal cut her a hard look, one eye almost swollen shut while the other glared as fiercely as an eagle's.

"Dougal, I'm sorry. I'll speak to Angus and —"

"No, thank you. I will speak to him myself." He sent a furious glare at the house. The front door, which Mary had left open, was suddenly caught by the wind and slammed shut with astonishing force.

Sophia shivered at the sky's heavy blackness and the chilled wind. "We had better hurry or —"

"You go. I am going to the stables. It would be best if I did not see Angus for an hour or two," Dougal said darkly. He turned on his heel and stalked away.

Sophia was left standing alone. Blast Angus for his temper! She ran up the stairs to the landing, to the sheltered portico. Almost instantly, the skies opened and it poured, sheeting so heavily that the barn was obscured from view.

Sophia barely noticed, for she was busy staring out at the storm. If MacLean grew this angry over a punch in the eye, how would he feel when she won back Mac-Farlane House?

"Good God, what happened to ye?" Shelton dropped the bucket of water he was carrying, unmindful that it spilled across the barn floor.

"I fell." Dougal picked up a brush and began to groom Poseidon.

Shelton gave a silent whistle. "Fell into what? A hammer?"

"Something like that."

Outside, the rain blasted down, rattling noisily on the barn roof.

Shelton frowned. "What's it doin' rainin'?" He clamped his mouth shut and regarded Dougal's black eye with new respect. "I see."

"You don't know the half of it." Dougal

gently touched his eye and winced. "Bloody hell."

"I have something to help wit' that." The groom disappeared into the tack room, and when he returned, he held a piece of raw beef.

"Where did you get that?"

"From town. I had it packed in ice fer yer supper."

Dougal slapped the steak over his eye, grunting. "Thank you." Outside, a low rumble of thunder laced through the rain.

Shelton took Dougal's arm and led him to a small barrel. "Sit here whilst I finish up the horses."

"I'm not an invalid."

"No, but how're ye goin' to charm Miss MacFarlane with one eye swollen closed? Ye need to let the swellin' fade."

Dougal sighed but stayed on the barrel, his head tipped back, the cold meat on his eye as Shelton unsaddled Sophia's horse, brushed it, stabled the two horses, then collected his dropped bucket and watered all of the animals. When he finished, he hung the bucket neatly on a peg and pulled up a barrel beside Dougal.

Dougal opened his good eye to find Shelton regarding him somberly. "What?"

The groom crossed his arms over his

chest. "I was just wonderin' . . . ." He jerked his thumb toward the roof.

Dougal closed his eyes again. "Yes, I caused the rain. I was furious about being attacked — from behind, too. I had just turned when her hulking ox of a servant hit me."

"Did the miss see it all?"

"Yes," Dougal snapped.

The wind lifted, and the great doors to the barn banged in protest, held in place by the ancient iron latch. The roof creaked and moaned as it strained mightily to let in the howling wind, but to no avail. Rain pounded on the ancient walls, leaks dripping onto the straw-covered floor.

Shelton sighed and stood. "I'll stir up the fire in the stove in the tack room. If ye're committed to this folly, then ye'll be wanting somethin' to eat before ye return to the house."

Where the delectable Miss Sophia was probably in the kitchen at this very moment, ruining his dinner. Despite his throbbing eye, Dougal reluctantly grinned. "You're right, I shall want my dinner first. And a bath."

"Which would be cold if ye got it in the house, I suppose?"

"And filled with itching powder, as well, if

they think of it."

"I'm glad we'll be leavin' soon," Shelton said grumpily.

Dougal didn't answer.

The groom frowned. "We *are* leavin' soon, aren't we, me lord?"

"I don't know yet."

"But I thought ye just wished to find out what that shyster and his daughter were up to."

"I did. They wish to trick me into tossing the deed back onto the game table so that they might win it."

"Then we don't need to stay another night."

Need? That was an odd word. Dougal didn't *need* anything. But *want?* That was an entirely different matter.

Shelton moaned. "We're not leavin', are we? I can see it in yer eyes. Ye're besotted."

Dougal snorted. "When have you ever seen me besotted?"

"Perhaps that's the wrong word," Shelton said morosely. "Challenged is more like."

Dougal moved the beef to a more comfortable position over his eye. "What's wrong with a little challenge?"

"Nothing, so long as ye don't lose an eye in the bargain!"

Dougal chuckled. "I won't lose anything,

I promise. Not an eye or the house." And definitely not his heart.

His smile faded. Where had that thought come from?

Shelton sighed. "I hope we don't stay much longer. Ye'll wish a bath this evening, and while I don't mind servin' as yer cook, I'm not washin' yer back."

"I won't ask it of you, I promise." Dougal took the beef off his eye and gingerly touched the swollen area. It was better already. In another hour or two, he'd be able to see out of it as well as ever.

A flash of lightning filled the cracks of the barn with light, followed almost immediately by a roar of thunder. Dougal sighed. The blasted curse was hard at work. He rarely lost his temper, but the events of the past few days had strained him to his limits, the crowning glory of Angus's attack making him reach the breaking point.

Dougal glanced at the barn doors as they rattled against the wind, rain beating steadily against them. It was his duty as a MacLean not to let the curse get the better of him; it was his responsibility as a man not to be bettered by anything or anyone — including the family curse.

Yet not only was he in danger of losing his temper, but he was also finding his hostess

172

far too engaging. Several times this afternoon, she'd let down her guard, and he'd glimpsed an entrancing woman. Not only was she charming, but there was a rare quality about her. He'd caught himself wishing their circumstances were different, that he could approach her as an equal, without the hidden innuendos and plots.

Dangerous thoughts, indeed.

For everyone's sake, it was time to end this. But first, he'd play one more game of cards with the delicious Miss Sophia. After all, what could a kiss or two hurt?

That decided, he rose from his barrel and went to prepare for his last evening with Sophia MacFarlane.

"He deserved it!" Angus said indignantly.

"Nonsense," Red replied calmly. "Sophia knows what she's about."

Mary snorted, plumping his pillow with far more force than necessary. "Angus, ye're a fool. Miss Sophia's always had more common sense than the average lass."

Angus scowled. "I'm not so certain the miss can muddle MacLean's thinkin' with her womanly wiles without muddlin' her own." Before Mary could respond, he added in an accusing tone, "Ye said yerself that the man was bonny enough to sup up with a spoon."

Red frowned. "I want my daughter to have her house back, but not if it places her in danger. Do you truly think this will do that?"

"Aye," Angus said.

"No," Mary said.

They glared at each other.

Mary said firmly, "Don't be thinkin' she'll go over the line. No one makes her do aught but what she wants." Mary moved to the windows, where she dropped the sashes and closed the curtains. "She's no fool."

Red knew far more about rakes than Mary or Sophia, and a man with MacLean's smooth charm and handsomeness might be more temptation than even his pragmatic, logical daughter could withstand.

Yet he also knew that Dougal was a Mac-Lean and family pride would bind him to a certain standard. Sophie was as lovely as her mother, just as talented, and just as strong-willed. She was a heady bundle who offered a challenge to a man just by breathing. Such a tempting bit might cause a man to lose his head enough to cross the lines of propriety, even when the cost might be great.

Out in the hallway, Sophia's door opened, then closed.

"There's the miss. I'll see if she'd like a tray before dinner." Mary whisked out of the door.

Red started preparing a short speech for Sophie about the importance of keeping a safe physical distance between herself and her guest. He was just working out a brilliant but poignant closing statement when Sophie walked into the room.

Red's welcoming smile froze, fell, and shattered. "Bloody hell! Ye can't wear *that!*"

"You, not ye," she corrected as she looked down at her gown. Made of heavy pale blue silk trimmed with cream lace, it fell in elegant folds to her ankles. The short sleeves were banded with a stripe of shimmering cream silk that matched the ribbon tied beneath her breasts. "What's wrong with this gown? I think it's lovely."

It *was* lovely, except for one item: the décolletage was quite a bit lower than her usual gowns. Worse, *someone* had sewn a small bunch of blue and cream silk roses at the lowest point, as if her breasts didn't draw enough attention on their own. "You can't wear that," Red said firmly. "It's too low."

Sophia sat on the edge of his bed and said placidly, "Red, my gown is the height of fashion."

"For a married lady, perhaps, but not for my daughter."

"Red."

He heard the rebuke and winced.

She laughed. "Need I remind you that I might persuade MacLean to play for the house this very night?"

Red brightened. "Tonight? Do you think so?"

"I hope so. I plan on flirting shamelessly, so it's a good thing you'll be up here."

"Flirt?"

"Naturally. I have to distract him while he's playing, and what better way than with a casual flirtation?"

"Distract him some other way!"

"What other way?"

"I don't know. You could . . . you could drop something on him." Red squinted thoughtfully. "Yes! Scald him with tea."

"During a game? I want him to finish playing, not leap up and run from the room."

"Then think of something else."

"I have thought of something else; I've thought of it all, in fact." She patted his hand. "If nothing else, you can rest easy knowing that MacLean's conceit wouldn't allow him to touch a woman who didn't wish it."

She had a point. Pride was a powerful motivator. No one knew that better than Red. He studied his daughter, noting that though she might *look* frivolous in her silk gown and beads, she was deadly sober. His little Sophie was no one's fool.

The trouble with Sophie wasn't that she wasn't capable; it was that she was so capable it was easy to allow her to determine her own way, right or wrong. She was so much like Beatrice that it sometimes pained him. Of course, Beatrice had been a horrid gambler, for she'd never been able to walk away from a challenge. Sophie was different . . . wasn't she? She *had* taken the loss of the house hard, far more than he'd expected. Was it possible that she had become fixated on keeping MacFarlane House, no matter the cost? All these years, as they'd worked to fix the house, it had never dawned on him that perhaps the best thing for Sophie wasn't the house. In dedicating herself to this place, far out in the countryside, perhaps his daughter had cut herself off from having any other future.

The thought disturbed Red. Had he allowed Beatrice's dream of having a stable home to become Sophie's prison?

Unaware of the fear in his heart, Sophia smiled, confident and composed as ever.

"Red, I know you would be happier wandering about Europe, but I am not you. This house —" Her voice wavered, and she paused a moment before going on. "This house is not just my home, it's the last memory I have of Mama."

"But she was never here," he said, frowning. "Lass, don't you have any dreams of your own?"

The question caught Sophia by surprise. Surely, the house was all she needed. "I don't know. I suppose I've never really thought about it."

"Once we have the issue of the house settled, I want you to think about it. Perhaps the time has come for you to live your own life, and let your mama's dream go."

Sophia stood. "I know what I want, Red. And I want this house."

"Of course you do; it's our dearest memory of your mama. But there's more to life than memories, and we'd both best remember that." Red smiled tiredly, taking her hand between his. "Stop looking as if you'd like to toss me from the window. Give me a hug, and go on to your dinner guest. Just remember that life does not begin and end with this house. If we win it back, good. If we don't, there's nothing that says we can't start again somewhere else and be just as happy."

Sophia forced a smile to her lips. "I'm certain we'll be happy here, where Mama wished us to be. Now, if you'll excuse me, I must attend to our guest." She placed a perfunctory kiss on Red's forehead, aware of his sharp blue gaze as she left the room.

Sophia closed the door behind her and leaned against it. What did Red mean? She was determined to win tonight. Then they could go back to their lives, while Dougal MacLean went back to his.

Strangely, she found herself overcome with an odd sense of loss. Today's ride had proven one thing: she and MacLean had more in common than she'd realized.

Sophia was beginning to think that in matters of the heart, she had more of her impulsive, romantic father in her than she'd thought. There was just something about Dougal MacLean that engaged her emotions.

She frowned. Perhaps the reason she experienced such a welter of confusing feelings was that he was a man of such contradictions — of lace and unapologetic masculinity, of humor and sensuality, of warmth and reserve. She sensed that despite his carefully presented exterior, he would ruthlessly do whatever he wanted. Which was why she *had* to win this wager.

She straightened her shoulders. Tonight would set the stage for her triumph. She'd lose the first few hands, though not by much; she didn't wish to raise MacLean's suspicions. That should be enough to draw him on. She'd already decided on the stakes, too.

Her heart thundering with a mixture of dread and exhilaration, Sophia smoothed her hair, adjusted her décolletage a bit lower, and sailed gracefully down the stairs, prepared to meet her enemy.

CHAPTER 10

There might come a day when ye'll find yer pride battling yer heart. Fer some, 'tis as bloody and fiery as only a war fer true love can be.

Old Woman Nora from Loch Lomond
to her three wee granddaughters
one cold evening

Outside, the rain poured, while the library was snug and dry. Dougal paused by the mirror over the fireplace and adjusted his cravat, ignoring the blue bruise and small cut beneath his eye.

Half an hour ago, he'd taken a hurried cold bath in a tub in the tack room. It was difficult maintaining his usual level of fashion without his valet, but even to his own critical eye, he appeared only slightly rumpled. With such a derelict house as a background, he doubted *rumpled* would be noticed.

He glanced about the room, noting again the exquisite molding that adorned the walls and mantelpiece. Miss Sophia and her minions had not been able to disguise that particular detail. Nor could they do much about the magnificent wood floors except cover them with badly worn carpets. He walked to the wall and ran his hand over the surface. A thick, waxy ash coated his fingers. "Clever girl," he murmured with a faint smile.

She certainly was that. Several times today, she'd surprised him with her knowledge, and not just of the land, though that was the topic for which she'd shown the most enthusiasm. Sophia MacFarlane loved her house and lands. Or, rather, *his* house and lands.

It was a pity they were vying for the same prize. Sophia had set them on a collision course with her nefarious plan to make MacFarlane House appear uninhabitable, and he was not a man to allow such chicanery to go unpunished. He owed Sophia a thorough set-down, and he was going to see that she got it.

A soft voice in the hallway made him look toward the door. He could see Sophia standing on the bottom step of the stairway, speaking in a low, urgent tone to Angus.

The huge ruffian towered over her, every line of his body stiff with outrage. He was not enjoying whatever message she was delivering, and judging by the set of Sophia's shoulders, neither was she.

Though Dougal couldn't hear their murmured conversation, he had the distinct impression that it was about him. Quietly, he walked closer to the library door.

"I am serious, Angus. No interfering."

Angus's gravelly voice contained a petulant note. "But, miss, ye can't mean that. Ye need me to —"

"I'm in charge here, am I not?"

"Aye, but yer father —"

"Would agree with every word I'm saying, and you know it. You'll be of much more assistance this evening if you'd keep Red company. He's restless since his accident, and a hand or two of cards would settle him down."

Angus rubbed his neck, shifting from one foot to the other, reminding Dougal of a small boy. Finally, the large man dropped his arm and said with a noisy sigh, "Very well, miss. I'll do as ye bid."

Some of the tension left Sophia's shoulders, and she nodded, her golden hair glinting from the sconces that lined the foyer. "Very good. Now, pray tell Mary to serve

183

dinner. I didn't have time to sneak any food from the kitchen earlier, and I'm likely to starve if we don't get this evening over with so that I can have some proper food."

Angus gave a reluctant chuckle. "Should I slip ye a piece of bread under the lamb Mary's burning?"

"Oh, yes, please bring me a slice with jam. Just disguise it on my plate."

"So long as ye don't think MacLean will see it."

"Him?" Her soft voice mocked. "He'll never know."

Dougal's jaw tightened.

Angus nodded. "Very well, then. Ye jus' remember that if things get out of hand, ye've but to yell, and I'll be there."

"I won't need you. I can handle Mac-Lean." Her voice lilted with laughter.

Angus chuckled and turned away.

Dougal stepped away from the door. Bloody hell, the chit made him sound like a fool.

Outside, the rain thrummed on the roof harsher than before.

So, that was the way she wished to play it, he thought bitterly. Forget this morning, when she'd seemed so pleasant, her laughter softening his defenses. She wanted one thing and one thing only: to steal the house he'd legitimately won.

Jaw set, Dougal waited for her entrance into the library.

Within moments, he heard the whisper of her silk gown, her light step, and then her honey-soft voice wrapped around him. "There you are!"

Dougal turned to face Sophia, and to his irritation, his body warmed in response. Her gown perfectly framed her delicate neck and throat, accentuated the rise of her magnificent breasts, molded her small waist, and draped sensuously over her hips, hinting at the perfection of her legs. The blue reflected the hauntingly lovely color of her eyes, and her golden hair shined magnificently in the evening candlelight.

She looked vibrant and gorgeous, her lips curved in a delicious smile, her eyes shimmering with humor and . . . caution, perhaps?

Her gaze met his, and she winced. "Your poor eye." She gestured helplessly, as if wishing she could make his black eye disappear.

He flicked an uncaring hand. "I'd forgotten it."

The faint scent of jasmine drifted up to envelop him as she regarded his eye with seemingly sincere interest. "I'm sorry it happened, but I'm glad you're not in pain. It doesn't appear to be swollen, just bruised." Her voice brushed over him, soft and sensual.

His body quickened even more, and he damned the pull he felt whenever she was in the room. When she wasn't there, he could think of her in a logical, calm manner. But the second she appeared, his body flamed to life, and he had to fight for control.

Damn, but he hated this stirring of attraction. He usually enjoyed it, but because of her deceit, he felt betrayed, which was ridiculous. He was not given to excess emotion, and he had no intention of feeling anything but lust.

He forced his lips to curve into a smile, keeping his expression cool and distant. "I was beginning to think I would be eating my delightful meal alone."

She shrugged, the movement sending her breasts perilously close to leaving their thin silk prison. "I am sorry if I'm late; I spent some time with my father."

Normally, Dougal would have been displeased to have been kept waiting, but he found that he didn't care. Right now, he couldn't think past the lush curve of her breasts.

He proffered his arm. "Shall we dine?"

"Of course." She placed her fingers on his arm and smiled up at him. "I'm famished."

As was he, though not for food. Bloody hell, just the feel of her hand on his arm, the occasional brush of her breasts against him, sent heat crashing through his carefully held reserve.

He forced himself to ignore it and escorted her into the dining room. With a distinct sense of relief, he assisted her into her chair and retreated to the other side of the table. He had to regain his sense of control; he'd be damned if he'd let her see how strongly she affected him.

Why in hell *did* she? It wasn't as if he hadn't been with a woman recently; he'd stayed in Stirling for three weeks for just that reason. Perhaps it was because he knew all of her attention sprang from an ulterior motive? Would she even have given him the time of day if not for her desire to win back her house? In a way, it was a definite snub.

Dougal wasn't used to such treatment, and he found himself oddly fascinated. Attraction and denial made a heady combination, and he was burning with the desire to conquer it — to conquer *her.*

His control was even more sorely tried when he was forced to watch Sophia's full, sweet lips close over the bowl of her spoon as she pretended to eat the soup placed before her, talking easily. His body flamed anew, hardening to the point of readiness.

Worse, the loud rain caused her to lean forward whenever he spoke, suspending his breath as her breasts pressed against the dangerously low edge of her gown.

Though he absently listened as she spoke of this and that, Dougal could not look away. The creamy, round fullness of her breasts claimed his attention; the shadowed valley between them made his fingers itch to discover more. He'd love to lean forward and trail his lips along that lush line of naked skin, and —

Blast it, he was far too experienced to be affected by a woman in such a way! She'd insulted him before dinner, laughing at him with a mere servant, yet he couldn't hold on to his anger. Outside, the storm faded until only a faint *drip, drip* from the eaves remained.

The gold of her hair as the candlelight flickered over it . . . the soft rose of her cheeks . . . the intriguing hollows at the base of her neck . . . With each laugh, each gesture, she inflamed him more, made him burn to see, to feel, what lay beneath her silk gown.

The door banged open, and Mary set down a thick slab of dry, burned lamb, heavily peppered until it was inedible. Dougal watched as Sophia surreptitiously found the jam and bread discreetly tucked to one side of her plate, then made a show of cutting it as if it was a bit of the burned lamb.

He waited until she lifted the fork to her lips, then captured her wrist, her skin warm beneath his fingers.

Her gaze flew to his, her lips trembling the faintest bit.

"Strange," he said, rubbing his thumb over her wrist. "I don't seem to have jam and bread on my plate."

Anger flickered in her eyes, and she pulled her wrist free. "I am sure it was an error. Shall I have Mary bring you some?"

"Yes. Two pieces, please."

Sophia's delicate brows rose. "I thought you *liked* Mary's cooking."

"I do; I just love bread and jam more."

Plainly unsatisfied by his answer, she reached for the bell pull and tugged it. When Angus appeared in the doorway, she frowned. "You were to stay with my father."

"He's asleep, so I came t'help Mary," Angus said, triumph in his gravelly voice.

"I see. Very well. Please bring some bread

and jam for Lord MacLean."

Dougal wasn't surprised when the butler stomped back in moments later and said in a voice heavy with satisfaction, "There's no more jam to be had."

"Or bread?" Dougal asked, knowing what the answer would be.

"Nor bread," Angus said with a smirk.

Dougal flicked his hand in the butler's direction. "Then you may go."

Angus's smile faded, and he glared at Dougal until Sophia said softly, "Angus, that will be all."

The butler scowled but obediently tromped from the room.

"He loves me," Dougal said simply.

Sophia's lips twitched. "I doubt that."

"No, no, I'm certain of it. He's constantly staring at me and cannot seem to stay away. But the most telling symptom is the way he gets upset when I pay attention to another woman."

She laughed, a sweet, light peal that made him smile in return. "It sounds as if you've had experience in this area."

He shrugged. "I have never suffered from a lack of attention. When I was younger, it was quite heady, but later, I realized that most women attach themselves to a man because they want something."

"Your wealth?"

"Or marriage. Or to brush against the magic of the curse."

Her gaze flew to his.

"Allow me to explain it to you." He leaned forward, allowing his gaze to drift over her as he spoke. "Long ago, my family was known for two things: their success in gaining wealth and their horrid tempers."

"Sounds as if things haven't changed much."

"Oh, we've grown far milder over the centuries. One of my ancestors, a man of great pride, lost his temper while bargaining with the village healer, a beautiful woman who was rumored to be half fairy."

"Naturally. There is always a fairy or a witch involved in these sorts of stories."

He smiled, then continued, "The disagreement grew, and my ancestor said some very unkind and untrue things, as people who do not control their tempers are wont to do. In return, she cursed him and his family. Every time they lost their tempers, storms would gather."

"That could be a boon in dry weather."

"Ah, but it is a curse, so there is a catch. Though we cause the storms to gather, we cannot make them cease. Raging torrents of rain can cause mudslides and floods; light-

191

ning is dangerous; and then there is the wind . . ." He was silent a moment, thinking of the many times he'd struggled to control his temper. "Fortunately, a normal flare of anger seems merely to cause storms of an average variety."

"Like today's?"

"Yes. It is only when we completely lose control that horrible things happen."

She glanced at the rain-spattered windows and looked back at him. "It's true, then," she said with calm acceptance.

"Yes, it's true. The only way the curse can be lifted is if every member of a generation does a deed of great good."

"Great good? What is that?"

He smiled. "No one knows. Which is why the curse has never been lifted."

"Does the curse affect your entire family in the same way?"

"There are some slight variations. When my brother Gregor grows angry, it tends to hail and snow."

"He has a cold disposition?"

Dougal almost laughed. "He used to, but life has warmed him up. Now he's happily married to a woman he met when they were children. They were best friends until a year ago, when they were stranded together at an inn for a week."

"Stranded?"

"By a snowstorm."

Her lips formed an O, which was distracting, to say the least.

Dougal forced himself to continue. "When my sister causes the weather, it's usually over a very limited area, and there is the distinct scent of lilacs in the air."

"I would think you'd have all learned how to control your tempers by now."

"It's not as easy as you might think. I, for example, grow especially furious when people play me for a fool." He offered her a bland smile. "Fortunately, that doesn't happen often."

Her lashes dropped over her eyes. "And your other brothers?"

"Hugh is very even-tempered and rarely gets angry, but when he does —" Dougal shook his head. "You wouldn't wish to witness that."

"And what of your eldest brother?"

"Alexander has the worst temper of us all but also the best control. I can remember only one or two times when his control slipped, and it was horrid. One time, an entire village washed away, cottages and all. He was nineteen at the time and took it very hard."

She absorbed this, saying after a time, "I

imagine you are all a bit guarded."

They were deeply guarded — especially since Callum's death. Quick to bring to laughter and equally quick to anger, Callum had been the family darling. It had been his hot temper that had finally put him in a situation that caused his death.

Dougal forced the unwelcome thoughts aside. "I am usually not quick to anger, and had Angus not surprised me today, I would have been able to react differently."

Sophia's gaze rested on his injured eye. "I would say a black eye is just cause for a bit of anger."

"Alexander would have maintained his temper and made his point another way. I am not very good at that. I cannot let things be."

"Neither can I," Sophia confessed with a faint smile. "Red says no one can make a stand in an empty road any better."

"Well, I owe our grim friend for this afternoon, and I'll not forget it."

Her smile faded. "You don't seem the type of man to hold a grudge."

"I am *exactly* the type of man to hold a grudge, my dear." His gaze locked with hers. "You might say it is a family trait, too."

She sent an uneasy glance at the window, and Dougal tossed his napkin onto the table. "Come. Let's retire to the library for some wretched sherry."

She looked at her bread and jam. "But I haven't yet eaten."

"Don't tell me you didn't get enough of that delicious onion soup?"

He pulled her chair from the table, watching with a satisfied smile as she dropped her napkin beside her plate and stood.

"Very well," she said.

He proffered his arm, pulling her hand through until she was cozily tucked against him, her breast pressing against his arm. He was so much taller that he could see directly down her gown to the delicate chemise underneath. The fine lawn was decorated with a tiny rosette that echoed the larger one on her gown.

Desire flashed through him. By God, he was going to enjoy this evening! He was going to enjoy pressing his little scheming hostess into improprieties she'd not soon forget. He didn't need a storm to make his point; he had his own powers of persuasion — and he'd use them all on her.

He led her to the library, to the table holding the sherry. "Will you do the honors?" He leaned forward and added in a low voice, "Or perhaps you'd like us to do it together — your hand under mine, your fingers wrapped about the neck of the decanter as we —"

Color flooded her cheeks, and she said in a breathless voice, "I will be glad to pour us some sherry — though I'm surprised you wish for some more."

"It is wretched, but your cook has ruined my palate. When I return to London, I won't know good port from bad, burned meat from raw, and don't begin to talk to me about soups."

She chuckled. "I'm sorry there was no more bread and jam."

"Not as sorry as I was. But so long as there is sherry in that decanter, I will make do." He walked to the door and closed it, the sound loud in the room.

Her color deepened. "Why did you do that?"

"Because I don't wish that brute of a butler to storm in here if I make you laugh. You don't mind, do you?"

She did mind; he could see it in her stiff posture. But she merely murmured an agreement and busied herself with the decanter and glasses.

Dougal watched as she poured them both a generous amount.

She was lovely in the candlelight, the warm glow turning her hair a more mellow gold, touching her skin with peach, tracing the plump line of her mouth. Dougal's body tightened, and he fought the urge to sweep her into his arms and bend her with the fury of his passion.

But he would not give her that satisfaction. He would make her want *him* — wildly, desperately, with every bit of the desire he could see in her turquoise eyes. And he'd do so using the very weapon she thought to use against him: her skill at cards.

He took a hard gulp of sherry, letting the acrid taste clear his thoughts.

He turned to Sophia and smiled. "Let's while away the time with some cards. Would you enjoy that, my love? I'm very certain I would."

CHAPTER 11

Beware the man who's quick to give ye jewels and gold. There's always a hook in such sweet bait!
Old Woman Nora from Loch Lomond
to her three wee granddaughters
one cold evening

He saw a light flare in her eyes, though she tried to hide it behind the tilt of her sherry glass. After taking a sip, she said in a careless voice, "Certainly. That will be a pleasant way to spend the evening."

He took the cards out of their small ivory box on the table. "What shall we wager on this evening?"

She smiled flirtatiously. "I still haven't won back my mother's jewels."

"I shall place them on the table again."

Her excitement was palpable. "Excellent. Then I suppose the next question is . . . what would you have of me?"

There was the faintest quiver to her voice. Good. She *should* be uneasy.

He ran his gaze over her insolently. That was the problem with Sophia's plan: it put her at a distinct disadvantage until the moment she won all — a moment that would never arrive. But she didn't know that, and there was power in knowledge.

"Let me think about our wager for a moment. Shall we be seated?" He gestured to the table.

"Of course." She brought the decanter and her glass to the table and sat down, her silk gown rustling as she moved. Her eyes were unnaturally bright, the thick lashes casting shadows over them.

Dougal sat as well, imagining kissing the sherry that lingered on her lips. The time would come soon. "Do you wish to shuffle the cards?"

She nodded, quickly picking up the cards. The firelight caressed her pink cheeks, warming her skin until he wished he could touch her.

She shuffled the cards, her fingers flying over their worn surface, then set them on the table. "Well? What is the wager?"

Dougal captured her hand, and her lips parted, her breath quickening as he turned it over. Her hand was well shaped and patrician, with graceful fingers, but calluses marred her palms, roughening the skin.

She curled her fingers closed. "Shall I name the wager myself?" she asked with asperity.

He stroked his thumb over her wrist, where her skin was as smooth as it should be. It was a shame life had forced her to perform her own chores. Did she ordinarily do all of the cooking and cleaning? He'd gathered that Mary and Angus were on loan from the squire's house until Sophia managed to fleece Dougal from his rightful winnings. After that . . . would she go back to her life as it had been before?

A pang of regret flickered through him, and he released her hand. "I know what I wish to wager."

She tucked her hand away, her cheeks suspiciously bright. "Do your worst, Mac-Lean."

He reached into his pocket and pulled out both the bag of jewelry and the deed to the house.

Sophia's gaze was glued to the large, folded paper. "You brought the deed."

"I didn't wish to leave it in my room."

Her cheeks flushed. "No one here would steal it from you, if that is what you were thinking."

"Of course not. I am merely cautious by habit." Dougal rested his fingers on the deed. "Hm. Where should we begin?"

"With the deed to the house." Her voice was breathless.

"I believe . . ." He allowed his hand to hover over the deed, before moving on to pick up the bag of jewelry.

Disappointment flashed over her face.

He smiled. "Shall we begin with these? Perhaps the earrings."

"I'm interested in it all," she replied shortly. "At one time."

"Not so fast, my dear." Dougal pulled the earrings from the bag and tossed them to the center of the table. Tangled together, the sparkling jewels slid on the slick surface until they rested in front of Sophia.

"Well?" Dougal asked. "What will you stake against them?"

She pursed her lips. After several long moments, she said, "I will wager my hairpins. *All* of them."

Remembering how her unbound hair had caressed her curves and clung to her breasts, flowing down almost to her waist, his groin tightened. "Your hairpins, then. But on our next hand, I shall want something more."

She smiled faintly. "Let's see who wins this hand, shall we?"

They played their first hand in relative silence, Dougal watching her every move. She won the first hand and, to his reluctant amusement, immediately exchanged the small pearl earrings she wore for the diamond set. The gems were beautiful, but her eyes were more so, and he decided he wanted to see her completely naked, wearing nothing but the diamond set.

Determined to win the next hand, he tossed a bracelet onto the table. Once again, she offered her hairpins, and Dougal, though wishing for more, accepted. She had the loveliest hair.

She lost the next hand, which was no surprise. She could hardly expect to entice him to toss the deed to MacFarlane House onto the table by seeming too easy to beat or by beating him outright. No, she was far too intelligent for that. But so was he.

He had been to enough gaming hells to know how things would progress. His devious Sophia would allow him to win most of the hands tonight, to build his confidence in his own skill and to promote a healthy underestimation of hers. She needed a good shock, something to rattle her confidence.

When she lost the hand and started unpinning her glorious hair, tossing the pins onto the table with impudent nonchalance,

Dougal said, "Perhaps we should spice up our next wager."

A wary look entered her blue eyes. "How?"

"By wagering your mother's necklace against . . . your clothing."

She froze, her arms over her head, her eyes wide. "My clothing?"

"Yes. Your gown — against your mother's necklace." His body was already hard at the thought of her standing before him in nothing but her chemise and stockings.

Sophia lowered her arms with a teasing smile. "I doubt it will fit you."

A surprised laugh broke from him. "That *would* be a sight. But to be crystal clear, if I win this hand, you will disrobe for me."

Sophia's mind raced, as did her pulse. Beneath the gown, she was wearing stockings and a chemise, so it wasn't as if she would be completely undressed.

And the benefit in losing this wager — and she fully intended to lose it — would be the opportunity to tease Dougal even more. To torment him with the possibility of what might happen, make him desire her until his thoughts were muddled and his head swimming.

Much as hers were right now. Blast it, she should have eaten something before drinking the sherry! She caught Dougal's gaze, and her cheeks heated at the intensity of his look.

"Well?" he asked.

Sophia picked up the cards and shuffled them with an expert twist of her wrists, her fingers flying, in an attempt to calm herself.

She had to be careful; this restless excitement was all too addicting. She'd never felt more alive. The air seemed crisper, the cards felt even silkier, the scent of the sherry floated sensuously about them. But even more, she was aware of Dougal's intense gaze. Of the strong line of his jaw. Of the way his dark blond hair fell over his brow, shadowing those intriguing eyes until they appeared smoke green.

Finally, she replaced the cards on the table. "I accept. The necklace for the removal of my gown."

She could almost feel the heat that flared in his eyes. "Deal the cards."

They played with quiet intensity, no sound but the flick of the cards against the table. Finally, Sophia was down to her last play. She hesitated, agonizingly aware of the man who sat across the table from her, his burning gaze rarely leaving her face.

There was an almost physical pull from him, as if he were silently willing her to give in to the wild thoughts now filling her mind.

Her spirit seemed to have awoken from a long sleep. Her soul reveled in the danger of this moment, in the very impropriety, and leapt willingly into it. Her blood burned with the challenge of maneuvering him into giving her what she most wanted, most desired.

She felt a crazed desire to laugh. *This* was why her mother had stayed away from Red's games. Not because she hadn't liked them but because she'd *loved* them.

Sophia took one last look at her cards, made her selection, and placed them on the table.

Dougal looked at them, so hard with desire that he could barely focus. She had a paltry pair of jacks. He inhaled deeply, then placed his cards beside hers. "I win."

She regarded him from beneath her lashes, the look seductive and promising. Damn, she was a heady wench. Under other circumstances, there was no telling what this might have led to, for he couldn't imagine ever tiring of her.

Unfortunately, fate had dealt them a short hand, and they were doomed to a brief, but brilliant relationship. He would have to be satisfied with that.

Dougal took another drink of sherry, the liquid burning his throat. It was traditionally a sweetish drink for gently bred women, but this brew was amazingly potent. He placed the glass back on the table and said softly, "How do you wish to do this, my love?"

She slowly stood. "I cannot believe I agreed to such a foolish wager."

"You thought you'd win."

"I always think I'll win," she said wryly.

He nodded blindly, mesmerized by the way the silk gown clung to all that was soon to be revealed. He stared at the curve of her breasts, full and round, imagining how they'd fill his hands. He could easily span her petite waist, and the curve of her hips seemed made just for his hands, as were the intriguing shadows beyond.

She slowly pushed aside her hair, the golden strands clinging to her neck and shoulders. He didn't blame them; he'd be loath to part from such glorious skin himself.

As she met his gaze, he was caught by the seductive light in her eyes. By Zeus, she was *enjoying* this. Savoring it, even!

As if to confirm his astounded thoughts, a smile touched her lips as she reached for the ties at one shoulder. Her diamond earrings glinted as she turned her head to the side. She slowly tugged on the ties, making them fall sensually over her shoulders.

His body ached with desire, and he grasped the arms of his chair to keep from reaching across the table and yanking her forward. Bloody hell, but he was enraptured, caught as if by a fairy queen from some legend of old.

She slowly slid her gown down one shoulder, smiling seductively, her blue eyes so bright they seemed almost silver.

He reached out, but she stepped away. "No," she said, her voice husky. "You didn't say anything about touching."

Damn it to hell! Why hadn't he done so? Dougal ground his teeth but forced himself to lean back in his chair. "Very well. I will not touch you."

Sophia saw the strain as he attempted to hold in his desire. Heat flooded her, her breasts tingling in a most unusual way. He wanted her badly; she could see it in every line of his body. She shivered with a mixture of her own desire and the heady realization of her power.

She loosened the ties on the other side and let the gown fall. It slid down her body, a sensuous flow of silk and lace that landed in a blue and cream pool at her feet.

Dougal's breathing grew harsher; his eyes shimmered with something raw and brutal.

Her white chemise was simple and service-able, with a drawstring neckline adorned with tiny rosettes and a single flounce about the bottom. Though it fell past her calves and the fabric was substantial, she felt exposed and naughty and wildly excited.

She peeped under her lashes at Dougal, who gazed at her with raw desire and clear masculine appreciation. His gaze roamed over her, lingering here and there, his mouth pressed in a hard, hungry line.

Though her first impulse was to cover herself, she lifted her chin boldly instead.

Dougal thought he would go mad. He gripped the edge of the table, his knuckles white. She stood before him, only one layer of thin fabric between him and paradise. And oh, how she looked like paradise — a mischievous angel with a body made to be tasted and teased, a mouth made for loving and laving, her golden hair caressing all of the places *he* wanted to caress. He ached for her as he'd never ached for any woman.

She nervously stroked a long lock of her golden hair, threading it through her fingers over and over, making his groin ache. If only she would do that to him. He envisioned her pale fingers stroking his skin, her fingers wrapping about his shaft as she . . . He closed his eyes against the temptation simply to *take* her, make her his.

But closing his eyes just made things worse, for his imagination took her luscious image and began to do all sorts of delicious things to it. He groaned, realizing that he could fight the storms more easily than fight his desire for her.

"Dougal?" Her smoky voice wrapped around him.

Dougal gripped the arms of his chair. If he let go he might reach for her, and if he touched her, he didn't know if he could maintain his control. The thought chilled him to the bone. He could not trust himself another moment.

He forced his eyes open and was engulfed anew by her. He loosened his jaw enough to speak. "Go."

"But —"

"Go!" His voice crackled like lightning.

Her eyes clouded, but no tears appeared. Instead, her chin lifted, and she bent, gathered up her gown, and retied it. Then she spun on her heel and swept to the door as if she were royalty.

When the door closed behind her, Dougal let out a huge breath, his heart pounding as if he'd been running uphill. His head bowed, he forced his stiff fingers to release the table. Good God. What had he done?

He wanted to take her, taste her, revel in her golden hair and lush body, and — And then what? Could he take her once and just leave? Or would this spell she was weaving consume him all the more?

He flexed his fingers, wincing as the blood flowed back into them. Another part of his body was just as stiff and likely to become just as painful. "Bloody hell," he muttered. "This is madness."

Sheer and utter madness. If he didn't leave soon, he might not be able to do so at all.

He stood abruptly, overturning his chair. He would pack his bags tonight and leave first thing in the morning. He'd ride straight to his sister's house and plunge into whatever gaiety she had planned, distracting himself from his endless absorption with a pair of pale turquoise eyes and the softest rosebud lips he'd ever seen.

CHAPTER 12

There comes a time when a man has t'decide if he's made of gold or iron. Ye might think this would be an easy decision t'make, but not every woman wants a man who has more shine than use.
          Old Woman Nora from Loch Lomond
                    to her three wee granddaughters
                              one cold evening

Sophia entered the kitchen the next morning, breathing in the wondrous smell of fresh-baked bread.

"Good mornin', miss," Mary said, sending a warm grin her way. "Ye're up early this morning."

"I had trouble sleeping." Before Mary could ask, she quickly added, "I'm worried about Red and the house."

"Ye're doing the best ye can. Did ye manage to talk his lordship into playin' cards again last night?"

"Oh, yes. I did." And had successfully inflamed MacLean to new heights. She could still see the raw hunger on his face as he sent her away; that's what had kept her up the rest of the night. That and the shock of her own reaction to being naughty.

She'd done something no respectable miss would do, but when had her life ever been governed by respectability? Mama had laughed at such notions, saying such rules were made to bind woman into subservience to their families. What mattered wasn't being respectable but being true to her own heart.

Sophia wasn't certain about her heart, but the rest of her body had definite ideas about what it wanted. She hadn't been prepared for the surge of power that rippled through her on seeing his reaction. And with that surge came the knowledge that she wanted him, too.

This was how Mama must have felt when she'd run off with Red after knowing him for only a few days. Of course, the difference was that she'd fallen in love. All Sophia had was lust — but oh, what a lovely, rich, and delicious lust it was!

She'd never really understood what the excitement was all about. She'd heard the maids giggling over their beaus and listened to the local romance gossip, but until now, she'd never understood how someone could throw away an orderly life for simple physical attraction.

Now she did. She'd tasted the power and felt the sheer exhilaration. She'd been unable to sleep because, for the first time in her life, she was too excited. Excited about life, about waking up, about being with Dougal, pushing him yet further into offering the deed to the house in a card game. She felt *alive.*

Tonight would be the night; she was certain of it. And then, once she'd won the house —

Some of her excitement died. After she won the house, Dougal would leave, and she and Red would continue as they'd always done.

A hollowness pressed against Sophia's chest. But that was what she wanted, what she'd been fighting for all along, wasn't it?

Mary, standing by the window, suddenly dropped her frying pan, startling Sophia from her thoughts. "Miss! It looks as if MacLean's leavin'!"

"What?"

"His man has both of the horses saddled, and their luggage is strapped to —"

Sophia dashed out the door and into the

yard, her gaze locked on Dougal. He stood by his horse, dressed all in black except for a brilliant white cravat, his elegant riding coat cut just so, his black boots polished until they shined, a gold tassel decorating each.

He turned as she approached, his dark green gaze sweeping over her, his tawny hair falling over his brow and shadowing his expression.

Blast the man! How dare he pack his bags and ride away after all the work she'd done! Worse, how dare he do it while looking so damned appealing?

Sophia marched up to him. "Where are you going?"

"Good morning, Miss MacFarlane. I'm afraid I must be going."

Miss MacFarlane? "I thought you'd stay another day, at least."

His gaze lingered on her mouth. "I was expected at my sister's days ago, but —" His green eyes warmed for a moment. "I allowed myself to become distracted."

"Yes, but we haven't finished —"

He captured her chin and lifted her face to his. "Are you certain you want us to 'finish'?"

His touch ignited a maelstrom of desires and feelings, but her pride stiffened her back. She would not let him see how much he affected her; she *refused.*

He dropped his hand, a bitter smile on his lips. "I thought not. There's nothing more to be said, my love." His voice was as cold as his touch had been hot. "My solicitor will be arriving within the month. You and your father may stay until then." He swung himself up on his horse and gathered the reins, flicking a glance her way. "I will be in touch regarding the house."

He couldn't just leave — not after all her work. He'd ridden in arrogant and cocksure, and now he was about to leave the same way.

Anger, pure and hot, flooded her veins. She planted her fists on her hips. "What's the matter, MacLean? Are you afraid?"

His brows snapped down, his eyes glinting dangerously. "*What* did you say?"

She lifted her chin. "I asked if you were afraid. If that is why you're sneaking out like a thief in the night?"

"It's morning, and I'm no thief."

"No, but you *are* afraid, aren't you? Afraid of me."

Dougal's expression darkened even more. "You don't know what you're saying."

"Yes, I do." She leaned close to say dismissively, "You are afraid of what our card

215

games might cause you to lose."

Dougal's body tensed at the words, making Poseidon jolt forward. How dare she accuse him of being afraid? The thought of it raged through him.

Yet in the back of his mind, a small voice whispered, *She's right. You are afraid of what you'll lose, only it's not about the house. It's about your self-control.*

Dougal slung himself down from the horse and faced Sophia. She refused to back away but stood her ground so that he was but a few inches from her.

She glared at him. "I saw your face last night. You want me, MacLean. Admit it. You're afraid I'll offer myself for the house, and you won't be able to resist it. And then . . ." She smiled smugly. "And then you'll lose."

The morning sun slanted across her face, illuminating her flawless skin. Her golden hair had a delicious tumbled look to it; her eyes were bright and clear. Even the faint circles only emphasized the color of her icy blue eyes.

He wanted nothing more than to scoop her up, toss her over his shoulder, take her into the barn, and *show* her exactly what he was feeling. And that was the problem: he felt far too much where Sophia was concerned. His passion alone could burn down the entire place; he didn't dare find out what would happen when they were both aflame.

He had to resist this, had to fight off the temptation she threw with her words.

Dougal turned coldly from her. "Whether I want you or not, I am leaving. I came to see the house, and I've seen it. There is nothing more to be said."

Sophia grabbed Poseidon's reins, turned to Shelton, who stood gawping at them, and tossed the reins to the groom. "Here! Your master and I have something we must speak about." She turned to Dougal. "And if we don't speak here, then I suppose I shall just have to find your sister's house. That shouldn't be very difficult."

Bloody hell, the woman was determined. "Damn you!" Dougal snapped at Sophia before turning to the waiting groom. "Walk the horses. I won't be long." He turned and strode away, his boots ringing on the flag-stones.

Sophia hitched up her skirts and scampered after him like a milkmaid. By the time he paused at the garden gate, she was even more hot and cross.

He opened the gate and went in, leaving it open for her but not offering to wait.

Sophia's anger simmered higher, but she lifted her chin and hurried up the path until she'd passed him. Puffing for breath, she briskly led the way to a bench beneath a tree, where she turned to face him.

He stood, feet planted apart, arms crossed over his broad chest. "What in the hell is this all about?"

"It's about me. And this house. And everything that's happened."

His gaze darkened, but he didn't move. "What, then?"

Suddenly, she wanted to tell him everything — how she'd worked so hard, fought to make the house into the home Mama had always wanted it to be. How in the space of one careless minute, Red had lost it all and how she desperately wanted it back. But more than that, she wanted to tell Dougal how his presence had changed things, disrupted her life, and made her aware that MacFarlane House wasn't the beginning and end of the world. She still wanted the house back, but now . . . now she wanted more.

But what? What *did* she want? She rubbed her forehead. "This is complicated."

He gave an impatient sigh. "Damn it, Sophia! I'll give you one minute and no more. What in the hell do you want?"

She spun on her heel and paced back and forth, struggling to find a beginning, pausing now and then as if to speak, then shaking her head and pacing again.

Dougal's irritation slowly faded, the knot in his chest easing as he watched her. She was a passionate woman; it showed in every stride she took, every emphatic move of her hands, every sparkle in her blue eyes. He gave her another moment and then said in a milder voice, "Perhaps I should just leave after all."

She whirled on him. "No! I'm just trying to find the right words, and I — oh, it's complicated!"

"Lies usually are."

She wetted her lips. "Lies?"

He raised his brows.

She sighed, her shoulders slumping, an expression almost of relief crossing her face. "You know."

Dougal nodded.

"Everything?"

He nodded again.

"How we tried to conceal the house's value? And disguised the beautiful paneling in the library? And —"

"Blocked up the chimneys and hid the good furnishings and served me food a dead man would refuse."

She bit her lip. "I'm sorry about that."

"No, you're not. You wanted me unhappy and uncomfortable."

"Well, yes — but not *very* uncomfortable. Only enough that you'd decide the house wasn't valuable."

"So that I would toss the deed onto the gaming table after you spent so many evenings luring me thither?"

She flicked an impatient hand. "And here I thought I'd been so devious."

"You were. I accidentally overheard you talking to Angus the day I arrived."

Her hands balled into fists. "You've known since the very first day?"

"Yes."

"Yet you pretended not to know anything."

He shrugged. "I thought to enjoy the show. I'm fortunate I overheard you because otherwise your plan would have worked."

Her gaze locked with his. "Would it?"

As much as he hated to admit it, he said, "Yes."

She pressed a hand to her temple. "Blast, blast, blast! I — I don't know what to say." She dropped her hand and faced him. "Red should never have wagered the house. It wasn't just his but mine as well."

"And you, my love, should never have made my bed so damp and lumpy. But don't worry; I only slept in that bed once, the night I arrived."

"Where did you sleep last night?"

He smiled. "I joined Shelton in the tack room. We found a cot and added some blankets; it was quite comfortable."

Her cheeks blossomed with color, and she sank onto the bench with a shaky laugh. "I can't believe you've known all along, which means we did all of that for nothing." She looked up at him. "Why didn't you say something?"

That was an interesting question, one he'd asked himself. He didn't like the answer, either: he'd wanted her to tell him. The thought made him frown. Why did he care if Sophia lied to him or not?

Perhaps it was a matter of pride.

There was no more reason to remain. He had received her confession; what more could he want?

Sophia asked, "I don't suppose you'd be willing to forgive my *faux pas* and stay a while longer?"

"So you can entice me into throwing the deed onto the table in a game of chance?"

She met his gaze boldly. "Yes." She stood and crossed the space between them, tilted back her head, and said in a silken voice, "And I would wager myself."

Dougal's body stiffened. The soft breeze teased the tendrils about her face and caressed her skin, bringing her faint scent to him. His gaze raked over her face, her eyes, her plump lips, her delicate throat, and beyond to the rounded swell of her breasts and hips. He remembered kissing her neck, tasting her after winning the first game. His lips still warmed at the memory, his body aflame yet again.

He wanted this woman as he'd wanted no other, but that was the reason he had to leave. He couldn't afford to care; and the way his spirit roared to life when she was about alerted him to that very danger. They were alike, the two of them. They lived for challenges and dared to defy life when they could.

His blood heated, and he had to curl his hands into fists to keep from reaching for her, from molding her soft, pliant body to his. She was so small and yet, in her own way, dangerous. She threatened his peace of mind, his equanimity, and his strength.

Dougal glanced up at the sky, where remnants of yesterday's storm still cast shadows over the dew-covered shrubs.

That is what happens when you care too much. That is what happened when Callum died and you thought you'd go mad with grief.

If you begin to care for anyone else, it will just make you weaker.

Even now, he had to fight a shudder at the storms he'd caused after Callum's death. There had been no stopping them, and it had been a miracle that no one had died. Riding his horse through the rain-swollen land, trees overturned and roofs ripped away by the winds, houses burned down by lightning, Dougal had seen the stunned faces of the villagers, had seen their disbelief as they looked at their ruined houses and lives. Worse, he had seen their fear.

Never again, he'd vowed. He would never allow another person in. He couldn't afford to.

"Dougal?"

He closed his eyes, refusing to give in to that warm, tempting voice.

"Dougal, just one game. That's all I want."

"No," he said harshly. "I wo—"

She kissed him, standing on tiptoe, her arms around his neck, her curves molded to him.

Dougal was lost at the first touch of her lips. Raw passion surged through him as he lifted her to him, holding her closer. He was aware of a thousand things at once yet couldn't form a single coherent thought.

The softness of her breasts as they pressed against his chest, the roundness of her derriere as he cupped her to him, the way her gown caught on his coat as he lifted her higher still, his mouth possessing and taking without cease.

Sophia had never been kissed in such a fashion, and oh, how she loved it! This was what the poets wrote of, what the maids had whispered about, what she had missed her entire life until now. Passion. Pure, unbridled passion. It thundered through her, filling her, completing her.

She was soaring, lifted by the heat of Dougal's embrace, urged on by his seeking hands. He broke the kiss only to trail his lips across her cheek to her ear. She shuddered with delight as he nipped at her lobe, shivers dancing over her skin.

She moaned and clutched him tighter, wanting more, needing more. Suddenly, he lifted her in his arms and carried her to the bench, where the shrubberies hid them from prying eyes. He tucked her onto his lap and cupped her chin with one hand as he lifted her lips to his once more.

She felt flame and fire, heat and sensuality, deliciously aware of the clinging silk of her gown, the faint rustle of lace at her breasts as Dougal's seeking fingers slid over her, the cool air on her toes as her slippers dropped to the grass.

She couldn't seem to get close enough. She tightened her hold around his neck, seeking more.

Responding to her urgency, Dougal molded her to him, his sensual kiss burning through her, into her, making her moan as she opened for more. More of him. More of the kiss. More of the intoxicating feelings that grew with each moment.

She felt the slip of his tongue over her teeth and shivered delightedly.

Dougal's hard mouth teased hers while his hands roamed freely, sliding over her hip to her waist and then up to her breast. He cupped her breast through the thin gown, his thumb finding her nipple and teasing it to aching hardness. She moaned and pressed closer still.

"Me lord?" came Shelton's raspy voice from the gate. "Are ye there?"

Sophia's eyes flew open, but Dougal didn't stop his explorations.

The gate creaked open, and then came the sound of booted feet walking hesitantly down the stone path. "Me lord? Should I walk the horses some more?"

Sophia pulled away, and Dougal reluctantly allowed her. Her entire body was aquiver, and she couldn't stop her hands and legs from trembling. She was on fire for more and couldn't seem to get her brain to work properly.

Dougal discovered that Sophia's ploy had worked and he had indeed changed his mind about leaving. He would *have* this woman. He'd play her game, win, and slake his lust. *Then* he'd leave, calmly and without emotional fanfare.

He set Sophia on the bench, where she attempted to right her clothing with hands that shook. Pleased, he said quietly, "Wait here." Then he made his way back to the pathway, where he found Shelton.

Relief flooded the groom's face. "There ye be, me lord. I was just wondering if the horses should be —"

"Leave them saddled, but remove my portmanteau. We'll take them for a ride before it gets too warm."

Shelton's face fell. "Remove yer portmanteau? Are we not leavin', then?"

"No. We are staying one more night."

"And after that?"

Dougal lifted his brows. "Go."

The groom flushed and scurried off.

When Dougal returned to Sophia, she was smoothing her gown back into place, unaware that a long curl of hair had come undone. Her cheeks were flushed, and her mouth was kiss-swollen.

A swell of satisfaction made him grin. He would burn this powerful yearning out of his blood with a good, solid night of passion. Then, when he left, Sophia Mac-Farlane would have no doubt about who had the upper hand.

"Sophia, I will stay."

Her smile trembled a bit, but she lifted her chin. "I was hoping you'd say that."

Hesitation flickered through him; there was something heart-wrenching about the way she looked, a touch of vulnerability in her gaze. He was imagining that, of course. She was the daughter of a notorious gambler and had traveled through Europe in the company of hardened rakes.

And the cool manner in which she comported herself could not be mistaken. Her actions spoke of her experience more than anything else: she'd prepared a plan to trick him into a game of chance and had been willing, even eager, to offer herself as the opposing stake. How could such a woman be an innocent?

Still, it would not do to leave such a concern unspoken. "Sophia, I do not dally with innocents."

Her gaze flickered, but then she flashed a

calm, knowing smile. "I am no innocent, MacLean. I know exactly what I'm doing."

He relaxed. Of course. No innocent could have so boldly stood before him in just a chemise, flashing that taunting smile. He'd slept fitfully because of that smile last night, dreaming of taking her over and over again.

Her eyes gleamed through her thick lashes now. "Dougal, I hope you don't take this the wrong way, but . . . are *you* an innocent?"

He blinked, too stunned to answer.

"Because if you are," she continued, laughter filling her voice, "then perhaps you *should* leave this morning."

"I will be glad to prove my experience this very evening. Will that suit you, Sophia?"

She nodded, her lashes shielding her expression from him. "It depends on who wins what, doesn't it? In the meantime, I will show you the house as it really is. I cannot undo everything, but I can show you some of the better qualities that Angus and I managed to hide."

"Done. But first, I am going to take Poseidon for a ride. He needs the exercise." And Dougal needed the cool breeze to regain his control. He crossed to Sophia and captured one of her wrists, then lifted it and pressed a kiss to her bare skin.

Her smile quavered but remained. "You, my lord, are giving me goose bumps."

"Every beautiful woman deserves to be clothed in no less." With a tug, he pulled her against him, her full breasts pressed against his waistcoat, her hips brushing his.

She looked up at him, her eyes mysteriously shadowed by her lashes, her cheeks a rosy pink. "MacLean, don't you think we should at least —"

He silenced her with a kiss, sliding his hands around her waist to hold her against him. She melted into him, giving herself to the passion as if his fire had ignited hers. She pressed against him with reassuring eagerness, her arms twining about his neck, pulling him nearer.

Dougal was once again afire. He stopped thinking, stopped considering, stopped everything but enjoying the kiss that consumed him.

Sophia stirred, her hands pressed to his chest. He loosened his hold and looked down into her flushed face. "Yes, my love?"

"I — I should go. Angus will come looking for me if I don't return to the house soon."

"But I hadn't finished yet."

Her lips quirked in a smile. "That was a long kiss."

"Longevity is one of my gifts."

She wasn't quite sure she understood him, but his expression sent a riot of heat over her face.

Dougal chuckled and ran a finger over her cheek. "Such beautiful skin. Such lovely color."

Sophia pulled away, and with a reluctant grin, he released her.

He followed her to the path, then ran a finger across her swollen bottom lip. "You are right, my love. If we were to continue, I might not be able to stop at just a kiss."

The words were more promise than threat, yet she shivered. What was wrong with her? Her limbs felt leaden, her tongue unable to form words, her mind a blank.

Dougal's finger slid to her chin, and he lifted her gaze to his. Warm humor filled his green eyes. "But I have never played a more enjoyable" — his gaze lingered on her lips — "game."

"Nor I." She found herself leaning toward him, her gaze locked on his lips. Firm and perfectly carved, they had felt so good, so hot, on hers. She shivered at the thought. Just one more kiss. What would that hurt? Just one, and —

"I will return after I've taken Poseidon for a ride." He dropped his hand, turned, and walked down the path, leaving her aching and feeling absurdly alone.

Sophia had always enjoyed her solitude, but this was neither pleasant nor peaceful. It was painful and empty, filled with yearning and a tumble of disjointed emotions.

She half walked, half stumbled back to the bench, her heart thudding wildly. She'd had no idea a kiss could affect one like that. No wonder men were so addicted to it! She'd never realized how powerful passion could be.

She let out a shaky sigh and sat up straight. She couldn't afford to get lost in such things if she wanted to win tonight's game. She had to focus on the cards and on counting.

If she wished to be successful, she had to remain clear-minded. A good strategy took in not only consideration of the enemy but also one's own weaknesses. And apparently she was far weaker than she'd known.

She had to keep her wits about her, which meant she'd have to avoid these kisses that left her breathless and unable to think.

She closed her eyes and shivered.

CHAPTER 13

As soon as they hatch from the egg, ye worry about yer wee ones. The trouble comes in knowing when to push yer little birdies from the nest and when to hold them in and sit on 'em.

Old Woman Nora from Loch Lomond
to her three wee granddaughters
one cold evening

Dougal leaned against the barn, the evening breeze stirring his hair, his gaze on the house before him. He absently noted the quality masonry and the beautiful inlay of marble on the front steps and how the windows caught the light as the sun slid out of sight.

Shelton picked up one of the saddles and carried it to a stand in the fading light. He pulled a brush from a nearby bucket, opened a small jar, and soon he was rhythmically polishing the leather.

Dougal ignored him, his mind focused on the residents of the house before him. Or, more truthfully, *one* resident. One golden-haired, impish, tempting armful of woman.

After Sophia had persuaded him to stay, he'd taken Poseidon for a run — mainly to cool his own unruly body. He'd also examined his motives for staying in that wretched house.

At first, it had been mere curiosity, wondering what Sophia and her minions were about. Then it had been the challenge of a beautiful woman, which he'd never been able to ignore. But finally, it had been Sophia herself. He'd become fascinated by her, admiring her spirit and determination.

A smart man would have turned on his heel and left. A truly smart man wouldn't have taken the risk of looking at Sophia as he did so. But Dougal luxuriated in beauty, and he couldn't help but look at her.

He loved her golden hair and had dreamed of it draped about them as she sat astride him, riding him to ecstasy. He imagined it wound about his hands as he took her in his huge bed at his London town house. He saw the thick, silky curls spread across the silk sheets in his house outside Stirling.

Since he'd met Sophia MacFarlane, he'd thought of little else. But tonight would change all that; he'd finally be freed of all these what-might-be's.

"Looks t'be a warm night," Shelton said as he rubbed the saddle's pommel.

Dougal shot him a glance. "You don't know the half of it."

Shelton spit on his rag and rubbed a leather strap with vigor. "Maybe not. But I do know that ye've been lookin' a mite distracted these last days. More distracted than I've ever seen ye."

Dougal shrugged. "I've had a lot on my mind." Even while riding this morning, all he'd been able to think about had been the feel of Sophia's lips beneath his, of the feel of her full breasts through her gown, her hips brushing his —

He moved restlessly, anxious for the evening to begin officially. He pulled a watch from his pocket and flicked it open. Five-fifteen. He still had an hour and fifteen minutes before dinner.

He'd spent the afternoon with Sophia as she gave him the "unabridged" tour of the house, and Dougal was amazed at the quality of wallpaper beneath the coating of soot, the fine furnishings in the attic, wainscoting that had been painted to hide its fine grain, a marble floor that had been covered with ugly carpets, doors that had been made to screech, and floor planks that had been pried until they creaked.

Sophia had been quiet as she'd shown him the true state of MacFarlane House. In a way, it was sad to give such a stately and magnificent home to his nephew, who was a mere child. It was a house to be lived in, laughed in, and loved in.

Dougal had thought about this as he followed Sophia through the house, Angus clumping behind them. Dougal had been forced to settle for merely watching her, her rounded bottom drawing his gaze as he followed her up and down the hallways and stairwells.

His groin tightened at the thought, and he flicked his watch open again.

Shelton clicked his tongue. "Ye keep checkin' yer watch so often, ye'll bring on bad luck. Are ye worried ye'll be late fer dinner?"

"No. I'm playing cards with Miss Mac-Farlane. I'm wagering the house."

Shelton dropped his rag. "Ye're playing fer the house? But ye won it just a month ago! Why, this land is worth more than yer estate near Stirling!"

Now that he'd toured the land and knew the true condition of the house, Dougal was tempted to agree. The deed to MacFarlane

House was worth far more than he'd originally thought.

Shelton shook his head. "Ye're moonstruck, me lord. Moonstruck and fairy-pinched."

Dougal snorted. "I have my reasons for wagering it." He looked back to the house, noting a figure in one of the upstairs windows. "When we leave tomorrow, I'll still have the deed tucked into my pocket. See if I don't."

Shelton picked up his rag and shook it out. "I shouldn't have let ye speak to the miss in the garden this morning. I just *knew* it would mean we'd be here yet another day."

Dougal grinned. "She's beautiful."

"I've never seen one more so," Shelton said truthfully. "Which is why ye need to have a care. She'll fill yer mind with fritters, and the next thing ye know, ye'll be playing a jack to a three and tossin' in yer London house, as well."

"I shall have a care. And now, I should get ready."

"Very well, me lord. But if ye lose the house —"

Dougal raised his brows.

Shelton sighed. "Never mind. Ye have so many houses, one less won't hurt ye none."

Dougal's pride would certainly notice the loss. That was yet another reason he had to win — and to do so in a way that settled the situation between him and Sophia once and for all.

Meanwhile, up in her room, Sophia had finished her bath and was dressing for dinner.

Her gown was a rich and heavy blush-colored silk, which in the golden candlelight appeared the exact hue of her skin. Its only ornamentation was a wide pale blue ribbon that tied beneath her breasts, and she'd found a pair of jeweled slippers that matched.

If she'd had any doubts about the gown, Mary's reaction would have soothed them. The maid had gaped openly, then clasped her hands together and said in a reverent tone that Sophia looked like an angel. That wasn't quite the look Sophia had been hoping for, but she thanked the maid.

Mary pinned Sophia's hair into a wild tumble of curls that fell over one shoulder, then stepped back and looked her over. "Gor," Mary breathed. "Ye look as fine as a fiddle, ye do."

"Thank you," Sophia said. "Should I wear my pearl set with this? The false diamonds are too bold."

"I wouldn't wear nothin' more than what God gave ye. Trust me, miss, ye look perfect."

"Thank you, Mary. I must admit I'm a bit nervous about tonight."

"I don't blame ye. I daresay his lordship is the same. He stands to lose the house, while ye —" Mary paused, a frown resting between her eyes. "What are ye wagering, miss? I never thought of that."

Sophia turned away to face the mirror. "Red said I could write markers." Of course, Dougal had refused to take them, but that was no one else's problem but hers.

Mary's brow cleared. "Well, so long as he's fine with that. Ye'll have to promise his lordship a right pretty amount."

"You could say that."

She shook her head. "One o' ye is goin' to leave this game mad enough to spit fire."

Sophia smiled. "It won't be me."

"I daresay MacLean would say the same," Mary said dryly. "Are ye goin' to see yer father afore ye go downstairs?"

"Yes. He should be awake now."

"He is, but barely. The doctor's kept him dosed up good." Mary smoothed her apron. "While ye're seein' to Mr. MacFarlane, I'm going to finish dinner. A *good* dinner."

Sophia sighed with relief. She didn't want to drink sherry on an empty stomach tonight. "Thank you, Mary."

The maid snorted. "It will be nice to fix a proper dinner. I'm servin' the first course in fifteen minutes."

Sophia gathered a thin silk shawl and draped it over her elbows, then made her way to Red's bedchamber.

"There ye are," he said in a sleepy voice. "I see you've dressed for dinner already. Come and let me have a look at you."

She obediently came to stand beside the bed.

He narrowed his gaze, but his eyelids kept slipping shut. He patted her hand weakly. "Sorry, lass. My eyes are a bit woozy from this blasted laudanum."

"Then sleep." The butterflies in her stomach buzzed uneasily, but she ignored them. She could do this; she just knew she could. "I can handle MacLean."

Red chuckled. "Och, just like me, you are. I love a challenge."

Sophia held his hand a bit tighter. "I'll win the house back for Mama. I promise."

"Good lass." His eyes drooped again. "Visit before you retire to bed. I want to know how it goes."

"I will." She placed her hand on his

forehead. "Sleep, Red. Mama's house will be safe."

He gave her a sleepy smile, his breathing deepening as he drifted off to sleep.

Sophia quietly closed the door and leaned against it. She'd win the game because she had to. She could do no less.

Holding that thought firmly in her mind, she walked downstairs to where MacLean waited.

Dougal replaced his glass beside the decanter of brandy. He'd found it sitting on the tray that usually held the sherry. He would have to ask Sophia about the wine cellars. If they were stocked with brandy like this, he might wish to purchase the entire stock.

He glanced at the clock over the mantel. She was late. He frowned and turned and looked out the window, the glow from the candles reflecting his outline and the room behind him. If he moved to one side, he could see himself dressed in his best coat, the white gleam of an intricately tied cravat, his hair still damp from his bath, his face tense. Dougal rubbed a hand down his jaw, suddenly remembering the feel of Sophia's cheek beneath his fingers. His body hardened instantly, and he turned from the window and took a fast gulp of brandy.

It didn't help. Not even a little. He'd hoped the alcohol might burn some of the heat from his blood; he was so taut with suppressed desire that he ached with it. Tonight that desire would be answered . . . or destroyed.

A sound from the hallway told him that Sophia was approaching, and he smiled wolfishly. They'd have their dinner, and then . . . He walked toward the hallway.

Her nude-colored gown rippled in the light, caressing first her thigh, then her hip, as she moved down the stairs as light and graceful as a sprite. She looked like a sprite tonight, the color of warm skin and naked sky.

Unfortunately, seeing Sophia looking as dewy and innocent as an angel did nothing to assuage his roaring frustration. It just inflamed him even more.

Bloody hell, was he already so weakened by her that he couldn't even control his reaction to her mere presence? Angry at himself, he growled, "There you are. How lovely of you to display your wager so prettily for me." The sneer in his voice tasted like metal.

As he spoke, her bright smile disappeared, and her cool voice demanded an apology. "I beg your pardon?"

She should. She should get down on her knees right now and beg him to forgive her scheming soul. Unfortunately, the thought of Sophia on her knees before him incited his lust even more.

He would go crazed if he did not touch her, taste her, *possess* her.

Seeing her standing before him dressed as luxuriously as any princess, as beautiful and sensual as any courtesan, he knew without a doubt that one way or another, he *would* have her tonight. Then this infernal wanting would end, and they'd be free to go their own ways, back to normalcy.

She met his gaze now, her expression coolly composed. "You will be glad to know that Mary has made something special for dinner."

"Something edible, I hope."

Her lips twitched. "Absolutely."

"Then it's doubly a pity that I don't want dinner this evening." The hunger that roared through him had nothing to do with food.

"No dinner? But Mary —"

"Are you hungry?"

She gave an odd flicker of a smile. "I couldn't eat anything now if my life depended on it."

Her admission relaxed his taut nerves. She

was as affected as he was. Good. That's how it should be.

He lifted a strand of her hair to his lips, the silken lock releasing a subtle fragrance that made his body tighten yet more. "Sophia, I am done waiting. Let us play our game and see where our futures lie."

She looked as if she might argue, but then her eyes narrowed. "Dougal, you've been drinking."

He shrugged.

She sniffed. "Brandy."

"It was on the sideboard when I arrived. I've only had two glasses, so I'm not shot in the neck yet."

A considering look flashed in her eyes, and Dougal knew what she was thinking: if he were drunk, she would have the upper hand. She didn't know that the MacLeans could hold their drink better than most.

She smiled and took his arm, leaning against him. "I'll send word to Mary that we've decided not to have dinner. She'll be upset, but it cannot be helped."

"Into the library, then." Suppressing his excitement, Dougal savored the warm pressure of her breast against his arm, the faint scent of jasmine wafting from her hair. God, she was a tempting morsel. He looked down at her, his gaze caught by the gap of her gown over her breasts and the elegant line of her shoulders.

As they reentered the library, Dougal pulled her hand from his arm and kissed her fingers. Her lips parted, a startled look in her eyes as she quickly stepped away, pulling her hand free.

Dougal watched her with interest. There were times when Miss Sophia MacFarlane seemed a cool, collected woman of the world. Then there were other times when he wondered if she'd ever been properly kissed.

He smiled. She'd been properly kissed at least once. "Allow me to find us both a bit of refreshment. There's nothing here but brandy."

"Brandy will do; Red has taught me the finer aspects of it."

Of course. Dougal crossed to the sideboard and picked up the decanter. "There's just enough left." He fixed them both a drink and brought them to the table where she stood.

She took the glass from his hand. "Now that we have our 'dinner,' shall we play?"

"By all means," he agreed. He pulled out her chair.

She smiled, an enigmatic smile that inflamed him. If she did not have a care, he would take her there on the table. Which he might well do anyway, once he'd won.

He ran his hand over the smooth surface, wondering if the legs were strong enough. He could picture her there, with her silken gown pushed up to her hips as he —

"Dougal?" Her husky voice brought him back to the present.

He forced the image away and assisted her into her chair, placing his hands on her shoulders and leaning down to say near her ear, "May the better player win."

She turned her head, her lips but an inch from his. "May she indeed."

Dougal smiled, then took his seat opposite. "Shall we play whist, for a change?" At her nod, he added, "We should play a few hands to warm up a bit. Unless, of course, you're in a hurry to cede to me now."

She colored delightfully. "No. Let's play a few practice hands. Shall we say . . . three?"

That would give him more time to appreciate the picture she made in the provocative gown. And to imagine her without it. "Very well."

"Excellent," she said, regarding him from beneath her lashes. "I will be *very* nimble when we play."

Her words sent a flood of desire through

Dougal, making him all the more determined to win.

The first hand went well for him, Sophia
losing, but barely. He watched her expressions, noting the tension around her mouth.
She desperately wanted to win, yet she
couldn't help watching him the way he was
watching her, a certain hunger in her eyes.

Which sparked an even deeper one in him.

The second hand went to Sophia, and he
noticed that there was none of the hesitation that had marked her previous games.
The little minx had been leading him along
the entire time. Even though he'd known
that, seeing it pricked his pride anew.

The last practice game was fraught with
tension. Every card turned added to the
palpable excitement in the room. Dougal
was aware of every flicker of Sophia's
eyelashes, every rise and fall of her breasts.

Dougal slowly but steadily gained. Finally,
Sophia turned over her last card and let out
a deep sigh. "I lost."

He heard the uncertainty in her voice.
"You seem surprised."

Her frown was quick and fierce. "I am.
No matter how much I play, I cannot get
used to losing."

Neither could he. Dougal reached into his
coat pocket, pulled out the deed, and tossed

it onto the table. "Enough practice. Let's do this."

For a long moment, Sophia stared at the deed. Then she picked up the deck, shuffled the cards, and offered them to Dougal to cut. He did so, and she dealt the cards. Dougal watched her carefully but detected no irregularities.

When he picked up his cards and looked at them, a surge of delight raced through him. He would win; he knew he would. He glanced through his lashes at Sophia and noted her paleness. Perhaps her hand wasn't as good as she'd wished . . . or was she bluffing?

She asked him for discards, and Dougal waved her off. Her brows snapped down, and she looked at him suspiciously, then discarded two of her own cards and drew two more.

When the hand finally ended, Dougal placed his cards faceup on the table. "I believe I take the trick."

She regarded his cards a long moment, then placed her own on the table beside his, saying nothing.

Dougal stared at her cards. Three queens. She'd won.

Disappointment and unfulfilled desire raged through his veins, his pride stinging bitterly. He'd lost it all — the house and Sophia. Damn it all, Shelton had been right; he should have left this morning.

Sophia couldn't believe it herself. She'd won — MacFarlane House was hers again! For an instant, pure and blinding triumph rushed through her. Then she caught Dougal's black gaze.

There was nothing left to keep him here now. The thought was as sudden as it was devastating. She was supposed to be exhilarated at her win, yet she felt as if she'd lost instead.

She reached for the deed and held it between her fingers, waiting futilely for a feeling of completion. Once Dougal left, life would go back to the way it was. She'd rise in the morning, fix breakfast for Red, then once he left to visit some friend, she'd work in her gardens. Then it would be time for lunch. Afterward, she might read a book or clean, dusting and such. After dinner, when Red returned, she would do embroidery or retire to bed with a book while Red tinkered with something out in the barn until late at night.

At one time, that had been all she'd wanted, but it was no longer enough. Now she wanted something more precious than a mere house.

Over the years, her sadness over Mama's death had been replaced by a deep loneliness. She hadn't realized it, but with Dougal's arrival, she'd suddenly had someone other than Red to talk to, someone interesting and enticing. Someone who would be leaving first thing in the morning.

She looked at the deed. Mama had wanted them to make the house into a home, but she wouldn't have wanted them to miss out on *life*. Her own vibrant choices were a testament to that.

A warm hand closed over her wrist, and Sophia looked across the table into Dougal's eyes. Slowly, inexorably, he pulled her forward.

His face was grim; his gaze never wavered from hers. She should have been offended at his insistence, but instead, she found herself leaning toward him, bending across the table, the deed forgotten.

His green eyes met hers, unfathomable and cold, so dark that they appeared black. "One kiss," he said, seductive and intent. "Or . . . are you afraid?"

CHAPTER 14

*Sometimes, the best ye can do is jus' toss
yer fears to the wind and tell the truth.
Even if ye have to lie to do it.*
Old Woman Nora from Loch Lomond
to her three wee granddaughters
one cold evening

"I am not afraid of anything." She yanked
her wrist from his grasp, placed her hands
on the table, and rose. "Not even you."

She was magnificent, staring disdainfully
at him even as her chest rose and fell with
the desire that bound them both. Yet in her
gaze was something else — like him, she
wanted *more.* The house wasn't enough.

Remaining in his seat, Dougal reached for
the cards and placed the deck before her.
"Prove it."

Her hands were fisted on the table, and
he could see her struggle — the part of her
that desired him and the part of her that

feared that desire. He knew that feeling; he was fighting the exact same battle this very moment.

Her lips curved into a damnably seductive smile as she picked up the deck. "Highest draw wins."

"Wins what?" he asked, his hands fisted.

Shivers traced through Sophia at the hoarseness of his voice. "A kiss, or something more. And the winner decides when to stop."

He raised his brows. "Sophia, are you certain about this?"

Her gaze dropped to the deed on the table before her. "I am very certain."

"Then you may go first."

"I should reshuffle the cards." She did so, her mind whirling as quickly as the cards. If she lost this hand, Dougal would take his kiss and then . . . leave.

The thought made her throat tighten until she couldn't swallow. She had to win this hand; she simply *had* to.

She glanced at Dougal, whose gaze was on her face rather than her hands. That would help. Red had shown her more ways to win than just counting the cards. While she never would have cheated to win back the house, it wasn't so bad when the stake was a kiss . . . or the very intriguing "something more."

Smiling a little to herself, she shuffled the cards quickly, manipulating the cards on the top with each flick of her wrist.

"There." She set the cards back on the table, palming a card as she did so. "Who shall go first?"

He regarded her a long moment, assessing, measuring.

She tingled all over, forcing herself to say in a normal voice, "Dougal?"

"I'm sorry; my mind was wandering. Please go ahead."

She started to reach for the deck so she could position the card as she wished, when Dougal grabbed her wrist.

"No."

His voice made Sophia freeze in place. His mouth was almost white with controlled anger, his eyes blazing a deep, endless green.

Outside, the wind lifted, swirling the curtains in the windows, ruffling the cards on the table, wafting heat from the candle flames.

Suddenly, he pulled her forward, out of her chair, across the slick surface of the table.

"MacLean!" she cried, grasping at her captured wrist, but to no avail.

His lips were just inches from hers. He

lifted her captured wrist and brought it to her eye level, the hidden card now visible.

Outside, the wind whipped to life.

His eyes glittered with fury. "So this is how you won the deed."

"No! Dougal, I —"

The shutters banged as the rumble of thunder echoed in response.

Sophia's gaze locked with Dougal's. There was nothing she could say. Nothing she could do. She lay half across the table, her wrist imprisoned in his large hand, her face mere inches from his.

Outside, the thunder moved closer. The wind blew harshly into the room, spinning the loose cards from the table. They spiraled up, then down, dancing on the wild wind.

"Why?" Dougal asked, his voice the crack of a whip.

Sophia's heart pounded against her throat, and she opened her mouth. "I —"

"No, don't say anything," he said bitterly. "You'll just lie to me, tell me what you think I want to hear."

He stood, oblivious to everything but his anger.

He hauled her up against him, trapping her to his chest, his body as hard as his expression. "This was what you'd planned all along, to steal from me by making me so wild with lust that I could no longer think."

She wedged her hands between them and pressed against his chest. "No, no! I did no such thing! I — I wanted the house back, but I did not cheat you out of it! I swear, I only —"

"Don't speak. You've been tempting me from the beginning, throwing yourself at me like a courtesan."

Oh, God, when he said it like that — "Dougal, please. You have to understand —"

A crack of thunder drowned out her words, lightning blinding her momentarily, the whip of a vicious wind snuffing every candle and leaving them in near darkness.

"Damn you," Dougal snapped, his voice vibrating oddly through her. "You are no better than your father — a gambler and a thief."

"Dougal, I only cheated now, for the kiss."

His jaw clenched white. "You expect me to believe that?"

Looking into his face, she knew that it was futile to explain anything right now. He was too angry, and the situation looked damning, even to her.

Lightning threw Dougal's harsh face into relief, and he looked like a beautiful avenging angel, come to exact a horrible justice.

She shivered at the sight as a crash of thunder cracked so close that the ground shook. With a muffled exclamation, Dougal bent his head and kissed her.

It was brutal, insistent. Despite her raw fear, Sophia opened to him. She couldn't stop it, any more than she could hold back the wildness of the storm.

She did the only thing she could do — the only thing she wanted to do. She gave in to Dougal's passion and allowed her own to flow free. Like the storm, it charged through her, and soon she was wanting more, needing more.

With a groan, Dougal lifted her to the table, her bottom sliding over the slick surface as he laid her among the tossed cards. She sank beneath him, feeling as wild as the wind, as powerful as the lightning, as much a part of the earth as the thunder that rumbled across it.

She could feel his hands as he slid her skirts up, past her knees, to her thighs and higher. His warm fingers found the tops of her stockings, and he stripped them from her, tearing them in his hurry.

Thunder crashed again, the lightning revealing Dougal's face set with determination, anger, and blatant desire; he'd never looked so handsome.

The table was hard against her back, but she didn't care. All she felt was him. She was engulfed by him, consumed by him, surrounded and completed by him. Every fiber of her cried out for his touch, and she craved him as she'd never needed another.

He pushed aside her chemise and stepped back to loosen his breeches. The momentary loss of contact made Sophia mad with desire. She writhed against the table, feeling wanton and exposed and yearning for more. Impatient, she hooked her heels about his waist and pulled him closer, seeking him.

Dougal's bared skin brushed her. Her heart thundered as loudly as the storm that crashed about them. The rain poured thirstily, the wind tormenting her as it brushed over her writhing body.

For a taut moment, he held himself at the edge, his face showing the strain of maintaining his control. She read the question in his green eyes and, in answer, grabbed his shirt with both hands, locked her legs about him, and yanked him forward.

A strike of lightning lit the room as Dougal sank into her, his gasped yell of triumph blending with the thunder. Yet as loud as the thunder crashed, Sophia's surprised cry of pain rang out clearly.

Dougal stopped, buried deep inside her, his gaze burning into hers. She saw the accusation there but would have none of it. This was what she'd wanted. She grabbed his shoulders and writhed against him, urging him deeper.

Thunder roared overhead, Dougal moving with it, his face contorted with desire and fury. Sophia opened beneath him, the pain subsiding as she lifted her hips to meet him, thrust for thrust.

Sophia clutched him to her, tears welling as she savored his fullness inside her, soothing her ache, making her yearn for more. And more. And yet more.

As he began thrusting into her, the pressure inside built. She writhed against him, seeking, always seeking, though she didn't know what.

Suddenly, a tidal wave of tingling pleasure crashed over her. She arched up, her eyes closing as she rode the crest of the feelings, gasping for breath. Her body convulsed with intense pleasure, her legs locked furiously about Dougal's waist as he gasped her name, then collapsed on her.

Outside, the thunder rumbled.

They stayed where they were, Dougal between her thighs, her legs locked about his waist, her arms about his neck.

Sophia hid her face in Dougal's neck, soaking in his warmth as reason slowly returned. Where did they go from here? Where *could* they go? He'd leave at first light, and she'd never see him again.

She'd lost in every way a woman could lose.

Dougal stirred and lifted himself on one arm. Sophia allowed him to rise, reluctantly slipping her arms from his neck.

He rested on his elbow and looked down at her, his eyes hidden by the dark. "Tell me, Sophia . . . was this part of the plan, too? Were you to seduce me if you were caught playing your tricks? Blind me by passion so that I wouldn't demand what is rightfully mine?" Thunder roiled overhead, the rain drumming down.

His gaze narrowed. "You told me you were not an innocent. Perhaps you didn't really want the house after all but a wealthy husband." He laughed bitterly. "If that was your intention, my lady, I'm afraid you've failed in that as well."

"No!" Sophia's sadness welled into irritation. "There was no plan other than to lure you into playing cards. I should have told you I was a virgin, but I —"

"Enough," he snapped. A crack of lightning punctuated his words. "I don't want to hear any more lies. I don't even know why I asked."

Damn him! She'd just given him her virginity, her very being, and he couldn't be bothered to listen to her.

"Let me up!" She pushed him away and scrambled to get up, yanking her skirts down over her sticky thighs, her hands trembling as she adjusted her gown. The wind blew across her, making her shiver as she faced the chill of his disdain.

She looked about the room for her shawl and found it pooled beneath one of the chairs by the table. She tossed it over her shoulders and marched to the windows to close them, uncaring that the rain sprayed her gown and hair. Lightning flashed as she struggled with the last window, and something caught her eye — an odd light, glowing fiercely against the black night.

Frowning, she peered through the rain, her hands gripping the window. The glow grew, casting enough light finally to show itself. "Dougal! The barn is on fire!"

CHAPTER 15

Ne'er back down from a compliment, an insult, or a conundrum. An honest woman knows there's little difference amongst the lot.

Old Woman Nora from Loch Lomond
to her three wee granddaughters
one cold evening

Hours later, Dougal stood beneath the overhang of the barn, only a faint haze of smoke seeping out the doorway and disappearing in the rain. He rubbed his neck wearily. Damn the lightning. Damn it to hell, along with his own raw temper.

He closed his eyes, which burned still from exposure to the smoke and heat. The lightning had hit the barn dead center, splintering the major support beam and sending sparks into the dry hay stored in the loft. In no time at all, the entire thing was ablaze.

Thank God for the heavy downpour. Without it, the barn would have been lost.

Shelton ran through the rain to join Dougal under the overhang. The groom wiped his face with a blackened hand, leaving streaks down his grizzled cheek. "The horses are tucked away in the shed. It's a tight fit, but they seem to know 'tis what's best for them."

Dougal nodded.

When Sophia had alerted him to the fire, he'd yanked on his breeches and boots, tucking in his shirt as he ran from the house. Thank goodness he hadn't run into Angus until a few minutes later, and by then, they were all too busy to do anything other than work together to save the horses.

Sophia had run out too, Angus following. They were drenched to the bone within moments. Dougal had shouted at her to leave, but she'd refused, helping Shelton with the horses while Dougal and Angus worked to save the barn.

Dougal reached out and let the water from the roof pour over his hands, washing the grime and soot from his arms. "Thank you for your help, Shelton. The horses would have been lost without you."

"I was jus' doing my job." Shelton sent a sidelong glance at Dougal. "That was a sudden storm. I was layin' on me cot when it just seemed to burst out of nowhere."

Dougal didn't answer. He'd allowed his lust for Sophia to overcome his caution, and this is what had happened. He glanced at her bedchamber window, remembering her this evening — lush and passionate, stealing his breath and his control at the same time. It had been a night he'd never forget, and not just because of their incredible lovemaking. It was because he'd finally found a woman whose passion matched his own. A woman who leapt at a challenge as quickly as he did. A woman he could never have — because somehow, over the past week, a bond had formed between them. A bond he'd done his damnedest to avoid.

Worse, because of her lies, he'd unwittingly taken her innocence.

He gritted his teeth and said shortly, "Shelton, we'll be leaving with first light."

"That's what ye said yesterday. And the day afore that, and the day afore —"

"There will be no change of plans now."

Shelton looked at the open barn doors, where smoke curled out to disappear in the rain. "It's a good thing the barn is yers already."

"None of this is mine. I lost it in the card game."

"Ha! So that's what tickled yer anger bone. I was wonderin'. Did ye lose the land, too?"

"I lost everything." Everything that mattered.

Dougal looked back up to Sophia's window and wondered if he should say goodbye. It would be polite, but . . . no, he couldn't do it. He'd just leave a note and send his man of business with a check to cover the cost of rebuilding the barn.

Damn his temper! Damn it to hell. He turned to Shelton. "Did you save our things from the fire? The tack room was engulfed when I arrived."

"Aye, I got most of our clothes as I went."

"Excellent. Angus said he'd have baths drawn for both of us so we don't have to sleep smelling like charred wood."

"That's generous of 'im," Shelton said brightly. "Did he mention anything about food?"

"Yes. Mary is preparing some meat and cheese."

"Then that's where I'm headin'. Are ye coming?"

"I want to wait until the smoke completely clears and make sure the barn doesn't burst back into flames."

"Do ye want me to —"

"No." He managed a bitter smile. "If anyone deserves to stand guard, it's me."

Shelton's brow lowered. "Me lord, ye didn't direct the lightning."

"Neither did I control my temper — and that *is* my responsibility."

"Me lord, ye can't —"

"Enjoy your meal. I will be fine here." At the groom's concerned look, Dougal added in a firmer voice, "Go!"

Shelton sighed. "Very well, me lord. I'll be back after I've had a nibble."

After the groom left, Dougal went back into the barn. Rain still poured in from a huge hole overhead, and smoke curled along the floor. Fallen timbers, blackened and broken, lay scattered about, much like his pride.

Once he left, he would never look back.

From her bedchamber window, Sophia watched Dougal disappear inside the barn. She started to reach for the latch to warn him to be careful, but he wouldn't welcome such a gesture. He wouldn't welcome any gesture from her at all.

She'd seen Dougal's face during the fire and recognized the guilt he felt for causing it, because she felt the same way. She'd known of the curse and had purposefully pushed him to the limits of his control.

Blast it, if only she'd thought — But she hadn't, and because of that, Dougal was shouldering blame that was far more hers than his.

She'd yearned to talk to him, but whenever his gaze passed over her, his coldness had halted her. Tomorrow. Tomorrow she'd catch him alone, and then they'd talk. Perhaps she could make him understand why she'd made the decisions she had.

But not now. As she watched him walk into the barn, her heart pressed heavily in her chest. He was leaving. She could see it in the set of his shoulders, the purposeful way he moved.

A tear landed on the back of her hand, which rested on the windowsill. She looked at it with surprise; she hadn't even known she was crying.

Lips suddenly quivering, Sophia turned from the window and threw herself onto her bed. There she let the tears fall, her growing sobs muffled by a mound of pillows.

Beatrice came to Red that night. As always, she slipped into his room when he was deep in a dream.

Ah, his lovely Beatrice! He never doubted

that it was her, even when the light shining from her face obscured her features. It was enough to feel her presence, to hear her sweet voice as she whispered that she was watching over him and loved him still.

As always, whenever she came, Red felt a powerful mixture of pleasure and pain, of companionship and loneliness, of all he'd had and all he'd lost.

She drifted above his bed, her white robes fluttering, her golden hair touched with a halo of light just like in the pictures in his mother's old Bible.

"Red." Her voice rushed over him with the heat of longing and the coolness of pure water.

Though he knew he couldn't touch her, he couldn't help lifting his hand. "Och, Beatrice. I've missed you."

A smile touched her tender lips, and she sighed. "I can see you do. You've been a busy man this last month."

She knew he'd lost the deed and her jewels. Swallowing hard, he said, "My love, I made a mistake, but Sophia fixed it all. I was just try- ing to —"

"Our daughter is not happy."

There was accusation in the soft voice.

"Aye, she's suffering. This man, Dougal MacLean —"

"The one who won my house from you in a card game?" A faintly waspish note was in Beatrice's voice now.

Red winced. "Yes, yes. I can see you know all of that, so I won't bore ye by repeating it."

Her arms crossed over her angelic robes. "Why is our daughter not happy?"

Red shifted uneasily. "I don't know."

"Our daughter must go to MacLean."

Red blinked, though his eyes were still closed. "But . . . he left two days ago."

"And how long has Sophie been moping about?"

"Since the barn burned down, the day before yes — oh." Red considered this. "I would think the same thing, but she seems angry whenever I bring up his name."

"She's hurt."

"I don't know. She hasn't said two words about him since he left. My love, I don't mean to question your judgment but —"

"Do you see this?" Beatrice pointed to the shining halo over her head, a spark of amusement in her shimmery voice.

"Aye," he answered, his own lips trembling in a smile.

"Then stop your blathering, you foolish man. Our Sophie must follow her heart, and that means she must go after MacLean."

Red's smile faded. Follow her heart? And

go after MacLean? "Beatrice, does that mean
—"

But when he raised his eyes again, she was
gone.

Red awoke with tears streaming down his
face, yet his heart sparkled. If he tried very
hard, he could hear Beatrice's voice now,
sweet and cultured, her face so like their
dear Sophie's, heart-shaped with a rosebud
mouth and bright blue eyes, skin of cream,
and masses of golden hair. Beatrice had
been a beauty, there was no doubt about it.
What's more, she'd left behind a powerful
father, several grand mansions, and dozens
of servants, all for him. She'd always said it
had been no hardship to leave behind her
easy life and soft living, but it had taken
Red years before he truly believed her.

He'd met Beatrice's only surviving parent
once. After the wedding, her father had
come to the inn where they were staying,
newly wed and filled with love. He'd come
in a carriage and eight, the most beautiful
horses Red had ever seen pulling a carriage
so fine a prince would lust after it. Beatrice's
father had not come to give them his blessing but to tell his daughter in no uncertain
terms what he thought of her behavior.

White-lipped and eyes sparkling, Beatrice

had listened to her father's words, and then, with the air of a princess, she had taken Red's arm and dismissed the old man. Red-faced with anger and vowing never to speak to her again, the pretentious fool had stomped away.

Red had watched that magnificent carriage pulling out of the innyard, awed that even the trappings on the horses were covered in silver and gold. Beatrice had laughed, saying a carriage was a carriage and a bossy old man was a bossy old man. But the visit had made Red treasure her love all the more. No woman was ever more loved, no man more blessed — especially after Sophie came to them.

There had always been a special bond between Sophie and her mother, and Beatrice had been fiercely protective of her daughter. Now Beatrice had come to him with a message, one he dared not ignore. The whole mess put him in a bit of a quandary, for he didn't know enough about MacLean to entrust Sophie to him.

Red scowled. To take such a gamble with his own daughter? It was a damned shame he wasn't well enough to travel, or he'd take her to see MacLean himself.

He turned his head and looked out the window, where a heavy rain beat down steadily. "Beatrice," he whispered. "Are ye sure?"

In the silence, he thought he heard her dear, sweet voice whisper back, *"Yes, you lummox."*

And in the darkness, Red smiled.

Morning finally arrived. Just like the two nights before, Sophia hadn't slept more than an hour or two at most. Every time she closed her eyes, she saw MacLean's blazing look of . . . contempt? Anger? She was no longer certain. All she knew was that her heart had broken into pieces.

Downstairs, she heard Mary's voice raised against Angus, something about wet firewood. Outside, the steady beat of rain muffled any hopes of cheer. Sighing, Sophie rose, washed her face and hands, and put on her clothes. Every movement was an effort, and when a slight twinge reminded her again of the library and MacLean, she pressed her hands to her eyes and tried to think of something else.

She resolutely left her bedroom, vowing to leave her sadness behind. Chin held a smidge too high, she plastered a smile on her face and entered her father's room.

He'd been looking pale after his injury, but today he appeared different. His eyes had their old sparkle, his face was relaxed, and a genuine smile curved his lips.

"You look to be in fine fettle," she said, bending down to kiss him. "You didn't look this youthful when you were well."

He chuckled, his blue eyes twinkling up at her. "Perhaps an angel healed me last night."

She laughed. "That and some pixie dust, and you'll be up by tomorrow." She took a seat beside his bed and smiled. "How did you sleep?"

"Fine, fine." He searched her face. "Lassie, you look exhausted."

She shrugged. "I didn't sleep well."

"You haven't slept well since you won back the deed." He pursed his lips thoughtfully. "I'd have thought that would be cause for celebration, myself."

"It's the rain. It's been going on for three days straight, and it's making me blue as a megrim."

Red patted her hand. "Lass, you haven't been sleeping or eating. You're wasting away, ye are."

"You," she corrected. "And once this rain stops, things will go back to normal."

"It's not the rain, Sophie."

"Then what is it?"

"Dougal MacLean."

She yanked her hand from her father's

grasp. "I don't know what you're talking about."

"You have feelings for this man," Red insisted.

"I do not!" she said hotly. "Dougal Mac-Lean is an arrogant, conceited, hard-headed arse."

"Your mother, bless her soul, often said the same of me. Still does, in fact, in her own way. But that doesn't explain why you're pining away."

"I am *not* pining away."

"Very well. Then what *are* you feeling?"

Sophia twisted her hands together. "I'm . . . I'm embarrassed. I was angry and hurt, and so was he. I didn't have the chance to explain why —" She flushed. "It's not important."

"It *is* important, or you wouldn't be so upset. Lassie, there's only one thing to do: go after him."

Sophia blinked. "What?"

"Go after him and have your say, whatever that is. Time's passed, so you'll both be calmer. Perhaps he'll be in more of a mood to listen."

Tears filled her eyes. "No," she said quietly. "He'll never be in the mood to listen to me. Red, I — I cheated."

Red blinked. "Ye did what?"

"Not when Dougal and I were wagering on the house, but afterward, when —" She caught her father's gaze and blushed. "It doesn't matter."

"What were you wagering on?"

She sighed. "A kiss."

"Damn it to hell!" Red clamped his lips together for a long moment before asking, "And what were you wagering this kiss against?"

She bit her lip.

"Och, lassie," Red moaned.

"Now you know why I cheated. I didn't wish to lose. I was afraid I might like it too much."

Red slapped a hand over his eyes and muttered under his breath, "Och, Beatrice, what do I say to that?" He dropped his hand. "Look, I don't know if this is the right thing, but some people might think it is, so I'll take a chance. MacLean is at his sister's house, which is a mere day's ride from here. Pack your bags, and tell him what you need to tell him."

She twisted her hands together. "And the deed?"

"What of it?"

"I think . . . I think he deserves to keep it. We did everything to attempt to trick him. At the time, it seemed important, but now . . ."

"Lassie, do you mean that?"

She nodded. "We could sell the brandy in the cellar and use it to begin again somewhere else."

"And you'd do that? Move away from this house?"

"At one time, I thought the house was everything, because it represented Mama. Now I wonder if perhaps you and I aren't what represents her the most."

Red clasped his hands to his chest and looked at the ceiling. "You were right all along, my love!"

Sophia frowned up at the ceiling. "Red, what —"

"Never mind. Lass, I agree with you completely. If it'll give you some peace, then give the deed to MacLean, and speak your mind."

"And then?"

He took her hand. "And then come home, and we'll pack our things." He smiled and released her. "Now, go. Tell Mary that she and Angus are to travel with you and to watch you like trained hounds."

"But I can't just show up on MacLean's sister's doorstep and demand to see him! It would take me a whole day to get there, and —"

"Yes, you can. And what's more, I daresay his sister will invite you to stay. She's known for her generosity, but if she doesn't, I know plenty of people around Stirling. I'll write the directions to one of them for Angus in case that should happen."

Was Red right? Would she never have any peace if she left things as they were? What if MacLean wouldn't listen to her? What would his sister think if she showed up uninvited, looking like some sort of brash female chasing down Lady Kincaid's brother?

Sophia's cheeks burned at the thought, but no more than her heart ached. What a horrid coil.

The culmination of the passion that had simmered between them since their first meeting had been inevitable; she'd known it and had desperately wanted it. She only wished it hadn't come in the midst of such a horrid misunderstanding.

If she didn't explain everything to him, he would forever think the worst of her, and that was the most painful part.

She swallowed and said, "Red, you are right. I'll tell Mary to pack right away."

"You'll take Angus with you, too. For protection."

She started to protest, but he held up a

hand. "If you leave within the hour, you can make it by nightfall. With this rain, I wouldn't wait longer. The stream is close to covering the bridge already."

Sophia had to smile. "Anxious to get rid of me?"

"Aye. I'm tired of seeing your long face over the breakfast table."

She laughed a little. "Red, I don't understand. Why are you so insistent about this?"

"Because if anyone knows the cost of lost opportunity, it's me. Sometimes you have to grab life by the horns and ride it, even if it tries to throw you. I don't want to see you spending the rest of your life wincing every time you say this man's name."

Which she would do. She felt stripped, exposed, raw. Red was right; if she didn't have her say to Dougal, she'd spend the rest of her life regretting it. "Red, I love you."

He beamed. "You ought to. I'll expect you back within a few days with a full report."

"Of course. But who will care for you while I'm gone?"

"I'll stay with the squire."

She stood and dropped a kiss on his cheek. "Good. I'll go and pack now."

"When you get to Lady Kincaid's house, don't leave until you've had a chance to talk to the man, even if you have to drag him by the ear. It may take a bit of persistence."

Sophie grinned, feeling better already. "That I have in abundance."

CHAPTER 16

A man who thinks he doesn't need women is a man damned to cold sheets, lumpy porridge, and the bitter taste o' loneliness.
Old Woman Nora from Loch Lomond
to her three wee granddaughters
one cold evening

"I am quite out of patience with him." Fiona Kincaid set her teacup on the small tray with a decided click. "Dougal's been in a horrid temper since he arrived."

"I like him better this way," Fiona's handsome husband retorted. "He barely said a word over breakfast."

She gave an exasperated sigh. "I'm surprised you two don't get along better, as you're very similar." Jack's flat stare made her add hastily, "In *some* things."

"In very *few* things." He glanced out the windows at the wet garden. The rain had fallen so hard that many of the flowers had been beheaded, their wet petals strewn over the puddle-filled paths. "It's been two days, and it's still storming."

Fiona poured more tea into her cup. "The weather definitely came from him. I could feel it the second he arrived." She made a face. "I had quite given up on him showing for our house party; almost everyone has already left."

"I hope they all leave soon." Jack's gaze traveled possessively over Fiona. "I don't want you subjected to hostess duties any longer than necessary."

She smiled at her husband. "Other than Dougal, we've only four guests left, so there's not much for me to do. Unfortunately, most of the eligible ladies have gone, which leaves Dougal without a dinner partner. Seating will be awkward."

"Seat him beside the judge's wife. That would make her happy, at least."

"I will do no such thing!" Fiona said hotly. "That woman is a virago. I only invited her because her husband has been doing some wonderful work with the orphanage in Hampton, and I wished to re-create his methods here in Stirling."

"From the way Mrs. Kent kept asking when Dougal would arrive, I suspect there's a bit of history between them."

"I wouldn't be surprised. To give him credit, Dougal hasn't been encouraging her, though he could hardly do so with her husband present."

"If he were interested, Dougal wouldn't let that trivial detail keep him away." Jack caught his wife's reproachful look and laughed softly, caught up her hand, and pressed a heated kiss to her soft palm, then curled her fingers over it. "Fiona, my love, as much as I adore you, I cannot stand your brothers. Any of them."

"Gregor is much nicer now that he's married. Even you must admit that."

"Only when Venetia is with him. When she's not, he's as annoying as ever."

Fiona's lips quirked into a smile, her green eyes gleaming. "Rather like you, I hear."

"Who has been carrying tales?"

"Everyone." She placed her hand on her husband's cheek and smiled up into his blue eyes. With his dark auburn hair and devastating good looks, "Black Jack" Kincaid had once been the scourge of London's polite society. Now he was her own personal scourge, one she couldn't imagine living without.

He chuckled and dropped his napkin onto the table. "I believe I shall go to the nursery and read a story to our son. Would you like to come with me?"

She smiled and stood, taking her husband's arm. "Of course! He's getting so big. I can scarcely remember when he was a wee babe, and —"

A soft knock sounded on the door, and Perkins, the butler, entered. "Pardon me, but a Miss MacFarlane has arrived for your brother, Lord MacLean. Unfortunately, he has not returned yet."

"Returned?" Fiona frowned. "Where has he gone?"

"I believe your brother went for a ride immediately after breakfast." The butler looked disapprovingly out at the rain.

Jack sent Fiona a quizzical look. "I wonder if we're about to meet the reason for Dougal's ill temper."

"I wouldn't be surprised. Jack, do you mind if I meet Miss MacFarlane by myself at first?"

"Of course. I'll see you when you're done with your interrogation."

"I am not going to interrogate anyone!"

Jack grinned. "Of course not. You're just going to ask questions." He cast a glance at Perkins. "Lady Kincaid will be with our guest shortly."

"Yes, my lord." The butler bowed and left.

Fiona frowned at the steady beat of rain

against the window. "Dougal will catch his death, riding in such a rain."

Jack shrugged. "He made it; let him swim in it." He pressed a kiss to his wife's forehead. "I'll be curious to hear about this woman."

Fiona absently nodded. If what Jack suspected were true and Miss MacFarlane was the cause of Dougal's gloom, then woe betide the lady!

Chin high, she swept into the entryway. Standing in the center of the hall was a woman with gray curly hair and freckles, broad as a barn and dressed as a servant. Fiona almost tripped over her own feet. Surely, this was not the sort of woman Dougal pursued? But perhaps . . . perhaps it was true love. Was *that* why Dougal had been so surly?

Fiona gathered her scattered wits and put a polite smile on her face. "Miss Mac-Farlane? Welcome to —"

A soft cough halted Fiona, and the woman before her pointed behind Fiona.

She turned around and knew instantly that she was indeed facing the cause of Dougal's storms. Miss MacFarlane wasn't simply beautiful; the girl was breathtaking. Small and fairylike, she had golden hair and the most amazing pale blue eyes, a mouth as sweet and red as cherries, and a straight, patrician nose that most of London's debutantes would kill for.

Miss MacFarlane bowed gracefully. "Lady Kincaid, I'm Sophia MacFarlane. I came to speak with your brother about an important business matter. Is he here?"

The woman's soft voice was both hesitant and determined, and Fiona detected a bit of steel behind the delicate features.

"Miss MacFarlane, I'm afraid my brother is out at the moment. Perhaps you'd like to have some tea while we wait? He shouldn't be long." Fiona only hoped he'd be gone long enough for her to assess the mysterious Miss MacFarlane.

An hour later, Dougal returned to Kincaid House, his boots uncomfortably full of water. He handed his dripping overcoat and hat to Perkins, brushed his wet hair from his eyes, and headed for the stairs. Just as he reached the sitting room, the door opened, and his brother-in-law strolled out.

"Dougal! Just the man I've been wanting to see!" Jack said, a broad grin on his face. "I'm glad you've returned."

Dougal eyed him narrowly. "Why?"

Jack's dark blue eyes twinkled with mirth. "Are you thirsty? Perhaps you should come into the sitting room and have some tea with

Fiona . . . and her guest."

Dougal scowled. He didn't want tea. He also didn't want Fiona trying to cheer him up. Ever since he'd arrived two days ago, he'd found himself at odds with everything. Nothing made him happy: not good food, not the flirtation of a pretty woman, not seeing his sister or his nephew. Nothing dispelled this heavy gloom.

All he could think about was Sophia Mac-Farlane and how she'd looked when he'd last seen her. As usual, the thought made his heart burn, and he silently damned her to hell yet again. "Pray make my excuses to Fiona. I want to bathe and change before dinner," he said curtly.

What he really wanted was to drown his thoughts in a decanter of Jack's best port. Scowling, he turned back to the stairs, then heard a voice drifting out of the sitting room like down on the wind.

She's here. Dougal came to an abrupt halt, every fiber of his being on edge, waiting, ready, wanting . . .

He pushed past Jack into the sitting room.

Sophia was perched on the edge of a settee, holding a teacup and saucer, facing Fiona, who was regaling her with tales of Little Jack. At Dougal's entrance, Sophia set down her cup and sprang to her feet, her face burning with color.

Dougal stopped before her. He'd never thought to see her again. Over the last few days, he'd told himself that things were exactly the way he liked them and that he'd been recuperating from his potent desire for her.

Now he knew he'd been lying. He wanted her just as badly now as he had the first time he'd seen her. Wanted her with a fierce fire that refused to be dampened.

And she felt the same. He could see it in her eyes, feel her desire as it pulsed across the space to him.

Fiona coughed delicately.

Aware that his sister's curious gaze was flickering between them, Dougal forced himself to bow. "Miss MacFarlane."

She sank into a quick curtsey. "Lord Mac-Lean."

Dougal couldn't take his eyes off her. She was paler than before, with faint circles under her eyes. Had he hurt her when — He turned to Fiona. "I need to speak to Miss MacFarlane."

Fiona frowned, her eyes warning him that he was being impolite. "You'll have plenty of time for that this evening. I've asked Sophia to stay for the night, and she has agreed."

Stay? In the same house he was staying in? It had been pure hell trying to sleep before, but now, knowing she was there, under the same roof, her lush body — "No." The word was torn from him.

Fiona's gaze narrowed. "Dougal, this is my house —"

"And mine," Jack added flatly.

Dougal sent him a cutting glare.

Fiona sniffed. "If I wish Miss MacFarlane to stay, she'll stay."

Sophia lifted her chin. "I'm sorry you're averse to my visit, but I've already accepted your sister's kind invitation."

Dougal's jaw clenched. If she stayed, he might not be able to let her go. Damn it all, this was not fair!

Outside, the gray sky began to darken again, a rumble of thunder sounding in the distance.

Sophia glanced out the window, her face paling yet more.

"Not again," Jack muttered. "We're going to float away."

"Dougal," his sister snapped, "watch your temper!"

"I am," he said through gritted teeth.

Sophia made a sound of disbelief, and he glared at her, which was a mistake. The sight of her plump lips pressed into a frown caught him — lips he'd tasted, lips that had clung to his when he'd taken her on the table, surrounded by the heat of a summer storm. His body immediately burned, and he knew that he couldn't speak to her yet — not until he'd exhausted himself past the point of desire.

Dougal turned on his heel and headed for the door.

"Dougal, where are you going?" Fiona asked.

He didn't break stride. "For a ride."

"But you just returned!"

"I know, damn it." He yanked the door open.

"Will you be back for dinner?" Fiona called after him.

He didn't bother to reply, leaving the house without his hat, slamming the door behind him.

Scowling, he ignored the roiling thunderclouds and was soon riding wildly over the fields as if the hounds of hell pursued him.

"There you are!"

Dougal turned to find his sister hurrying across the entrance hall. She was dressed in a pink silk gown that flowed about her slightly plump figure. She'd gained a bit of weight when she'd had the baby, but Jack didn't seem to notice or care.

For an instant, Dougal envied Fiona and Jack. They loved each other in a way that was rare, accepting each other as they were. There was no deception or guile between them.

He sighed as Fiona looked him over from head to toe. "You're soaked! Dinner is in half an hour; you'll never be ready in time."

"So begin without me." He shrugged out of his dripping coat and handed it to a waiting footman.

Fiona glanced at the impassive footman, then took Dougal's arm and pulled him into the empty sitting room. She shut the door firmly. "I've been waiting for hours, and I deserve some answers. Who is Sophia, and why is she so important?"

"Before you begin, explain why you invited that woman to stay here."

Fiona crossed her arms, which, because of her small stature, wasn't a very threatening pose. "I invited Miss MacFarlane because I could see that there was something between the two of you."

"Something that I longed to avoid."

Fiona eyed him a moment, obviously fascinated. "Would you explain what you mean?"

"No."

She pursed her lips. "What if I promise to name my next child after you?"

Dougal lifted his brows. "Won't Jack dislike that?"

A smile quivered on her lips. "Yes. Which is why I thought it a wonderful inducement for you."

"I don't believe you'd do that."

"Well, I would," Fiona said firmly.

Dougal ran a hand over his wet face. "Fiona, I am wet through and through. If you wish me ready for dinner, I must change."

She sighed. "Fine. You aren't going to tell me anything anyway." She opened the door and told one of the footmen, "I requested a bath to be readied for Lord MacLean's room. Please have it sent up now."

"Yes, my lady." The footman bowed and left the hall.

"Dougal, I will hold the guests in the library for a little while, but do hurry, or dinner will be cold."

"I shall bathe with alarming quickness." When he'd been riding hell for leather through the rain, he'd been too angry to feel the cold. Now, standing away from the warm fire, he was chilled through and through.

"I don't know why I even try," his sister

said sourly. "That's what I get for taking pity on you."

"Pity?"

"Pity," she repeated firmly. "Look at yourself in the mirror. I've never seen such a long face. Now, go get ready for dinner, and don't dawdle." She turned and left, her gown fluttering behind her.

Dougal made his way up the stairs. Two footmen had just finished filling a large brass tub beside the fireplace, and as they left, he went to test the pleasantly steaming water.

Suddenly, he wanted nothing more than the hot bath soothing his aching muscles. Every inch of his body felt beaten and bruised.

He glanced at the clock and realized he had only twenty minutes to make his appearance. Walking to the tub, he tugged at his neck cloth and began to undress.

His own sister pitied him, he thought sourly. He didn't need any pity. He might be angry, but he certainly wasn't sad. He was *not* unhappy about the way events had turned out. The heaviness that pulled at his soul came from the feeling of betrayal.

He yanked his shirt over his head and tugged off the rest of his clothing, then went to the bath.

Fiona was a fine sister for all her busybody ways. She'd had the tub placed by the fire so that he'd have both warm air and warm water.

The tub itself was phenomenal, large enough for two and deep enough that he could sit upright with water almost to his shoulders. He rolled his stiff shoulders, wincing at their tightness. Sophia had him stretched as taut as a wire.

All day, he'd been haunted by the way she'd looked at him in the sitting room, as if her entire future rested on him and no one else — which was a foolish thought, indeed.

Why had she followed him? What did she want? He hoped he hadn't hurt her with his abrupt departure.

He clenched his jaw. Damn it, her feelings were not his problem. Ruthlessly pushing his thoughts aside, he was preparing to step into the tub when someone knocked briskly on his door.

Before he could answer, it swung open, and Sophia slipped into his room, closing the door quickly. "Dougal?"

She was dressed in a gown of vibrant blue shot through with silver that draped over her body, hugging the line of her hips and the lovely curve of her breasts. Her long hair was upswept, a diamond winking in the curls. Her chin was high, and she held a folded sheet of paper before her, almost like a shield.

When she saw him standing nude beside the fireplace, her lips parted, her eyes widened, and she took a startled step back, dropping the paper.

Surprised as well, Dougal couldn't move. He stood beside the tub, completely naked, one leg lifted to step in. The heat from the tub and the fire were nothing compared with the hot excitement that shot through his veins.

"What the hell do you want?" he asked harshly.

CHAPTER 17

Men are like rocks. There are times they cannot move 'less ye give 'em a wee nudge.
Old Woman Nora from Loch Lomond
to her three wee granddaughters
one cold evening

Sophia couldn't breathe at the sight of Dougal standing naked before the fire, the firelight licking hungrily at the shadowed muscles of his stomach and thighs, tracing the powerful bulges of his arms down to his well-formed hands. Their previous encounter had happened in the near dark, with occasional flashes of lightning, so it had been more about touch and taste than sight. Nothing had prepared her for Dougal's bared masculinity and his obvious arousal, which literally grew as she looked at him.

The sight stole all ability to think, all ability to breathe, all ability to do anything but stare.

She should have blushed and fled, but she couldn't. Her heart thudded harder, her fingers curling with the need to touch those hard muscles and feel the warmth of his skin beneath her fingertips. *God, he is magnificent!* Every tawny, muscled inch.

Dougal planted his feet wide, as if daring her not to stare at him. "Well, well, well," he drawled, his voice hot enough to start a fire of its own. "What are you doing in my room, Miss Sophia? Was this what you had in mind when you tricked my sister into inviting you here?" His eyes narrowed to slits. "Did you come to tempt me into making a fool of myself again?"

She licked her dry lips and said huskily, "I came to speak with you. We'll be with the other guests this evening and may not have time for private speech."

"And you could not wait until morning?"

"I will be leaving first thing in the morning."

His eyes glinted. "What is so damn important that you cannot wait?"

Her gaze dropped to his maleness, her mouth watering, yearning to touch his skin and see if it was as warm as it looked. To trace the lines of his muscles with the tips of her fingers. To melt into his arms and feel his lips over hers and —

He gave a muttered curse and suddenly strode toward her.

Sophia's eyes widened as he stopped in front of her, and she could see the irritation in his green gaze. "What do you want from me? *What?*"

She lifted her hand, then realized the paper wasn't in it. Blast, she must have dropped it. She looked around and saw it by her foot, so she bent to pick it up — pausing halfway when she realized she was at eye level with Dougal's very obviously aroused male member.

It was but an inch from her, the shaft smooth and hard and thick. This was what had given her such pleasure. Her entire body tightened at the thought, and she burned to reach out and touch it. Her hand lifted, and —

He caught her shoulder, his fingers tightening. "Sophia," he rasped.

Suddenly, she knew what he wanted. Knew it with all of her heart. The idea was indescribably naughty, which made her want to do it all the more.

She leaned forward, and slowly, ever so slowly, she kissed the end of his shaft.

Dougal took a shuddering breath as she

pulled back and retrieved the paper from the floor.

She held out the paper, unable to meet his gaze. What was it about this man that made her forget propriety?

There was a long silence, then Dougal snatched the paper from her. It crackled as he opened it.

"The deed?" He thrust it back at her. "I don't want it."

She met his eyes. "Neither do I."

His brows snapped together. "Why not? Wasn't this the reason you threw yourself at me —"

"I didn't mean for *that* to happen — any more than you did."

"I don't believe you."

"Then why am I here, giving you the deed?" she asked simply.

"Guilt?" His eyes had darkened until they were almost black.

"No," she said softly. "I feel many things, but guilt isn't one of them."

His gaze dropped from her face to the deed. For a long moment, he stood like that, his head bowed, the firelight playing over his dark gold hair, the paper crumpled in his hand.

Then he lifted his head. "We're like tinder before a flame. I don't know what this attraction is that flares between us." He shook his head ruefully. "I've never experienced anything like it."

Sophia's chest tightened, and she forced herself to look into his eyes so that she wouldn't be distracted by anything else. "I don't know what it is, either, but it's a little frightening."

He frowned. "That night, in the library — did I hurt you?"

There was such concern in his voice that she swiftly shook her head. "No. Of course not. It felt quite . . . good, actually."

"You told me you were not an innocent." His eyes were damning. "Why did you tell me that?"

Her cheeks burned. "Because I knew that if I told you the truth, you would leave. And I wanted you."

He searched her face, and finally, he nodded, his stern look replaced by a faint smile. "Fair enough. I understand desire if nothing else."

"Yes, you do," she said in a fervent voice.

He laughed softly, his eyes softening to a deep green. "You sound astonished."

"It was wonderful," she said simply. "Dougal, I am sorry for trying to trick you about the house. It was my mother's fondest dream that Red and I live there. He was on his way to Edinburgh to sell the last of her jewels to pay for a new roof, when he lost the house to you." She made a hopeless gesture. "He meant to help, but . . . it didn't work."

"Did it ever occur to you to explain that to me?"

She blinked at him. "Would you have given up your claim?"

His smile was dark and beautiful and made her yearn for him yet again. "You won't ever know, will you?"

Sophia shook her head and made the mistake of dropping her gaze. She found herself looking at his muscled shoulders and chest and at the trail of dark blond that led down, narrowing intriguingly as it ended — She slapped a hand over her eyes, her body burning.

She heard a soft chuckle, and his warm hand closed over her wrist, her entire arm tingling at the touch. He pulled her hand from her eyes, his expression sobering as he met her gaze. "You are an intriguing mixture of innocence and sensuality. I never know what to expect from you."

"I never do, either," she muttered, pulling her hand free. She wanted him so badly and exulted in that feeling. But she also knew the cost of throwing herself into the flames.

Every time they were together, it was becoming more and more difficult to distinguish between lust and love.

Love? The thought jolted her. Where had that come from? How could she possibly be in love with Dougal MacLean?

"We must rid ourselves of this desire." He handed her back the deed.

She took it without thinking. "How?"

He swooped her into his arms and turned, her gown sweeping over his arm. Sophia clutched at him, linking her arms about his neck, the deed falling to the floor once again. "What are you doing?" she asked breathlessly.

"What I should have done the second you walked into this room." His voice was almost a growl, though a faint smile curved his hard mouth.

He set her on her feet beside the tub. "Undress."

She blinked. "I beg your pardon?"

His green eyes gleamed. "You can't take a bath in your clothes."

"A bath? But dinner —"

"Can bloody well wait. Neither of us is a slave to society's rules, are we?" A challenge lit his eyes.

Something within her flared in response. She'd always enjoyed the freedom of her unconventional upbringing, the freedom that had allowed her to plan to live in her own house without a husband, the freedom that had led her to initiate a high-stakes game of chance with the man who stood naked before her.

He gave her a wicked, follow-me grin before he stepped over the edge of the tub, slid into the lapping water, and held out his hand. "Shall I help you in?"

She longed to join him, the feeling almost painful. But if she lost control and allowed him closer physically, could she continue to fight off the emotional ties that seemed to strengthen every time they were together?

She knew that once she was in the warm water, with Dougal's powerful arms about her, there would be no control, no thinking, just a crushing wave of *being.* She shivered deliciously.

The water sloshed as Dougal rose, naked and gleaming, and lifted Sophia, gown and all.

"Dougal!"

He held her over the water. "Well? Will you join me now?"

"Do I have any choice?"

"No." He sat down, settling her in his bared lap.

Her gown floated about her, the silver netting of her overskirt draped over the edge of the tub as her underskirts floated about them. Warm water soaked through her clothes and lapped at her breasts, making her nipples peak.

His arms tightened about her, and he pulled her back until her head rested against his shoulder. "There," he said, his voice warm against her ear. "Finally, you are where you should be."

For now. That was the way of men like Dougal; they were all yours . . . until tomorrow. That was all she'd get. But perhaps that would be enough. She was just realizing the truth about her own character, acknowledging the desire for excitement that had been dormant so long. Perhaps when tomorrow came, this was all she'd want, too.

Dougal tilted up her chin and smiled into her eyes. "Shall I scrub your back, my love?"

"Through my gown?" Sophia lifted an arm. Her gown was soaked and clung to her, streams of water running into the tub. A quiver of laughter tickled her. "Dougal, you are ridiculous! How am I to get back to my room dressed like this?"

He grinned at her, his teeth flashing whitely in the dim light from the fire. "You'll leave a trail of water."

"Which the servants will report to your sister."

"Fiona won't care."

Sophia lifted her brows. "You can't believe that."

"So long as I'm happy, she'll be happy for me."

She turned and regarded him for a long moment. He was devastatingly handsome, his eyes dark and mysterious. His mouth seemed carved from granite, drawn with such a definite line, his square chin a testament to his strength. His shoulders rose from the water, heavily corded with muscles. She could feel the hardness of him all around her, in his arms, his stomach, his legs, his —

Her eyes widened, and she scrambled to stand up, but Dougal was too quick. His arms tightened about her the second she tried to push out of the water. "Dougal, let —"

He kissed her. Not roughly as before but passionately, his mouth warm, his lips deliciously firm. The kiss burned through her, shattering her thoughts, rendering her incapable of thinking or feeling anything but him.

This was what she'd longed for, missed, and needed. She struggled to untie her

gown, growling when the wet ribbon knotted.

Dougal reached beneath her gown and
pulled the tie free. He turned her so that
she straddled him. Sophia shivered as his
fingers found her core beneath the clinging
material.

Ever so gently, he drew his fingers over
her. Again and again, his fingers barely
touched her, tracing a light path, sending
exquisitely delicious tremors through her.
She moaned, and her head fell back.

His arm tightened, though he didn't cease
his ministrations. She stirred restlessly, and
he increased the pressure of his fingers, driv-
ing her wild with need. Every touch made
her long for more; every tremor made her
yearn for release.

His breath was harsh, his chest rising and
falling rapidly as he slid his hands to her
hips and pulled her over him, his manhood
pressing against her. Sophia gasped with
pleasure as he entered her.

Then she was rocking back and forth, her
gown a floating blue puddle, her hands tight
on his shoulders. He thrust upward, holding her waist as he took her over and over.

The feeling built, and she moaned his
name, faintly aware of the water sloshing
onto the floor as her body rose and fell in

and out of the warm water, her nipples abrading against her wet gown in the most delicious way.

A low growl of excitement grew inside her, rising with every thrust, every move. When Dougal's lips fastened over her peaked nipple, she arched back as waves of exultation washed over her, pleasure unlike any she'd ever felt thundering through her.

She gasped his name, then hung on tightly as she slowly regained her breath.

He pulled her close as she recovered, his manhood still hard within her. Then he stood, taking her with him as if she weighed no more than a feather. He stepped from the tub, her soaked gown and hair streaming water onto the wet rug, and set her before the fireplace, where the warm flames stilled her shivers.

Sophia looked up at Dougal. Gone was the light-hearted philanderer; in his place was a man bent on seduction. Had she any sense, she would leave.

But having tasted Dougal's kisses, she knew that no house, no matter how beautiful or how dear, would ever fill her heart. She wanted this. She wanted him.

She didn't realize she was trying to loosen the tie of her gown until his hands closed over hers.

"Allow me." His voice, deep and rich, brushed over her ears, sending another shiver through her.

He quickly undid the tie and pushed her sodden gown from her greedy skin, leaving her clad only in her wet chemise and stockings.

Dougal discovered that it was possible to lose one's breath at the mere sight of a woman. God, but she was beautiful. The chemise clung to her curves, cupping each breast, molding her flat stomach, sliding along the curve of her hip to the entrancing length of her thighs. Her long hair was half drenched and clung to her neck and shoulders in dark gold tendrils.

But it was her mouth, red and swollen from his kisses, that held him speechless. Full and plump, it glistened moistly, beckoning him, daring him to taste it once more.

And he did. As he slowly rolled her chemise from her drenched body, he kissed her bared skin as it was revealed, inch by inch. She clung to him, her chest rising and falling quickly, her lips parted, her desire growing with his own.

Finally, he knelt before her and removed her stockings, then rocked back on his heels to look at her. The flickering firelight glistened on her damp body, smoothing over her curves, hiding her secrets in the shadows.

He placed his hands on her hips and pulled her gently down to where he knelt. She sank to her knees, joining him on the thick carpet, her breasts brushing his chest. Aflame, Dougal bent to kiss her as his fingers slipped between her thighs.

She gasped, her hands tightening on his shoulders. He slipped an arm behind her and lowered her to the carpet, never breaking their kiss. He pulled back only when he'd parted her thighs and pressed against her.

Awash in desire, he consumed her with his eyes even as he possessed her body. He reveled in the way she threw back her head, how her eyes closed as she moaned his name with each thrust, how she writhed against him in wild abandon.

His release burst from him with a cry, as wild as any storm his temper had ever produced. She cried out then too, arching against him.

Afterward, with the fire warming their bared skin, he kissed her softly, holding her tight. Though their breathing had settled to a normal rhythm, the air was still heavy with their passion. It was deliciously intimate, holding her naked body to his, her head tucked against his shoulder, her legs twined with his.

A man could get used to this, he thought — then stopped himself. He couldn't afford to care. His temper was dangerous enough as it was. His heart sank as he pushed the bitter thought away.

When a soft knock sounded on the door, Sophia started, but Dougal merely held her tight. "Do not enter," he called. "I am not dressed."

"Yes, my lord." Perkins's dry voice wafted through the door. "Lady Kincaid wished to remind you that dinner is being served momentarily."

"I'll be down shortly."

"Yes, my lord." The butler's steps faded.

Sophia sat upright. "He'll go to my room next!"

"And think that he missed you on your way to the dining room. We'll wait until he's gone, then I'll see you back to your room so you can change and go downstairs. If anyone says anything, tell them you got lost in the house."

"No one will believe that."

"It happens all the time. Lady Durant was once an hour late for that very reason."

Sophia's lips quivered with laughter. "I am sure I will enjoy appearing a fool to your sister."

He kissed her nose. "Come, let's get you to your room before she comes to check on us herself."

After he'd wrapped Sophia in his robe and bundled her off to her room, he discovered that she'd left the deed to MacFarlane House on his floor.

He picked it up and grinned at the soggy paper, soaked from their energetic bath. Shaking his head at the trouble the deed had caused, he laid it out to dry, then dressed for dinner.

CHAPTER 18

Don't let anyone say that men can do more than women. Just imagine how few bairns there'd be if men had to deal with life's true pains!
Old Woman Nora from Loch Lomond
to her three wee granddaughters
one cold evening

For Sophia, dinner passed in a blur. She was uncomfortably aware of her hair, pinned tightly to her head to hide the wet ends. She'd been fortunate that Mary had already left for dinner in the servants' quarters. In her dazed state, she couldn't have out-bluffed her maid's gimlet gaze.

And no amount of self-discipline could keep her gaze off Dougal now. He radiated sensuality just by breathing, a fact one of the other guests seemed all too aware of.

There were eight of them at dinner. Besides Fiona and her husband, Jack, there was a judge and his wife, a horse-crazed woman named Miss Stanton who talked of nothing but the ride she'd taken that afternoon, and a handsome gentleman by the name of Sir Reginald Barksdale, who stared at Sophia all evening as if perplexed by something.

It wasn't the unattached female, Miss Stanton, who fawned over Dougal but Mrs. Kent, the judge's wife.

The judge, a rotund, red-faced man with a jolly laugh, was a good twenty years older than his pert and lively wife.

Mrs. Kent laughed and talked in an outrageous fashion and blatantly attempted to flirt with Dougal. Her husband, meanwhile, was impervious to everything but the quality of his meal, regarding the whole party with a sort of fond tolerance.

Sophia felt no such charity of feelings. Every time Mrs. Kent lifted her big brown eyes to Dougal and smiled at him as if they had a secret, Sophia's blood simmered. Which was ridiculous, of course. She didn't *own* him, for heaven's sake. She'd just *borrowed* him, more or less.

Her gaze met Dougal's across the table, and he raised his wineglass and sipped as if silently toasting her.

Especially because she knew the sharp-eyed Mrs. Kent was watching, Sophia couldn't help lifting her own glass and silently saluting Dougal in the same manner. He smiled, while Mrs. Kent's fake smile hardened.

Not the sort to cede anything to another woman, Mrs. Kent was soon whispering to Dougal, placing her hand on his arm, and leaning forward so that her breasts pressed precariously against her neckline.

Sophia frowned. Good God, didn't the woman know she was making an absolute fool of herself? She looked like a —

"Miss MacFarlane," came a deep voice to her side.

Sophia turned to find Sir Reginald facing her. He'd been conversing with Miss Stanton about the merits of the various riding paths; now he'd made his escape.

He smiled. "I don't wish to sound impertinent, but have we met before?"

Dougal let out a derisive snort.

She sent him a warning look. "No," she told Sir Reginald. "I've lived a rather secluded life in Scotland and haven't traveled in almost twelve years; I doubt we could have met."

"That's odd. I'm certain I've seen you before. It's your eyes; they are quite remarkable." His gray gaze swept over her, a deprecating smile softening his expression. "I'm sorry if I've embarrassed you. We'll talk of other subjects. Have I mentioned that I have a monkey? He's an intelligent pet, and I used to travel with him everywhere."

As he continued on in this vein, she decided he was a very handsome man. His face was pleasant, his eyes a piercing gray, his chin firm, and his mouth well shaped, though he possessed none of Dougal's raw magnetism.

"I know where we met!" Sir Reginald said suddenly. "In Vienna! I was on my tour of the Continent." He frowned. "But it couldn't have been you. That was years ago; you would have been a child then."

"Perhaps you met my mother — she and I look very similar. She and my father traveled quite a bit before I was born."

"That's possible, I suppose," he said, as if not entirely convinced.

"Sir Reginald." Dougal broke in on their conversation, entirely against common etiquette. "Perhaps you mistake Miss Mac-Farlane with a dream." He let his gaze linger over her in a familiar fashion. "I often do."

Sophia's face burned. Fiona choked on her wine, and Jack patted her back, glaring at Dougal. The judge let out a snort of laughter, while Mrs. Kent sent dagger glances at Sophia, and Miss Stanton, oblivious to it all, asked for the salt.

Sophia knew Dougal was merely staking his claim. She was a well-enjoyed conquest to him, but nothing more, and that was exactly how she should think of him, too. Somehow the thought pinched her heart.

When they retreated to the drawing room, Sir Reginald made no move to leave Sophia's side, quizzing her about her life and travels. As Fiona joined them, Dougal shook off the cloying attentions of Mrs. Kent and also made his way to Sophia's side.

Sophia saw him approaching, and in an attempt to appear unaffected by his presence, she hurriedly said to Fiona, "That's a lovely necklace."

Fiona brightened, her slender fingers going to the large diamond. "Jack bought it for me when we learned I was expecting. I told him it was too dear, but he was determined."

"May I?" Sir Reginald asked, lifting his quizzing glass.

Fiona smiled. "Of course!" She took off the necklace and handed it to him, saying to Sophia, "Sir Reginald is something of an expert on jewels, especially antiques."

He looked up from the brilliant diamond

to say in a self-deprecating fashion, "You're far too generous, Lady Kincaid. The term *expert* implies far more effort than I'm willing to impart." He handed the necklace back to Fiona. "It's lovely."

"Thank you." She smiled playfully. "Can you tell me more?" At Sophia's look of inquiry, Fiona added, "It's a game with us. I try to stump him with the various pieces Jack purchases for me. Sir Reginald has yet to miss a guess."

Sir Reginald laughed. "Give me time, and I'm certain I'll fail."

Sophia had to smile. While he lacked Dougal's overwhelming masculinity, Sir Reginald seemed to be a nice man.

Fiona touched her necklace. "Well, Sir Reginald? What can you tell me about my new necklace?"

"First of all, it's not new. Judging by the clasp, I'd say it's at least thirty years old." He pursed his lips and added, "I'm not certain, but looking at the workmanship and the set of the diamonds, it's most likely the work of Rundell, Bridge, and Company, of London."

"You're right again!" Fiona exclaimed.

Sir Reginald bowed, looking pleased.

Dougal reached into his pocket to pull out a velvet pouch and handed it to Sir Reginald. "Tell us what you think of these. They are Sophia's."

"*Were* Sophia's," she corrected.

Sir Reginald looked at Sophia, his brows raised.

"I lost them in a card game to Lord Mac-Lean," she explained.

"Ah," Sir Reginald said, the delicacy of his expression making Sophia blush.

"However I obtained them," Dougal said smoothly, "perhaps you can give us an estimate of their true value."

"I would be delighted." Sir Reginald crossed to a nearby table and carefully slid the contents of the velvet bag out onto the surface.

"How lovely!" Fiona exclaimed as the delicate gold and diamond necklace spilled out. A bracelet followed, as well as some diamond hairpins.

"Fascinating," Sir Reginald murmured. He held up the necklace, his brows knitted. "What exquisite workmanship!" He traced a finger over the delicate filigree before he glanced at Sophia. "Would you mind if I took them to the lamp to examine them in a better light?"

She shrugged. "Ask Lord MacLean. They are his."

"No," Dougal said, his dark green gaze

burning into hers. "They are yours. I don't take what doesn't belong to me."

Did he mean the diamonds? The deed? Or *her?*

Sir Reginald held the necklace to the light, his expression intent as he looked at each piece. Finally, he returned, a crease between his brows. "Miss MacFarlane, where did you come by these?"

"They were my mother's."

Sir Reginald carefully slid the jewelry back into the bag. "They are exceptional. I've never seen the like." He frowned again, holding the bag cupped against him in a rather possessive manner. "Except . . ." His gaze narrowed, and he was lost in thought.

Fiona flashed a smile at Sophia. "It appears that you've finally stumped poor Sir Reginald."

He shook his head ruefully. "The workmanship is definitely Italian, but beyond that, I cannot say. They are markedly unusual pieces. In fact, they remind me of a very unusual tiara I once saw at —" Sir Reginald looked at Sophia, his gaze unfocused, as if he saw her and yet didn't.

She raised her brows. "Yes?"

He colored slightly and shook his head. "I'm sorry. That necklace and the way you were standing there with your head tilted just so made me think of a portrait I once saw of . . . but that couldn't be you, because—" He laughed awkwardly. "I'm sorry, I'm rambling."

"Sophia has that effect on people," Dougal said, holding out his hand.

With obvious reluctance, Sir Reginald returned the bag.

"Thank you." Dougal took the jewelry, and, grasping Sophia's wrist, he placed the bag in her hand.

"But you won these."

"They are yours. I have very little use for diamonds."

"How gallant," Sir Reginald murmured, looking from Dougal to Sophia and back.

Dougal turned and began to speak to his sister, so Sophia kept the jewelry. Unless she made a scene, there was little else she could do.

As if sensing her unease, Sir Reginald attempted to engage her in conversation.

Sophia barely noticed him; she was far too busy trying not to look at Dougal. Every time he moved or spoke, a tingle raced over Sophia's skin. Though she'd been well sated by their encounter, she found herself growing more restless.

She sent him a glance from beneath her lashes. He was amazingly sensual, from the way his dark blond hair spilled over his forehead to the deep green of his heavy-lidded gaze. She wished they were alone so she could trace his lips with hers once again.

But that was not to be. Just then, Mrs. Kent broke away from her obviously sleepy husband, attached herself to Dougal's arm with a determined air, and began to monopolize his conversation.

It was the chance Sophia had been waiting for. She excused herself to Sir Reginald and quietly pleaded a headache to Fiona, who immediately offered a tisane. Sophia refused and said that sleep would be a better curative than anything. Then, with her mother's jewels clutched in one hand, she escaped to the safety of her room.

In the morning, she'd leave. With her, she'd take just the knowledge that at least Dougal wouldn't think of her as a thief now. That was worth something, she told herself as she wiped a single tear from her eye.

Later that night, she heard the footfalls of a man's boots as they came down the hallway. They paused at her door. She knew it was Dougal; she could feel his presence as clearly as if she could see him. Sophia held her breath, clenching her eyes closed, hoping he would leave.

She couldn't possibly resist another seduction, but such a thing would only make leaving even harder, and she couldn't chance it.

After a long moment, he walked down the hall to his own room. When she heard his door close, she pulled a pillow over her head and cried herself to sleep.

Morning arrived, and a bleary-eyed Sophia came down the stairs wearing her traveling gown and cloak. Mary puffed behind her, carrying a portmanteau and a bandbox.

In the front hallway, Fiona was speaking to the housekeeper. She broke off as she saw Sophia and hurried forward. "Miss MacFarlane, you cannot be leaving!"

"I'm afraid I must be going."

"But the roads are nearly impassable."

"I managed to get here; I'm certain I'll manage to make it ho —" But she had no home now, so she amended, "Back to my father."

Fiona looked unconvinced, her green eyes dark with worry. "I can see you're determined, but you must at least stay for breakfast."

Jack came from the breakfast room, pausing when he saw Sophia and her maid.

Fiona gestured for him to join them, which he did. "Jack! Pray tell Miss Mac-Farlane that the roads are impassable."

"The roads are impassable," he replied immediately.

"And that she should stay at least another day."

"You should stay at least another day," he repeated, a twinkle in his eyes.

Fiona nodded. "And that she is more than welcome here."

"I am certain she knows that."

"And how we'd love to have her for another week, at least, and —"

Jack laughed and took his wife's hand. "Fiona, love, I believe Miss MacFarlane is very aware that we both wish her to stay."

Sophia had to smile. "I am very flattered, but we really must go. There've been so many unexpected storms that the roads could easily get worse."

Jack snorted a laugh while Fiona glanced up the stairs. "Haven't there been," she said grimly before returning her gaze to Sophia. "I am so disappointed you are leaving."

There was genuine warmth in Fiona's voice. "I am, too, but I must get back to my father, who has been ill. I was only to be gone one day, and he'll worry if I don't return immediately."

"I suppose you can't —"

"She's not going anywhere."

Sophia closed her eyes at the deep voice

from the top of the stairs. Her entire body had tightened at the sound, traitor that it was.

Dougal came down the stairs to stand before Sophia, his expression guarded and tense. "Fiona, Jack, would you mind giving me a few moments' private speech with Miss MacFarlane?"

"Will you attempt to persuade her to stay?" Fiona asked in a hopeful tone.

"Absolutely." His dark gaze never left Sophia.

"Very well," his sister said, taking her husband's arm. "Come, Jack. I'm famished."

He sent a stern glance at Dougal. "We will be in the breakfast room if we're needed."

"You won't be needed," Dougal snapped.

"Jack, stop it," Fiona hissed. She tugged him into the breakfast room and closed the door.

Dougal stepped forward to say in a low tone, "We must speak. *Now.*"

Sophia sighed. "Mary, wait for me here." She turned toward the sitting room. The door was open, though the room was dark. She went to the curtains and threw them open, then turned to face Dougal.

He closed the door. "It's gone."

"Gone? What's gone?"

321

"The deed."

She blinked, struggling to wrap her brain around this information. "But . . . you had it!"

"I know. It was in my room, spread out on a chair before the fire."

"On a chair? But . . . why?"

His lips twitched. "Somehow it had gotten quite wet."

Her cheeks warmed. "Oh."

"Yes." His gaze flickered over her, hot and possessive. "We must find the deed."

She pressed a trembling hand to her forehead, wishing she'd been able to sleep last night. The entire world seemed engulfed in a fog. "When did you discover it missing?"

"This morning. It was there last night before dinner. I didn't think to look for it afterward, but it must have been gone then. I'm a light sleeper and would have heard anyone who came into the room while I was there."

"I can't believe it." She rubbed her temple, her mind jolted into action.

"I think it had to be someone here in the house, either a servant or a guest. I don't know which, although . . ."

She looked at him curiously. "What?"

"I had left a bag of coins on the dresser,

and it wasn't touched."

"So it's probably not a servant."

"I wouldn't think so. Which leaves the other guests. You *must* stay until we discover who has the deed."

"Of course," she said with an impatient wave of her hand. "We'll need to talk to all of the servants and find out who they might have seen in the hallways last night, and —" She blinked.

"What is it?"

She yanked open her reticule. "I wonder if my jewels are missing, too. This morning when I picked up the bag, I thought it felt light."

"They were in two separate rooms. It's not very likely that —"

She turned the reticule upside down above her hand, and marbles rolled out onto her palm. "They're gone, Dougal. They're all gone!"

Sophia sent Mary back to the room with their luggage. She was not going to leave until she'd solved this mystery.

When Dougal suggested they not make the loss of the deed and the jewels known to the other guests yet, Jack had concurred, and Fiona had reluctantly agreed, protesting that none of her guests or servants was capable of theft. Sophia wasn't so certain.

Breakfast was a tense affair. Everyone who knew of the missing items was preoccupied, none more than Sophia. She surreptitiously watched the other guests. Sir Reginald was his usual bland self, but he had seemed interested in her jewelry the night before. That made him a prime suspect for that, but what of the deed? Who would want that?

Mrs. Kent laughed at something Dougal said, and Sophia's attention went to the judge's flirtatious wife. Had she taken the deed in an effort to gain Dougal's attention? She certainly seemed unscrupulous enough to try such a thing.

Miss Stanton was speaking to Sir Reginald, planning an outing of some sort, involving a ride to a nearby lake. Fiona sent Sophia a significant look before saying how lovely it would be if *everyone* were to get some fresh air this afternoon.

Naturally, the judge decided to take a nap instead, while Mrs. Kent did her best to discover if Dougal planned on riding before she committed herself.

When Sophia caught Dougal's gaze, he tilted his head toward the garden. She gave him a tiny nod, and for an instant, a smile shimmered in his green gaze.

Sophia shivered, thinking of their interlude

in the tub. Dougal was an incredible lover, and his pursuit of her was flattering. Would he have paid as much attention to her in London, where there were more available women? Or would she have been just one among a number?

The thought made her lips tighten, and she heard Miss Stanton ask, "Miss Mac-Farlane, is something wrong? You look a bit upset."

Miss Stanton's loud voice halted all conversation, and all eyes turned to Sophia.

"You *do* look ill, my dear Miss Mac-Farlane," Mrs. Kent said in a rather waspish voice.

"I'm fine, thank you. I was simply thinking about . . . about my lack of a riding habit! I didn't think to bring one, so I won't be able to ride out today." If *everyone* would go for a ride, then the way would be clear for her to search the house. She glanced at Fiona, hoping her message was received.

Fiona clapped her hands together. "I know a pretty stream that is only a few miles off."

"How few?" Sir Reginald asked. "I don't wish to be too far from the house, in case it rains again."

"Oh, not far," Fiona said evasively. "It's a lovely path, too. There's a good deal of shade, and the vistas are breathtaking."

"That sounds like just the thing," Miss Stanton said. "Who else is going?"

Sir Reginald smiled. "If you think you can do it, Miss Stanton, then of course, I shall attempt it."

"Good man!" Miss Stanton poured herself some more tea. "It looks as if the weather has finally broken, so it should be a pretty day to ride."

Sophia glanced out one of the tall windows and saw that the day beckoned bright and sunny.

"I hate to see anyone miss a ride," Miss Stanton continued gruffly. "Miss Mac-Farlane, I wonder if you could borrow one of my habits? I brought three."

The woman was at least eight inches taller than Sophia and as flat as a boy. "Thank you, but I'm not certain it would fit."

Miss Stanton nodded. "True. A pity."

Mrs. Kent turned her large brown eyes on Dougal. "And you? Will you be riding, too?"

"No. I must write a letter to my man of business in London." Dougal flicked her a cool look. "I trust that meets with your approval?"

Mrs. Kent flushed. "Of course."

"Then I shall see you after the ride."

Fiona's bright gaze turned to Sophia. "I'm sorry you'll be missing the fun, Miss Mac-

Farlane. We shouldn't be gone too long. Two hours, I should think." She stood. "Shall we all change into our riding habits after breakfast and meet back in the foyer?"

Everyone nodded, and she clapped her hands. "Excellent!"

"Perhaps I won't go riding after all," Mrs. Kent suddenly said, her gaze flickering between Sophia and Dougal.

Dougal shrugged. "Suit yourself. I, for one, will be locked in the sitting room." He met Mrs. Kent's gaze. "Alone."

Her face suffused with color.

"Mrs. Kent, pray come with us," Miss Stanton said, buttering a piece of bread. "The more the merrier, I always say."

Jack added, "There's a pretty little mare that would be perfect for you."

"Very well." Mrs. Kent rose and swept toward the door. "I'm going to change."

Miss Stanton wiped her fingers on her napkin and rose, too. "As will I. What a lovely outing it will be!"

Sir Reginald soon followed them.

Left alone, Sophia looked at Dougal. "After they're gone, we'll search their rooms."

"No. You will keep watch while *I* search the rooms."

"Dougal, I —"

"I won't take no for an answer." He glinted a disturbingly attractive smile her way and stood. "Now, if you'll excuse me, I'm going to the sitting room and make a show of writing my man of business to keep Mrs. Kent from deciding to stay after all."

With that, he was gone, leaving Sophia alone in the breakfast room.

CHAPTER 19

Och, me lassies! Ye've but begun yer journey. If I could show it all to ye now, ye'd never believe where ye'll be goin' and where ye'll end!
Old Woman Nora from Loch Lomond
to her three wee granddaughters
one cold evening

As soon as the guests had left, Sophia went to the sitting room. "You search Miss Stanton's room, I'll search Sir Reginald's," she told Dougal.

"No." He tossed down his pen and rose.

"Dougal, I'm not going to argue —"

"Good." He walked past her. "I'll search. You stay here and watch for anyone who might return early."

Sophia plopped her hands on her hips. "Dougal, that is not fair!"

He leaned down until his eyes were even with hers. "Is this fair, then?" He lifted her into his arms and kissed her madly.

Sophia melted against him, unable to fight the emotions that tumbled through her. She wrapped her arms about his neck and held him tightly.

Suddenly, she was back on her feet, and Dougal was on his way to the stairs. "Watch for the party to return. Someone could get hot or take a tumble, and they'd all be upon us before we knew it."

Sophia stood staring blankly up the stairs for an entire minute before it dawned on her that he'd used the kiss to befuddle her. Blast it all! She fumed to herself as she walked to the front window and stationed herself there.

Time went by. The clock ticked. A bee buzzed against the windowpane. Dust settled. After thirty minutes had passed, Sophia had had enough. She gave the empty lane one last glance, then went upstairs.

Dougal was probably in Miss Stanton's room, the one closest to the landing. She'd take Sir Reginald's room, since he'd seemed interested in her jewelry.

Outside his door, she looked up and down the hallway, then let herself in.

It was a pleasant bedchamber, with a huge dresser on one side, a large wardrobe on the opposite wall, and a bed so enormous that four people could fit in it. A large washstand stood to one side, adorned with a beautifully decorated washbasin and pitcher. The Kincaids certainly knew how to spoil their guests; every bedchamber she'd seen was a work of art and comfort.

Sophia quickly made her way through the dresser. Finding nothing of interest, she eyed a trunk that stood at the foot of the bed.

A large lock held it shut, so she used her hairpin to open it. When she pushed the top up, the trunk appeared to be filled with clothing.

Perhaps there was something hidden under the clothes. She was half-buried in the trunk when she heard a noise out in the hallway.

Heart galloping, she whirled toward it, listening. Another step sounded and then another. Sophia crammed the clothes back into the trunk. A small packet fell onto the floor and she scooped it up and turned toward the trunk.

Then the doorknob began to turn.

Sophia's heart pounded in her throat. She closed the trunk lid, dropped to the floor, and scooted under the bed. A roil of dust swirled up, and she pressed her hand over her nose to keep from sneezing.

She saw a man's boots quickly walk across the room. They paused in the center, then moved to the wardrobe. He opened it and began rustling through the items there.

Dougal! Blast it, she didn't want him to find her hiding under the bed like a frightened child. She'd just lie quietly and come out when he'd left.

She heard him close the wardrobe door and cross to the dresser. There was the sound of glass tinkling and other items being moved. Then he crossed to the trunk she'd been searching.

He began unpacking it exactly as she had. She wished he'd hurry; she was beginning to get an ache in her shoulder from lying on the hard floor.

Dougal suddenly paused, and in the hallway, Sophia heard heavy footsteps and a soft, masculine laugh. Sir Reginald!

Dougal crammed the clothes back into the trunk, closing the lid just before the door began to open. *Oh, God, please don't let him crawl under the bed!* To her relief, he dashed across the room and disappeared behind the curtains.

The door swung open, and Sir Reginald walked in. Sophia could see his dusty riding boots, followed by a smaller, more feminine pair. The door closed, and the two faced each other. Then she heard the sound of a passionate kiss, followed by a feminine moan.

Sophia's eyes widened. What was she supposed to do now?

As if he'd heard her thoughts, Dougal peeked out from behind the curtains. His blond hair was mussed from digging in the trunk, his eyes sparkling with amusement. Blast him, he had a clear view and knew who the woman was. As Sophia scowled, his gaze dropped from the couple to find Sophia beneath the bed.

Anger flared in his eyes. Sophia caught herself before she made an apologetic shrug. He wasn't in charge of anything. In fact, they were both in a fix, though she supposed that if she'd stayed at her post, none of this would have happened.

Suddenly, the bed sagged over Sophia's head as Sir Reginald and his partner collapsed together. They were making more noises now, articles of clothing falling to the floor as they disrobed. Sophia covered her face, wondering what she should do.

She couldn't stay here, but how to get out? She looked toward the door but decided they'd notice it opening. The only window was closed and was two stories aboveground, so that wouldn't work — not to mention she'd have to go through Dougal to reach it.

Sir Reginald's deep voice rang out. "Ride me, my sweet Regina!"

A woman's voice answered, "Oh, my love. I can feel you so well, feel you deep inside — ohhh!"

Good God! It was Miss Stanton! Sophia looked at Dougal to see if he was surprised. He was watching the couple in the bed, his brows raised. He glanced down at Sophia and smiled a little, his eyes twinkling.

Suddenly, a giggle tickled through her. She clapped a hand over her mouth as she heard Sir Reginald instruct Miss Stanton to use her whip on him.

Sophia clasped both hands over her mouth, but it didn't help. A giggle snuck out. For a paralyzing second, all was silent. Then Sir Reginald said hoarsely, "It's nothing, my dear Regina! Ride me, my darling!"

And it was on again. As Sophia tried to control her laughter, there was a sudden movement to one side, and Dougal slid under the bed with her.

She gasped. "How did you —"

"They were facing the other way," he whispered back. His teeth gleamed in the dimness.

Above them, the mattress began to buck,

and Sir Reginald's pleas and Miss Stanton's moans increased. Sophia remembered the first night she and Dougal had made love, the wildness and the passion. And then their time in the tub, the silken heat and the feel of his hands sliding over her wet body. She moved restlessly, and without warning, Dougal pulled her close and kissed her.

It was a wildly erotic moment. They were trapped beneath the bed, with two near-strangers making love above them, and she couldn't make a sound. She had to hold in a moan when Dougal's hand slipped to her breast and cupped her, his thumb rolling over her nipple and sending ripples through her.

Dougal had felt Sophia's burgeoning desire as she listened to the sounds coming from the bed, and he'd been more than willing to answer it. They couldn't take this too far without giving themselves away, but the moment was too erotic to allow it to pass.

Eventually, the couple above them stilled, their harsh breathing filling the room.

Sir Reginald gave a soft laugh. "That was lovely, my dear."

"As ever," she said in a breathy voice. She laughed, more of a purr, and rolled off the bed.

As the woman gathered her clothes,

Sophia held her breath, afraid she and Dougal might be found, but nothing so exciting occurred. Miss Stanton washed in the basin, dressed, and prepared to leave. The whole time, she and Sir Reginald carried on a conversation with an ease that told Sophia that this was a relationship of long standing.

"There. I'm presentable again."

"You're always presentable," he replied gallantly.

"Please, Reginald, don't." Though the words were petulant, the tone was amused. "This arrangement works because neither of us attaches any importance to it. Dressing it up will just confuse the issue."

"I apologize," he said immediately. "Did you get your scarf? It was on the dresser."

Miss Stanton crossed to the dresser, paused, and then picked up something from the floor. "A hairpin? I wonder how this came to be here."

Sophia's eyes widened. The pin she'd used to open the trunk!

"Let me see it." Sir Reginald rose from the bed and walked barefooted to Miss Stanton. "Hm. I don't know whose that is."

A *ping* sounded as Miss Stanton tossed the pin onto the dresser. "It's not Mrs. Kent's? I had the impression you two were becoming friendly before MacLean arrived."

"Mrs. Kent doesn't wear hairpins this color; her hair is too dark."

Sophia noticed that he didn't deny he'd been with Mrs. Kent.

"Then perhaps it belongs to the lovely Miss MacFarlane. You seemed very interested in her jewelry."

"I am."

"How interested? Enough to take it?" Amusement laced through Miss Stanton's voice. "I know how expensive you can be, Reginald. A man must live."

"I didn't steal Miss MacFarlane's jewelry," he said, though he seemed far from upset at her suggestion. "I thought about it, but in the end, I decided it belongs with its rightful owner."

"Have it as you will." Disbelief colored her voice. "I'm going to my room to call for a bath. Perhaps after dinner, you might join me for . . . a game?"

He chuckled. "Regina, you are insatiable. It is one of your best qualities."

There was a pause as the two kissed. Sophia looked at Dougal, whose brows were lowered, a thoughtful expression on his face.

Moments later, Miss Stanton took her leave, and Sir Reginald, apparently exhausted by his energetic activities, fell into bed and was soon snoring.

Dougal motioned for Sophia to stay until he could slip out and open the door. Checking Sir Reginald's snores, he motioned for Sophia to follow him. Then they were in the hallway, closing the door softly behind them.

Dougal grabbed Sophia's hand and pulled her into his own room, locking the door.

"I never imagined Miss Stanton and Sir Reginald together! Did you?"

"No." Still leaning against the door, his gaze locked on her, he frowned.

"What is it?"

"Something just dawned on me. They both knew the jewels were missing. I don't know if it means anything, but —" He shook his head. "It's probably nothing. I'll have to look into it."

"I hate it when you're mysterious," she said dryly. "Did you find anything in Miss Stanton's room?"

"Only a pair of men's boots. Now I know whom those belong to."

Sophia sank onto the settee by the fireplace. "Then we're no closer than we were before."

"We've other rooms to search." He glanced at the clock. "But the others should be returning soon."

She nodded thoughtfully. "Dougal, I can't stay much longer."

"Why not?"

Because she was beginning to find it difficult to imagine her life without him. Because every time he came into a room, she yearned for him. Because she was afraid life without him would be stale and lonely.

"Because my father will worry."

Dougal shrugged. "Send him a message and explain what's happened. He'll understand."

"No, he won't. But a message will ease his mind. I will send Angus home tomorrow, but . . . Dougal, even if we don't find the deed and the jewels, there's no reason for me to stay. Besides, none of it really belongs to me."

He watched her with a dark expression in his eyes.

What was he thinking? Sophia bit her lip. What she really wanted to know was what did he think of her? Did he respect her and accept that their passion was a gift?

She'd thought for a long time that happiness lay in MacFarlane House; now she knew that happiness lay within her own heart. All she had to do was find it. And there were times when, looking at Dougal, she wondered if she finally had.

But thinking of Dougal in terms of forever was a waste of time. He wasn't the sort of man to settle in one place. Men like him needed constant excitement, the steady roar of the ton, or travel to keep them happy. Did Dougal even believe in forever? And how could a woman ask such a question without appearing hopelessly in love? For she wasn't. She was merely in deep *like* — though a few more days in Dougal's presence could well send her over the edge.

Awkward as it was, if she wished to know how he felt, she would have to ask. She cleared her throat. "Dougal, why do you wish me to stay?"

"The deed and jewels are missing."

"And?"

His eyes narrowed. "And what?"

Embarrassment flooded through her, but she kept her composure. "I wish to know *all* of the reasons you want me to stay."

There was a long silence and then he answered, his voice abrupt, "I enjoy making love to you."

His answer sent her pulses racing, yet her heart panged hollowly. "Is there anything else? Any other reason?" She met his gaze straight on and knew from his frozen expression that he knew exactly what she wanted to hear.

His gaze flickered to the window beyond. She didn't know what he saw there, other than the ruined garden, but his expression hardened even more.

Finally, he looked back to her. "No," he said shortly. "I enjoy your passion, and I am determined to find the missing items. What else could there be?"

Sophia's throat tightened with disappointment. But what had she expected? She knew Dougal was a man of many dalliances; why had she thought their relationship different?

Well, no matter what the outcome of their relationship, she would not be sorry they'd met. He was a generous and skillful lover, and she was thankful for that at least.

She'd never known how important that was, but having tasted it once, she didn't think she'd ever be satisfied with a passionless relationship. When she married, she wanted compatibility *and* passion, though she couldn't imagine making love to anyone but Dougal.

Dougal caught her hand and pressed his lips to her fingers. "Don't look so forlorn." He tugged Sophia forward, pulling her into his arms. "For now, my little spy, we must plan our next attack."

"The judge's room?"

"Yes. We need to find a way to lure him

and his busy wife away from the house." Dougal traced a finger from her shoulder to the top of one breast.

Shivering at the sensation, she managed to say, "Do you really think we'll find anything?"

His fingers dipped into the low neckline of her gown, watching her face with a warm expression. "We won't know until we try." Before she could answer, he enveloped her in a kiss, and soon they were lost to passion.

It was magnificent, as always. But afterward, when Dougal was asleep, his arm warm over her, tears welled and slowly slid down Sophia's cheeks to the pillow.

The thought of leaving was lonelier than she'd ever imagined. Yet staying was not an option. Oh, she could sneak an occasional embrace with Dougal, but that was all.

Two days. Two days, and she'd leave and begin the process of forgetting Dougal Mac-Lean.

CHAPTER 20

When the wind blows from the north and the cold rains begin, I wonder what sort o' trouble the MacLeans must be in to have set loose the wrath o' the storms.
Old Woman Nora from Loch Lomond
to her three wee granddaughters
one cold evening

Sophia slipped out of Dougal's bed, pausing to look back at him. His tawny hair was mussed, his thick lashes crested on his cheeks, his sensual lips parted in sleep. He'd slept with one arm over her, and now, frowning, he gathered a pillow and hugged it in her place.

She reached out and gently brushed his hair from his eyes, smiling as he snuggled deeper into the pillow. He was painfully handsome, and she couldn't look at his large, well-shaped hand without thinking about that hand cupping her breasts, run-

343

ning up and down her back as she pressed to him —

She shivered and forced herself to turn away. She ached to toss her sense of self-preservation to the winds and slip back between the warm sheets, but she needed to think — and that was the one thing she couldn't do while wrapped in Dougal's arms.

He was a complicated man, tender one moment and demanding the next. There were times when their eyes met and she felt that she'd never want to be with another man. But then she'd remember what he was, and the thought would shatter.

Lips trembling, she quietly dressed, tiptoed to the door, and peered out.

No one was in the corridor. With a lingering look at Dougal, she slipped outside.

She was halfway to her room when she heard a doorknob turn. Without checking to see which door it might be, she hiked her skirts and ran.

She darted inside her room and closed the door, resting her cheek against the panel, panting as she strained to hear into the hallway. Were those footsteps coming toward her room or —

"Where have ye been?"

Sophia jumped and turned to find Mary

standing behind her, arms akimbo.

"Well?" the maid said, looking her up and down.

Sophia pressed a hand to where her heart had attempted to jump from her chest.

Mary's suspicious gaze whipped over Sophia. "Ye've mussed yer gown, too!"

Sophia looked down. The entire front of her gown was smeared with dust from where she'd hidden beneath Sir Reginald's bed. "Ah. I was looking for a — a — an earring that had fallen under the table in the, ah, sitting room, and the floor was dusty."

"Humph." Mary's disbelief was plain. "That might get dust on yer knees, but it don't explain the dust on yer bodice."

"I had to lie completely flat, as the ring had rolled under the table to the other side."

"Ring? Ye said it was an earring."

Blast it! "One or the other. I don't remember which."

Mary quirked a brow, and Sophia sighed, feeling like a child who'd been caught with crumbs on her chin during a missing-cookie hunt. "Mary, do you think I might have a bath?" She untied the ribbon at her neck and began to push the gown down her arms.

Mary came to help, whisking the gown away and bringing a robe. "I don't mean to complain, miss, but ye've been acting strange since we arrived." She held the robe open for Sophia. "Ye're fortunate I didn't brain ye with my dust pan when ye came in, fer ye scared me to death. What with there bein' a thief in the house and all, ye should be careful."

"How do you know there's a thief in the house?"

Mary lifted a brow. "Yer jewels are gone, aren't they?"

"How did you know that? I didn't tell anyone."

"I heard it from Sir Reginald Barksdale's valet in the servants' hall. He asked if ye'd found yer missin' jewels. I tried to tell him ye'd never lost them, that Lord MacLean must be holdin' them fer ye, but the bloke wouldn't listen. Finally, the housekeeper tol' me she thought he was tellin' the truth."

Sophia frowned. "How did Sir Reginald's valet know my jewels were missing?"

"I don't know, but he did. Kept asking me this and that about the diamonds, where ye got them, and if ye knew where they'd come from." Mary leveled a hurt gaze on Sophia. "It was a bit embarrassin', not knowin' they was even gone."

Sophia winced. "I'm sorry, Mary. I should have told you, but Lord MacLean and I were hoping to discover who took them. We thought that the fewer people who knew, the better our chances."

The maid nodded, looking slightly mollified. "I can see that. Is anything else missing?"

"The deed to MacFarlane House."

"Gor! Both the deed and the jewels are gone? At the same time?" Mary whistled, then picked up the dusty gown. "I don't know what the world's comin' to. Ye can't even leave a piece o' paper without someone takin' it into their heads to steal it, and — Miss? What's this? It was in yer pocket."

Sophia looked at the small bag in Mary's hand, a faint memory stirring. Ah, yes. The bag from the trunk in Sir Reginald's room. "Let me see that."

Sophia undid the tie to the small pink satin bag and pulled out the contents. Inside was a much crossed-out note that appeared to list the various houses belonging to the carl of Ware. Beneath it was the velvet pouch that had once held her mother's jewelry.

Sophia smoothed it between her fingers. *Sir Reginald.* Finally, she had proof that he had taken the jewels. But what about the deed? And why was there a list of the earl of Ware's houses? That made no sense at all.

She supposed she should tell Dougal. But every time they were together, they succumbed to the passion that flared between them. And each time, it seemed as if he stole more of her precious resistance.

She couldn't afford to lose much more, or when the time came to leave, she wouldn't be able to do it; she'd soon be in love with him.

Sophia bit her lip to keep it from quivering and pulled the robe tighter. She had to stop the continuing intimacy between herself and Dougal; all it did was deepen the feelings she was already fighting. Though he was right when he said it was pleasurable — she couldn't think of anything more so — that didn't make it a good idea.

Still, she couldn't help thinking wistfully of his warm bed, a bed that was now officially off limits.

Sophia closed her eyes against a wave of painful longing.

"Miss? Are ye ill?"

Sophia forced her eyes open. "I'm fine. I was just thinking . . ." She pulled her thoughts from Dougal and back to the velvet pouch clutched in her hand. It was difficult to care about her jewels and the deed, though. Everything seemed to have lost its flavor.

She caught Mary's worried gaze. "This came from Sir Reginald's room. I wonder if he'd disappear if he realized I know he took my jewels?"

"Don't ye worry about that. He wouldn't stir a step without Gilbert, his high and mighty valet." Mary crinkled her nose. "I was glad to see *him* leave this morning."

"Do you know where he went?"

"Aye. He was complainin' that he had to ride to Prestonhall, outside Edinburgh, and return in the morning with a note of some kind."

Sophia looked at the list in her hand. The second residence for the earl of Ware read "Prestonhall." And there was a distinctive tick mark to the side. "Did Gilbert say what he was to do there?"

"Nay. He was actin' all important-like, until I pointed out he should be miffed to be used as a courier." Mary smirked. "That got to him, it did."

Had Sir Reginald sold her jewelry to the earl of Ware? Or was that where he was traveling next and he was merely confirming an invitation?

It was a pity she couldn't discuss this with Dougal. She glanced at the closed door and sighed.

"I'm going to take your gown downstairs and have one of the maids brush it clean. While I'm there, I'll send up yer bath."

"Thank you." Perhaps after the bath, she'd feel more herself. Right now, she longed for peace and quiet and a return to her normal spirits. Anything rather than this horrid emptiness that weighed her down.

Mary opened the door, then hesitated. "Miss? How long do ye think we'll be stayin'? Angus is anxious to return home."

"We'll leave as soon as we find the deed. Send Angus to my father in the morning, and let him know we'll be here another day or two."

The maid nodded. "I will."

As the door shut behind the maid, Sophia paced the floor. As soon as she'd bathed and dressed, she'd send word to Dougal to meet her in the sitting room — with the door open, of course. There, safe from temptation, they'd discuss their strategy for confronting Sir Reginald.

They'd have to act quickly, for he might leave as soon as the valet returned from his mysterious errand. That was probably the only thing holding him here — except, perhaps, the charms of the enthusiastic Miss Stanton. Sophia could understand that, now knowing the power of Dougal's manifest charms.

The thought of never seeing him again, returning to MacFarlane House alone, seemed wrong and sad and — She blinked back tears and paced more quickly. Without Dougal, everything lost its color and flavor. Yet lately, she felt equally lonely when she was with him, because she wanted far more than he wished to give.

For him, excitement would always be over the next hill, around the next bend in the road, behind the next deck of cards. For her, peace and contentment meant home, wherever that was.

Yet now that she'd tasted true passion, how was she to go back to her old life? And how was she going to find the strength to walk away from Dougal MacLean?

Dougal awoke with a start. The room was still bright, but something was missing. He blinked sleepily, trying to think what was gone, why he was in the bed in the middle of the day.

Sophia.

He lifted himself on one elbow and looked at the empty bed beside him. The pillow still bore a faint impression of where she'd been, and he placed his hand over it as if he could still steal some of her warmth. Damn it, why hadn't she stayed? He sighed at his own foolishness and rested his cheek on the linens that bore the faint scent of her perfume.

Sophia MacFarlane was a remarkable woman. He thought of how furious he'd been when he'd seen her hiding beneath Sir Reginald's bed. Now that she was safely away, he found himself smiling. No other woman was as intrepid as his Sophia.

His smile faded. *His* Sophia? Where had that come from? Certainly, he was enjoying her; she was beautiful and winsome and had enough spirit for three women. She also ignited his lust with a mere glance from beneath those thick lashes. Remembering the passion they'd just shared, a jolt of hunger racked through him, so raw it almost hurt.

He'd never lusted so much for any woman. That was because it was more than just lust; it was — He frowned. What was it? Certainly, it was admiration. And caring. And . . . what? It couldn't be love. He would never fall for a woman like Sophia, whose attachment to MacFarlane House was so deep. He knew she loved that house and would have no desire to live anywhere else. Which was why her gift of the deed meant so much.

He absently slid a hand over the pillow, thinking of the softness of her skin, the silkiness of her hair. She was more than merely beautiful. There was a gentleness to her, an aura of comfort that made a man wish for things like warm beds, quiet dinners by a roaring fire, the peace of a home —

Bloody hell! He pushed himself upright. He knew what would happen if he cared too much, how his sometimes tenuous control would be weakened. He couldn't give in.

Earlier, Sophia had asked his reasons for wishing her to remain with him. He knew what she'd really been asking, for it had been plainly evident in her expression: she wanted to know whether he cared for her.

He'd almost said something he would have regretted, when he'd chanced to glance past her to the window beyond. Through the rain-streaked glass he'd seen his sister's beautiful tea garden, ripped apart by his temper. The roses had been scattered, their tattered petals strewn over the garden path, while huge limbs hung broken from the trees. Worse, Fiona's ornate fence was tilted precariously to one side, a blackened gash showing where lightning had struck.

The sight had painfully reminded him why he could not afford to care more for Sophia than he already did.

Scowling, he swung his feet over the side

of the bed and rubbed his face, aware of a deep desire to get up and leave forever, never looking back.

He smiled bitterly. He had that thought a million times a day lately, but every time, it was followed by another — that he would stay just one more minute. Or hour. Or day. It was his last time with Sophia, and he never wanted it to be over. *Weak fool!*

The murmur of a man's voice arose in the hallway, followed by a woman's lilting laugh. Glad for the respite from his unwelcome thoughts, Dougal listened closely. It was Sir Reginald, talking to Mrs. Kent. Sir Reginald was quite the philanderer.

Dougal stood and washed, then glanced at the clock: three in the afternoon. He was starving, having missed lunch. Had Sophia eaten already? He hoped so; she seemed so pale of late, and —

Damn it, Sophia was old enough to take care of herself. She'd gotten along fine before she'd met him and would do equally well afterward.

He had no doubt that one day, some country bumpkin would woo her until she succumbed. No doubt the fool would spend his days blessing the heavens for his good luck, too.

Irritation simmered through Dougal as he

grabbed his boots and stomped into them. He should be happy that Sophia wouldn't languish without him. Instead, he felt a burning resentment toward the mystery country bumpkin, a hatred deeper than any he'd ever felt. Dougal pulled a fresh shirt over his head and tucked it in, then donned a red waistcoat. He pulled on his coat as he left the room.

In the empty hall, he paused outside Sophia's room. He bent, leaning close to the door. All was silent. Then he heard the unmistakable splashing of a tub of water.

Sophia. Naked and wet. Water dripping over her bare skin, trickling down her neck and over her shoulders to caress her full, round breasts. Her blond hair would dip into the water, the wet strands clinging to her shoulders, curling around her delicate neck —

"Damn."

The splashing ceased. "Dougal?" Her voice was husky and hesitant.

Dougal straightened, his blood pounding in his ears. He reached for the knob, then stopped. He shouldn't do this. He should walk away.

But every muscle in his body yearned otherwise, and the memory of Sophia in the tub in his room, her skirts floating about her, her wet gown clinging to her breasts, her nipples hard and —

"Odd, I thought Fiona had put you in the blue room."

Dougal turned to find Jack leaning against the hall wall, watching him with amusement.

"What the hell do you want?" Dougal snapped.

"Your sister was surprised you didn't join us for lunch. She thought perhaps you were ill."

"I'm fine, as you can see. I merely took a nap."

"That's good enough for me," Jack said. "Unfortunately for you, Fiona will wish to hear it from your own lips."

Dougal stalked past his brother-in-law, taking the steps down two at a time. He found Fiona in the foyer, speaking with the housekeeper. She left the woman as soon as she saw Dougal and hurried up to him. "Where have you been?"

"Sleeping."

She frowned, her green eyes wary. "Dougal, I wish to speak to you. Jack, would you mind giving us some privacy?"

Jack looked Dougal up and down. "Are you going to berate him?"

"No."

"Chastise him?"

"No."

"Kick him out of our house?"

"No."

"Then I don't mind leaving." Jack turned a bland gaze to Dougal. "Be careful of listening at keyholes, old man. Some of these locks are rather rusty; you could cut yourself." He retired to the library, where no doubt a bottle of port awaited.

"Just ignore him, and come into the sitting room." Fiona turned, and he followed. She closed the door. "Did you find anything in your search?"

"No."

Her shoulders slumped. "Oh. I wish you had. Lunch was quite awkward. Sir Reginald must have asked me a million questions about Sophia; I think he suspects something."

"That we searched his room?"

"No, that there's something between you two. Mrs. Kent was especially vocal about neither of you being present for lunch."

Dougal didn't reply.

Fiona sighed. "We'd all have to be blind not to notice, Dougal. The second she comes into a room, you gravitate toward her like a moth to a flame. If it were any other man, I'd say you were besotted. But since it is you, I'd say instead that you are just playing." She looked at him pointedly. "Are you?"

No, he wasn't. But neither was he marking Sophia as his own for all time. "That's none of your concern."

Fiona placed her hand on his arm. "Dougal, it's clear you find Miss MacFarlane attractive. I had hoped it might be a different sort of relationship for you, but I haven't seen any evidence that that's so."

"How do you know how I feel for So— Miss MacFarlane?"

Fiona gave him a reproachful look. "If you cared for her, you would have been more cautious of her reputation."

Her words pinned him in place, causing a sinking sensation in his stomach. His sister was right. He'd been so taken up with pursuing Sophia that he hadn't taken care of her reputation, or her safety, either — or she'd never have ended up under Sir Reginald's bed.

It was totally unlike him and showed all too clearly the problems with dallying with innocents.

Regret burned through him. Had he been thoughtless? In many ways, he supposed so. But he couldn't seem to help it. She tantalized him with every breath, and he was as mad as a youth with his first love to have her.

"Dougal, are you listening? You must stop pursuing Sophia."

He knew Fiona was right. Yet, desperate to get away from the emotions bubbling to the surface, the thoughts he'd tried to hold back, he walked toward the door, saying, "I'll think about it."

"Dougal!"

He looked back at his sister.

"I know you and Sophia both wish to find the missing deed and the jewels, but you must have a care with her reputation. She's a good, beautiful woman, and she deserves all of the opportunities that will give her, including a good marriage."

Dougal rubbed a hand over his eyes. When he opened them, his sister looked at him with a stunned expression.

"You do care for her!"

Dougal scowled. "It doesn't matter what I might feel. I can't afford to care for her, Fiona," he said bleakly.

"You have to stop blaming yourself, Dougal. We were all angry when Callum died. You don't know that you were the one who caused that storm."

"Yes, I do."

She sighed. "You're not going to tell her

how you feel?"

"No." He paused, silence weighing him down. "But you're right, I have been selfish. I wanted to keep her here, so I —" He shook his head, his heart aching in the oddest way.

"What did you do?" she asked softly.

His throat suddenly seemed too tight, and he had to swallow before he could continue. "I should have sent her home right away, but I didn't wish her to leave."

Fiona took a step closer, her voice quiet. "Why is that, Dougal? *Why* didn't you want her to leave?"

Because I love her.

The thought crushed down upon him like the weight of a million bricks. For a second, he couldn't breathe, couldn't think. He loved her. Oh, God, when had that happened? And what in the hell was he supposed to do about it?

Once she had the deed and her missing jewels, she'd be on her way back to the home she so loved. And he would return to London and . . . nothing.

But nothing was better than guilt, which he'd feel every time he grew jealous or lost his temper, and the storms came.

Damn his greedy heart!

Fiona placed her hand on his arm. "Dougal, surely there's something you can —"

"No." He placed his hand over his sister's. "I should have left the second she arrived, but I knew it would be the last time I'd ever see her. The last time I'd ever *allow* myself to see her."

She sighed, her shoulders slumping. "Dougal, I'm so sorry."

"So am I." He gave Fiona a brief hug and, unable to speak, left. He was halfway across the great hall when the butler caught up with him. "Excuse me, my lord."

Dougal turned. "Yes?"

"A note, my lord. From Miss Mac-Farlane."

Dougal looked at the folded note for a long time before he opened it. *Meet me in the sitting room at five. I must speak with you.* She'd signed it with a delicate flourish that caught at his heart.

"Will there be an answer, my lord?"

Dougal tucked the note in his pocket, his fingers lingering on the place she'd signed her name. "Inform Miss MacFarlane that you could not find me."

"Of course, my lord."

Dougal left for the barn. A good, hard ride would stiffen his resolve, and when he returned, he'd make certain Sophia knew that their lively lovemaking was at an end.

That's all he had to do.

Yet as he walked to the barn, his steps lagged, matching his spirits. He knew then that no amount of riding would make him feel better. The question was, would anything?

The weight of his heart said no. As if in agreement, black clouds gathered on the horizon, ominous and heavy, yet strangely quiet.

CHAPTER 21

Ah, to be the one woman to make a man burst into the fury of love — that's the magic o' it all!
Old Woman Nora from Loch Lomond
to her three wee granddaughters
one cold evening

Sophia paced the sitting room. Dinner was but an hour away, so Dougal should be coming back from his ride soon. She had to tell him about her belated discovery from Sir Reginald's room. Why had he gone riding at such a time? It was maddening.

She paused by the window and looked out. Dark clouds hung over the horizon, but there was no wind. She shivered and turned away; she could smell the coming storm, the air tingling with anticipation.

A movement by the hallway caught her attention. Had Dougal come in through the back? She crossed to the door and peered out.

Sir Reginald stood in the hallway, handing his hat to a footman. Dressed in a riding coat and breeches, the white tops of his boots decorated with gold tassels, he appeared the epitome of fashion.

Should she try to find out more? Blast it, she wished she'd had the chance to speak to Dougal. Biting her lip, she stepped behind the edge of the doorway so Sir Reginald wouldn't see her.

As she did so, a man hurried into the hall from the servants' door, crossing toward Sir Reginald. Was this Gilbert, the valet? Small and wizened, he carried himself with an air of great importance. He bowed to Sir Reginald in an exaggerated manner.

"There you are!" Sir Reginald said impatiently. "Well? Did you bring word?"

"Yes, my lord. His lordship wrote you a letter." He glanced down his nose at the impassive footman. "Shall I await you in your chambers to —"

"No, no! Just give it to me now."

The valet, obviously unhappy to be deprived of his planned drama, produced a small envelope.

With eager hands, Sir Reginald opened it and scanned the letter quickly. "Excellent."

He tucked the letter into his pocket. "Thank you, Gilbert. That will be all."

The valet bowed again. "Shall I prepare your evening clothes?"

"Yes, please. Lay out the blue and silver waistcoat."

"Yes, my lord." The valet bowed yet again and left, though it was plain he thought he'd been poorly used.

Sir Reginald stayed where he was a moment more, his hand in the pocket where he'd placed the letter, his brow furrowed in thought. Finally, looking around as if just awakening and realizing he was still in the hallway, he turned and walked toward the stairs.

He couldn't leave! Sophia just knew the letter was proof of Sir Reginald's perfidy, doubtless an agreement regarding the sale of her jewels to the earl of Ware. If she could just get her hands on it, all would be proven. Impulsively, she stepped forward. "Sir Reginald?"

Sir Reginald started at the sound of her voice, but he dutifully smiled and bowed. "Miss MacFarlane! How are you this afternoon?"

Smiling, she beckoned him forward. "You are just the man I wished to see. I must ask you a great favor."

"Of course," he answered gallantly. "I am yours for any service you might request."

"I knew I could count on you!" She gestured to the sitting room. "Shall we step in here? My request is of a personal nature."

If she could get close enough to him, she could take the missive from his pocket. Her heart raced at the thought.

His brows rose, but he said, "I am the soul of discretion."

"I am certain of that." How would she maneuver close enough to be able to reach into his pocket undetected? "I, ah, need your opinion about an important matter concerning . . . well, it's about —"

"Hold one moment, and allow me to close the door," he said smoothly. "It will set your mind at ease." He crossed to the door, making a show of looking outside to make certain no one was nearby to see him close the door.

She frowned, realizing he thought she wished to begin a flirtation. Sir Reginald's opinion of himself was extreme, indeed, although . . . perhaps that was the way to get her hands on the letter. She could pretend to flirt with him and, when he was distracted, take the letter. Dougal would be astonished at her daring. She was, too, if she thought about it.

She turned away to smooth her gown and tighten the sash that tied beneath her breasts, then frowned. Though she'd thought her gown madly fashionable when she'd had it made, her stay here had proven that she was woefully out of fashion. Mrs. Kent's gowns were of much finer materials, the necklines more revealing, her shoes of a completely different cut from Sophia's.

Perhaps she should lower the neckline slightly. She gave a quick tug. That was better. Yet even as she had the thought, the neckline rose back into place.

Sophia frowned and jerked the gown again. This time, it went farther, and not only were the tops of her breasts visible but the lace of her chemise as well.

Sophia bit her lip. Well, that was certainly racier. She straightened her shoulders and lifted her head — and found herself looking straight into the reflection of Sir Reginald's eyes, watching *her* reflection in the window glass.

Oh, God. He'd seen her adjust her gown. Her cheeks flooded with color. But there was nothing for it; she either faced him now or later over dinner. Now would be better, since there was no one else around, especially Dougal with his eagle gaze and refusal to leave well enough alone.

Sophia smiled and turned to face Sir Reginald, then dipped a curtsey. "Thank you for being so gallant in attending me."

He inclined his head in return, his gaze never leaving her. "I am always at your service, Miss MacFarlane, no matter what." His gaze flickered over her, resting a moment on her lowered neckline. "Perhaps more so now than ever."

Her cheeks now burned hotter than the coals in the fireplace. She curled her fingers into the palms of her hands to keep herself from yanking her neckline back up. "I need your opinion on a small personal matter."

His gaze sharpened. "Oh?"

"Yes." She took a step forward, taking up the ends of her sash and threading them through her fingers. "Sir Reginald, you are a man of fashion."

He couldn't help but preen a bit. "I am held to be something of a connoisseur." His gaze flickered over her form. "Especially of things feminine. I must say, I like your style best of all the ladies present. It is quiet, unassuming." His gaze flickered over her hair and face, moving back to her breasts. "And damnably beautiful."

She managed a smile, fighting the urge to cover herself. To pass over the embarrassing moment, she went past him to the window, staring outside with unseeing eyes. "The weather is certainly unpredictable here, isn't it?"

"It's always unpredictable when the Mac-Leans are involved."

She turned to look at him. "You've heard the rumors of the curse?"

"I've heard them and believe them." He moved beside her. "Don't you?"

The pocket she needed to reach was on his other side, blast it. "Do you think one of the MacLeans might be angry now?"

He looked over her head to the gathering clouds, a frown settling between his eyes. "Yes," he said quietly. "One of them is growing more furious by the moment."

A fresh wind now tossed the treetops about, the grass rippled like an angry ocean, and the clouds filled the entire sky. She remembered the huge storm the night of the card game, and a deep shiver shook her.

She rubbed her arms to rid herself of the goose bumps that prickled up and down them. She caught Sir Reginald's amused gaze and dropped her arms to her sides. "I don't believe in curses."

"As you wish, my dear." He crossed his arms over his chest and smiled down at her. "Forgive me if I am wrong, but you seem to have a lot on your mind. Do you care to share it? I am happy to be of assistance in . . . *any* way I can."

With that opening . . . *In for a penny, in for a pound.* Sophia stood on tiptoe, threw one arm about his neck, and kissed him. While he stood stock-still in surprise, she found his pocket.

She had it! She slipped the letter into her own pocket as she released him. "I'm so sorry! I don't know what came over me, but —"

Sir Reginald grasped her head, bent, and kissed her back.

Sophia was stunned. He wasn't supposed to do that!

She struggled against him, but he mistook her attempt for encouragement and kissed her more passionately. Sophia tried to turn her face away, for Sir Reginald's kiss was nothing like Dougal's. There was no exciting, prickly heat dancing up her spine, nothing but the annoying press of his lips to hers and — Good God, was that his tongue?

She gripped his wrists and freed her head, gasping an outraged "Sir Reginald!"

He gazed into her flushed face. "You're a handful, aren't you, my love?"

"I am not your love. Release me at once." Her voice was frosty.

He laughed softly, his arms tightening.

"One of those, are you? That's fine with me. I like a chase."

"Sir Reginald, unhand me!"

"You kissed me first, love."

"That was an error."

"No, it wasn't." He flashed a smile. "I find you too charming by half."

"And I find you too annoying by far. If you do not release me, I cannot be held responsible for your well-being."

He chuckled at that. "A fiery little bundle, aren't you? I'll wager you like —"

She brought her foot down hard on his instep.

He yelped and released her, his face contorted in pain.

Sophia stepped past him, but he grabbed her arm and yanked her back toward him. "You tease!" he gasped.

She used her forward motion to shove him back, against the settee.

One moment, he was standing before her; the next, he was lying upside down on the rug behind the settee, his legs in the air.

Sophia gathered her skirts and ran for the door. She was only steps away when it flew open and Dougal stood in the opening.

He was dressed in his riding clothes, and she couldn't help but compare his elegance with Sir Reginald's flashy attire, with his exaggerated riding coat and gaudy gold-tasseled boots — which were still waving in the air.

Dougal's gaze narrowed on the man before he cut a glance at Sophia, his voice so cold it could chip ice. "What the hell is going on?"

The windowpane rattled, and the gathering storm rumbled.

Sophia grabbed Dougal's arm and tugged him back toward the door. She had to get them out of there before Sir Reginald realized she'd stolen his letter. "Come, let's see when dinner is to be served. I'm famished, and —"

Dougal shook his arm free, his gaze locked on Sir Reginald, who was rising. His hair was disarranged, his cravat sadly smashed, his coat and linens wrinkled. Any moment now, he'd start setting his clothing to rights and would discover that his pocket was empty.

Sophia said breathlessly, "Dougal, there's nothing to be seen here. Sir Reginald and I were merely talking." She sent Sir Reginald a quick glance. "Weren't we, my lord?"

He glared at her, adjusting his rumpled cravat. "Yes," he gritted out. "We were merely talking."

"And now I wish to change for dinner."

She stepped past Dougal, but his hand clamped about her arm.

"You are not going anywhere. Not until I know what's happened here."

Sir Reginald began to straighten his coat and cuffs.

Panicked, Sophia whirled on Dougal. "*Please,* I must —"

Out in the hallway, a commotion arose as new guests arrived. Over the babble came a voice she knew all too well.

"Red!" Sophia freed her arm. "Dougal, I must see why my father's here."

Dougal's gaze met hers. For an instant, she was lost in the green depths. She could see his desire for her, mixed with the anger that was building.

He released her. "Go. Greet your father. I'm staying here to have a word with Sir Reginald."

Fine. Let him deal with Sir Reginald. She nodded, a delicious shiver traveling through her as Dougal's possessive gaze burned into her.

He moved aside, effectively blocking Sir Reginald's departure.

In the great hall, Red balanced precariously on a pair of crutches, looking outraged. As Sophia began to cross to him, she realized his gaze was locked furiously on the other side of the hall.

Standing there was an old gentleman dressed in the epitome of decades-old fashion. His eyes were bright blue, and upon his head rested a powdered wig, the curls flowing down either side of his thin, wrinkled face. An extraordinary number of silver fobs and porcelain buttons glimmered on his puce waistcoat, which was edged with silver lace. A coat of fine silk hung from his thin shoulders, while his silk breeches were accented by striped stockings and ridiculously high-heeled shoes.

The old gentleman lifted his silver-knobbed cane and pointed it at Red. "You!" he intoned like an actor in a play. "I told you never to return to England!"

"And I didn't," Red snapped. "At least, not until my little Sophie wished to settle down, after her mother's death."

The older man thumped his cane and said in a voice that warbled with doom and emotion, "My Beatrice wouldn't have died if she'd been here in England and not in some drafty inn in a foreign clime. I hold *you* responsible for her death, MacFarlane."

His Beatrice?

"I took good care of her, I did," Red snapped, hobbling closer and ignoring the hovering Angus's murmured protests. "Beatrice loved me." He added grudgingly, "She loved you, too, but you were too stubborn to accept her as she was."

Sophia stared at the old man, stunned. "You . . . you are my grandfather!"

Red turned. "Sophie! I was worried to death about you, lass, so I came to —"

Sophia stepped around him, her gaze locked on the older man. "*Are* you my grandfather?"

The man stared at Sophia as if struck by lightning.

Red made a sound of disgust. "Aye, Ware is your grandfather, though a more worthless arse I couldn't name."

"You — you — you — !" The old man limped forward with his cane, his sallow face blazing with anger. "You've already stolen my daughter, MacFarlane. I'll not allow you to keep me from my granddaughter, as well."

Sophia looked squarely at her father. "You told me he was dead."

Red said through his teeth, "There was no point, for there's no meaner, more petty man in all of God's England."

"At least I'm not a wastrel," the old man snapped.

Red started toward the old man, but Sophia stepped between them. "Red, don't."

He looked as if he might burst into flames, then snapped, "I came to get you, Sophie. Have Mary bring your things, and let's go."

"I can't leave, Red. Both the deed and my jewels have gone missing, and I must find them."

"Missing? Where in the hell are they?"

"I don't know. I thought . . ." She turned her clear blue gaze to the old man, who stood watching her, his expression a blend of amazement and rapture. "I beg your pardon, but I take it that you're the earl of Ware?"

The old man's wrinkled lips folded into a faint smile. "Yes."

"Do you have my jewels and the deed to my house?"

The man reached into his pocket, pulled out her diamond set, and held it out to her.

She accepted the jewelry with bemusement. "Red, I believe introductions are in order."

Red audibly ground his teeth. "Sophie, this is your grandfather, the man who callously turned his back on your mama when she was but seventeen."

The earl stiffened. "My Beatrice ran away from home. She had no respect for her position." He looked at Sophia, and his gaze softened. "You look just like her."

"Thank you. It's . . . it's nice to meet you. I always wanted a grandpapa." She turned toward the sitting room, looking over Dougal's shoulder to Sir Reginald. "*You* told the earl I was here."

Sir Reginald nodded. "I hope you don't mind, but I borrowed your necklace to send to the earl."

The old man's head turned with a pleased expression. "Ah, there you are, my boy. Sir Reginald is my godson," he told Sophia.

Sophia was confused. "I still don't understand."

Sir Reginald said, "There is a portrait of your mother in the earl's London home. When I first saw you, I was certain I'd seen you before, but I couldn't remember where. Then I saw your jewelry, and I knew. To be certain, I sent the necklace to the earl. He responded just today." Sir Reginald put a hand in his pocket. "Blast it! Where is that letter?"

Sophia pulled it from her pocket. "I have it here."

Sir Reginald's voice lifted with amazement. "You took that from me? When we were —"

"Yes," she said, her color high. "I thought you'd sold my jewelry and that the envelope contained the payment. I wanted proof, so I took it."

"By kissing me?"

Outside, lightning cracked.

"You *kissed* him?" Dougal demanded.

"Only once."

"Actually, it was twice," Sir Reginald said softly.

Dougal punched him, sending the dandy flying into the wall, where he slid to the floor.

"B'God, that's a nice one!" Red cried. "MacLean, I'd like to see you in a real mill."

"Aye," the earl agreed. "He's got a good solid left."

"What do *you* know about boxing?" Red asked rudely.

"I've seen every large match for the last —"

Thunder crashed as lightning sent shards of light flashing into the great hall.

"That's enough," Dougal said firmly, noting Sophia's pale face. He shot a hard look at the earl. "Why are you here? You obviously aren't fond of MacFarlane."

"I came for my granddaughter."

"You can't have her!" Red snapped. "She's not a possession, you fool!"

The earl flushed. "I didn't mean to suggest she was. Damn you, MacFarlane, I've come to make amends!" He faced Sophia.

"My dear, I was a hothead when I was younger, full of pride. Because of that, I reacted badly when my Beatrice chose your father. I cut her off without a cent, telling myself that it was no more than she deserved. But after she left . . ." The old man's voice quavered. "I missed her so badly. I never knew how much I loved my daughter until she was gone."

Sophia nodded slowly. "I am certain she missed you, too."

Red hobbled forward. "She cried herself to sleep almost every night for a year!"

The earl's entire body seemed to sag against his cane. "I tried to find her, to find you, but you never stayed anywhere long enough. I sent men to France and Italy and anywhere I could think of, but to no avail."

There was a long silence.

Red frowned. "You tried to find us?"

"Yes. To apologize." The earl's lips quivered. "I never got the chance." He pulled out a handkerchief and dabbed at his eyes. "Pride is a horrible thing." He sighed.

Red nodded silently.

The earl limped toward Sophia. "I'd give everything I own to tell my daughter how I regret my pride. Since I cannot do that, please give me a chance to prove myself. I was not a good father, but I will do my best to become a good grandfather."

Red snorted. "That's a very pretty story, but you'll just do to Sophie what you tried to do to Beatrice — lock her up and deprive her of life."

"I was just protecting her!" The earl's lips folded. "Which I would do better than *you've* been doing. Sir Reginald just admitted that he's compromised Sophia, and I don't see you acting upon it. But I will." The earl sent a hard look at Sir Reginald, who was slowly climbing to his feet. "You, sir, will marry my granddaughter!"

"No, he won't," Dougal said softly.

Everyone looked at him.

"If anyone is going to marry Sophia, it's going to be me."

Sir Reginald rubbed his swollen jaw. "I believe Lord MacLean has a far more pressing claim on the lovely Miss MacFarlane than I. The man's in love with her."

All eyes turned to Dougal, but he saw only Sophia.

She took a step toward him, her eyes wide. "Dougal?"

This was it, the moment of truth.

"My love, I thought I could fight this, but I can't. I never thought I was a marrying sort of man, but now . . . it's worth the gamble."

Red grinned at Dougal. "Aye, lad, it is. Well worth it."

Dougal kept his gaze locked on Sophia. "I can't promise anything. I'm not given to staying in one place, and I've never considered myself the sort of man who'd be a good husband."

"Neither did I," Red said.

"Nor I," the earl said.

Dougal looked at the older men. "No?"

Red shook his head. "Our marriage wasn't always easy, and I won't say I didn't make any mistakes, for I did, and so did she. But we worked our way through them." Red's gaze softened. "If you love Sophie and she you, then you'll work things out."

The earl nodded, his eyes misty. "I loved my wife, too. She died when Beatrice was but thirteen. I suppose that's why I tightened my hold on her and wouldn't let her go anywhere. It hurt more than I can say, losing Mary, but I'd do it all over again if I could."

"Dougal?" Sophia asked.

He looked at her.

"Are you saying . . . that you love me?"

Her words plucked at his heart like a finger on a harp string. "Yes, Sophia. I love you. I love you more than I can say. I thought caring for you would weaken me

381

until I lost complete control over the curse. Now —" Dougal glanced at the window where the storm lashed outside, and gave a rueful smile. "Now I realize that not having you in my life would leave me with no control at all, and no reason to try."

She walked to him and lifted her face. "I love you, too." She took his hand and smiled. "And in my heart, I've already married you."

She stood before him, head raised high, her golden hair glimmering, her eyes bright with love. And he knew that she was right. Their hearts had made their pledge the very first time he'd seen her walking down the stairs at MacFarlane House.

"Sophia, I know how important your house is to you. I can't promise I'll wish to live there the entire year, but I'm willing to give it a try."

She smiled, but then it faded. "We've never found the deed —"

He reached into his pocket and pulled it out.

Her eyes widened. "You — but where — how did —"

"I thought if you believed the deed had been stolen, you'd stay."

"But the jewelry —"

"Was stolen the same day by Sir Reginald.

A coincidence that worked to my advantage."

Sophia was silent. Then her soft hand closed over his, and he knew what he had to do.

He dropped to one knee before her. "Sophia MacFarlane, though I've been every sort of fool there is, and though I've stolen from you and lied to you, as you've stolen from me and lied to me, will you please marry me? To keep me out of trouble, if nothing else."

She gave a hiccup of a laugh, her eyes moist with tears. "Only if you, Dougal Mac-Lean, will have me. After all I did to save MacFarlane House, I now realize that without people in it, the people I love, it's nothing more than an empty building. My home is with you, inside your heart."

Dougal swept Sophia into his arms and kissed her thoroughly. Then, laughing, he set her back on her feet. "Come, my love, let's find my sister. She spent a good part of the afternoon telling me what a fool I was. I have to show her that she was wrong."

"And you need my help to do that?"

"It would be a great boon if you'd cling to my arm and look absurdly happy."

Sophia chuckled. "I think I can manage that."

It was a noisy, contentious group that moved down the hall, as the earl and Red continued to snipe at each other, and Sir Reginald felt he needed to explain his improper embrace with Sophia even though everyone attempted to dissuade him.

As Dougal ushered them into the dining room, he wondered if Sophia's father and grandfather would both wish to stay at Mac-Farlane House with them.

But as he looked into Sophia's smiling eyes, he realized it didn't matter. So long as she was by his side, life would be a grand adventure.

And no man could ask for more.

We hope you have enjoyed this Large Print book. Other Thorndike, Wheeler, and Chivers Press Large Print books are available at your library or directly from the publishers.

For information about current and upcoming titles, please call or write, without obligation, to:

Publisher
Thorndike Press
295 Kennedy Memorial Drive
Waterville, ME 04901
Tel. (800) 223-1244

or visit our Web site at:

http://gale.cengage.com/thorndike

OR

Chivers Large Print
published by BBC Audiobooks Ltd
St James House, The Square
Lower Bristol Road
Bath BA2 3SB
England
Tel. +44(0) 800 136919
email: bbcaudiobooks@bbc.co.uk
www.bbcaudiobooks.co.uk

All our Large Print titles are designed for easy reading, and all our books are made to last.